HEART-RENDING REUNION
IN PARADISE

Across the crowded ballroom of Honolulu's finest hotel, Pat Carey saw the handsome young officer and gasped. It was Cameron Fulton!

Into her heart surged the aching memories of two years ago. Their first rapturous meeting, their whirlwind courtship, her breathless assent to marriage . . .

And then her panic at marrying a man she hardly knew. Her cowardly note containing her broken promise. Her flight to her aunt's estate in Hawaii . . .

And now, here he was before her in the flesh. Her heart lurched with sudden hope . . . had he come all the way to Hawaii to find her?

Bantam Books by Emilie Loring
Ask your bookseller for the books you have missed

EMILIE LORING

BRIGHT SKIES

BANTAM BOOKS · TORONTO · NEW YORK · LONDON

The names of all characters in this novel are fictitious.
Use of a name which is that of a living person is
accidental.

*This low-priced Bantam Book
has been completely reset in a type face
designed for easy reading, and was printed
from new plates. It contains the complete
text of the original hard-cover edition.*
NOT ONE WORD HAS BEEN OMITTED.

BRIGHT SKIES

*A Bantam Book / published by arrangement with
Little, Brown and Company*

PRINTING HISTORY

*Little, Brown edition published November 1946
2nd printing .... December 1946
3rd printing .... March 1947*
Grosset & Dunlap edition published September 1948

Bantam edition / September 1965

2nd printing ... October 1965	7th printing ...... May 1968
3rd printing .... January 1966	8th printing . November 1968
4th printing .. December 1966	9th printing ...... May 1969
5th printing .. December 1966	10th printing .... March 1970
6th printing .. December 1967	11th printing . November 1975

*Bantam Books are published by Bantam Books, Inc. Its trade-
mark, consisting of the words "Bantam Books" and the por-
trayal of a bantam, is registered in the United States Patent
Office and in other countries. Marca Registrada. Bantam
Books, Inc., 666 Fifth Avenue, New York, New York 10019.*

1

THE *lanai* was cool and full of shifting green shadows. Far out the ocean broke against a coral reef in geysers of foam and spray. From where she sat in a fan-back, lacy wicker chair Patricia Carey watched the paddling, swimming surfers on a sea sparkling in stripes of emerald, sapphire and, where the sun warmed it, rosy gold, which curved into white-plumed surf as it rolled beachward. It was such a day as the gods are prodigal of in Honolulu. The bowl of the sky was a deep blue with slowly sailing white clouds whipped into fringe at the edges by the same fragrance-laden trade wind that was waving the banyan leaves in the court beyond. Distant pale blue mountains lifted peaks into the sky, and nearer at hand Diamond Head, with its fluted cones, dipped into the iridescent sea.

Pat glanced at her wrist watch. Four o'clock. She was to meet Sally at this hotel at ten minutes before the hour. As usual her aunt was late. Two army men in khaki were crossing the *lanai*. Were they the speakers? The thin gray-haired man with hard-bitten features had three stars on his shoulder. The taller, much younger officer, with a face the shade of bronzed leather, with crossed rifles on his lapel and a colorful array of ribbons on his tunic, was a colonel. He looked like—blood surged through her in a scorching tide. It *couldn't* be Cam. It was, if this wasn't just another dream.

"Attention!"

Patricia's incredulous brown eyes, which had been fastened on the face of the younger man, flashed to the General as with the sharp order he halted in front of her. The Colonel, a foot behind, moved up both hands as if boosting something. Had combat fatigue left him a little mad or was he taking this opportunity to practice his daily dozen?

"Young woman," the General warmed to his subject. "What d'you mean by sitting there like a bump on a log in the presence of officers?"

Officers! She had forgotten she was in WAC uniform. So, that was what the Colonel had meant by his calisthenics? His eyes were as impersonal as if she were one of a company passing inspection while every nerve in her body was vibrating like a violin string, her throat was tight, her heart was pounding. Apparently he did not intend to recognize her. Okay, if that was the way he wanted it. On her feet, heels together, eyes on the General, she brought up her hand smartly in salute.

"Sorry, sir. I forgot, sir."

"Forgot. Soldiers don't get away with forgetting. Take her name and company, Colonel, and report to her commanding officer." He turned to reply to a man with gray hair and ample waistline who introduced a woman dressed in a gaily flowered pink *holoku* with a white gardenia in her sleek black hair. The music of brasses and drums beating out "Stars and Stripes Forever" drifted from the hotel. The Colonel drew a notebook from his pocket.

"Name?" he demanded.

"Patricia Carey."

"Company?"

Her thoughts ran round her memory like a squirrel in a revolving cage.

"Step on it, Carey. I'm due inside. Don't you know where you belong? Did they forget to teach you that as well as that a private stands in the presence of an officer? What's your company?"

His complete ignoring of what had happened between them burned up the sense of guilt which had been her companion for two years. Boy, I'll bet men under your command have to "step on it," she thought before she stammered:—

"D—D Company, s—sir." There *must* be a D Company she told herself frantically. She gazed up at him with exaggerated wistfulness. "Please excuse me this time, sir? Don't report me."

That had shocked him out of his impassivity, had brought a flash to his clear hazel eyes, dark color under his bronzed skin. Had she put her appeal across? This wasn't a man to be cajoled. Not the gay companion she had known. There were deep creases between his nose and the corners of his mouth which had been chiseled into a stand-and-deliver line, a touch of platinum in his dark hair at the temples. Lines deep as if etched with a sharp tool radiated from the corners of his eyes. Why not? He had had two years on the battle front, the last devastating years of the war. His nose was large and clean-cut. He was still sensationally good-looking.

Walter Pidgeon type, only younger, a whole lot younger and leaner.

"You're not listening, Carey."

His deep, authoritative voice sent shivers along her nerves, brought the tightening ache in her throat, the hot sting of tears behind her lids she hoped she had outgrown. Perhaps he could clap her into the guardhouse for being in a uniform she was not entitled to wear, perhaps it would be the pay-off for what she had done to him.

"No, sir. Yes, sir. Sorry, sir. Please repeat what you said, sir."

"One 'sir' in a sentence will be sufficient, Carey. I said I had orders to report you to your commanding officer. One of the first things a soldier learns is—"

"Pat, my *dear.*" A slight woman, smartly dressed in amethyst crepe, wearing a *lei* of purple and violet pansies, and a purple flower in her white hair, sent her voice ahead as she crossed the *lanai.* "Why aren't you in the ballroom with the other models?"

"Because you told me to meet you here, Aunt Sally."

"General Carrington! Colonel Fulton!" Sally Shaw's voice was a squeal of dismay as she recognized the men in uniform. "Why aren't you inside? Oh dear, won't anything go right if I am a minute late? Go in, Pat, quick."

Patricia downed a natural impulse to remind her aunt that ten minutes was a long time more than one and entered the hotel. Why hadn't Sally told her she knew the principal speaker? Where had she met Cam Fulton? Why shouldn't she know them? She had invited them to speak at this fashion show put on by one of the big mainland *couturiers* for the first time since '41 to raise money for the Disabled Vets Club she had organized. She had persuaded her niece to model the WAC uniform in place of the real WAC who had been transferred to another post at the last minute.

From the wings she watched the professional models walk with measured tempo, grace and style across the stage to the accompaniment of the muted strings and brasses of the Royal Hawaiian Band. The black-haired girl with the brilliantly painted mouth was showing play clothes. The girl with titian hair in the silver gauze frock, modeling the evening line—formals were being worn low and long again—turned to the right, to the left, smiled her bright, meaningless smile.

Something about her flashed a series of two-year-old pictures on the screen of Pat's memory. She was back at the southern Post where she had gone to be maid of honor for a college friend, the daughter of the C.O. The day of her arrival she had met Lieutenant Cameron Fulton. The attraction between them had been an electric spark which had flamed into love. He had told her that first evening as they danced to the music of "Sunday, Monday and Always," at the inn where she was staying:—

"I've been looking for you. You're my dream girl come true." She remembered the effort it had been to laugh, when every pulse was throbbing in response to his persuasive, lovable voice, to answer gaily:—

"I'm amazed that a C.O.'s aide wouldn't think up a more original line, Lieutenant."

"It isn't a line. I've never said that to a girl before. I've never had a girl." His grin disclosed perfect teeth. "Believe me—darling?"

She had nodded. Her voice wouldn't come. Heavenly days followed with all the time he had off duty spent with her, a week in which they had loved and laughed, which had held a sense of high adventure. She remembered the night before the wedding. He was driving her back to the C.O.'s house after the rehearsal at the chapel. She had reminded:—

"I've given you my case history; in case you've forgotten, here is a transcription: I'm really New England, Massachusetts, to be explicit. Since my parents died ten years ago, I've made my headquarters at Silver Ledges in Honolulu with my father's sister, Sally, who married an Islander, John Shaw. Now that I am through college I have signed up for Red Cross work whenever and wherever they want to send me, I am also a Nurses' Aide; but you have told me nothing about yourself."

He had gathered her into his free arm. Her head had quite naturally settled against his shoulder.

"Now we can talk. I've been so knocked in a heap by my love for you that I haven't thought about myself. Here's the story:—

> My name is Norval; on the Grampian hills
> My father feeds his flocks; a frugal swain,
> Whose constant cares were to increase his store,
> And keep his only son, myself, at home.

That was the first declamation I learned at school. Scooped a prize for it. Pretty good, what?"

"Good! You'd be a sensation on the screen," she had responded lightly to counteract her emotional response to his rich voice. "To switch from the poetical to the practical, just what does that burst into verse mean?"

"That my father owns large cattle ranches in Montana, with an oil field or two on the side, though he is anything but a frugal swain; that I had to fight and die before he consented to a law course for me—he wanted me to succeed him on the ranch; but, I have convictions as to what an honest lawyer can accomplish for his state in politics. If I can carry them out I have a lifetime job."

A not too gentle poke in Pat's side snapped the memory film.

"Hey, WAC. Here comes the bride. Gee, but she's a knockout!" the WAVE at her right whispered.

To the soft music of the Wedding March from *Lohengrin* the bride floated across the stage, her gleaming white satin frock deftly simple, her veil a drift of mist over her pale gold hair, her eyes a dream of happiness.

The bride at the Post had looked like that, pale gold hair, if minus the dreamy eyes, Pat remembered, and she remembered that after she had tossed her bouquet of white lilies which her maid of honor caught, Cam had maneuvered that same maid of honor to the garden. All his gaiety was gone, he was in grim earnest as he laid his hands on her shoulders.

"Those solemn words 'to love, to cherish as long as you both do live,' have been echoing through my mind. That's what I want to do, love you, cherish you, darling. Marry me tomorrow? If nothing new breaks I can get ten days' leave and a special license. We can have that bit of heaven together, at least." She recalled the unbearable tightening of her heart as she looked up at him for an answer to the question she dared not ask, What does "at least" mean?

"Will you marry me?" She had pressed her face against his shoulder and nodded in reply to his husky whisper. And then—

"Snap into it, WAC!" It was the excited voice of the WAVE again. "Here's where we make our grand entrance. Gee, but we're getting a hand."

The Colors and their escort took stage center. The models in smart frocks formed a semicircle. The chairman introduced the General, touched on the fact that he and Colonel Fulton had been in the advance wave of infantry to reach the Normandy beachhead on D Day and among the first to enter Germany.

Under her lashes Pat regarded Cam Fulton in the front row of seats. Had seeing her set his memory flashing back as it had hers? Was he remembering the frantic letter she had sent to his quarters in which she had told of her sense of panic when she realized that she had consented to marry and spend her life with a man she hadn't known was in the world a week before?

"I'm starting toward Honolulu at once, back to my Red Cross job. My aunt, Mrs. John Shaw, will know where I am. *Please* don't follow me now. Give me time to think. I mean it."

That last must have given him a laugh, as if a man in the army were free to follow a girl halfway round the world. She hadn't told him that the memory of the bride's flirtatious interest in him had set her wondering if already she realized she had too hastily promised to marry her groom, that she, herself, had taken the reminder as a watch-your-step warning. And after all, she hadn't returned to Honolulu. She had been sent to the European theater. He hadn't answered her letter. Why should he? Why want a girl who was a quitter?

The music of "The Star-Spangled Banner" crashed into her troubled reflections. The audience rose like a vast varicolored wave and lifted fervent voices in song.

As she stepped into the ballroom, Phil Ruskin, her aunt's brother-in-law, a brown-skin Islander, impeccably attired in afternoon dress, hailed her.

"Hi, Pat! You looked like a million even among those professional models. Lady, you're beautiful with your heart-shaped face and shining brown eyes." He tucked her hand under his arm. "Come on to the tea room and partake of the cup that cheers as you draw the line at the cup which inebriates. You need a bracer after this ordeal. Boy, but it was boring, except that General Whosis. He was mercifully brief."

Over his shoulder she glimpsed her aunt, the General and Colonel standing together. The Colonel's eyes, cool, indifferent, met hers. A tingle of apprehension shivered along her nerves. The certainty that she had her fight against heartache all to do over dried her throat.

She looked up at the man beside her. Why couldn't she love him now that Cam had lost interest in her? Suppose he were slightly on the stuffed-shirt side? Suppose he had a narrow, rather tight mouth that suggested chronic disapproval? His dark good looks, to say nothing of being the son of one of the most influential women in Hawaii, one of the most competent sugar technicians in the Islands, on his way to be a delegate to Congress, made him a noticeable and talked-of figure wherever he went.

"How about the drink, Pat?"

"I can't, Phil. I must change to street clothes. I don't belong in these. I may be haled to the hoosegow for wearing them."

"Okay, okay. Why did I fall for a gal with a New England conscience? The real reason you won't come with me isn't because you prefer those officers talking with sister Sal—or is it?"

"Officers! As if officers weren't my daily diet," she countered gaily.

"The Fashion Show was a smash hit, wasn't it, Pat?"

Two hours later, at her aunt's eager question, she turned from the glass wall which made the *lanai* an extension of the living room. The window revealed velvet lawns tinted pink in the afterglow, gay flower borders, the iron door of a bomb-proof shelter among golden shower trees, a rock wall blazing with red Bougainvillia, the round crater of Diamond Head where it thrust its bulk out into the blue and green sea. Color. Gorgeous color everywhere.

"It was a grand show, Sally."

She crossed the room and perched on the arm of a wing chair covered with a bird-of-paradise chintz. From the muted radio came a man's voice singing, "Don't Fence Me In." The mirror above the fireplace reflected Sally Shaw's short white hair, her charming, youthful face with its saucy turned-up nose, her silver-gray costume and the dog collar of lustrous pearls at her throat; gave back Pat's lime-green frock and the copper lights in the sleek swirls of short chestnut hair, the outsize diamond leaves at her ears; a Renoir that Sally had brought from Paris, a gorgeous rug on the floor she had bought in India; the end of a piano; a portion of filled bookshelves, all of light wood, highly polished; a red teakwood table laden with ivory carvings from China, and silver boxes from everywhere, and a bowl of yellow roses on a marqueterie desk.

"I repeat, it was a grand show and did your little Patricia get a shovin' round. Relax, Madam Shaw, while I relate the adventures of Private Carey."

She told the story of the afternoon. Through her mind ran an undercurrent of thought—"Did Cam tell Sally of our meeting at the Post?"

"When the General roared—and I mean roared—'Take her name and company, Colonel,' I thought I would be arrested for being in a uniform I had no right to wear."

"You were there as a model. You put it on in the dressing room, didn't you?"

"I did, but you told me to wait for you in the *lanai*. Our three-star dictator didn't give me a chance to explain. Why are those two officers on the Island?"

"Temporary assignment to Schofield Barracks. Had I

known of the misunderstanding about the uniform I would have straightened it out this afternoon. They are dining with us. I will explain when they come."

"Is the Colonel who took my name to report dining here *tonight?*"

"Yes. Don't hold it against him, Pat, he was merely obeying orders. The General will understand when I explain about the WAC uniform. I've known Sam Carrington since dancing-school days back in our home town, He's peppery but basically warmhearted and tender."

"Is that imposing Major General your onetime adorer, Sammy Carrington?"

"He is." Sally Shaw snapped off the radio commercial. "We quarreled. Smarting with the hurt of what I thought was his injustice I married John Shaw, whom I met on a visit here. Rebound, you've heard of it—that and the magic and beauty of this Island world hypnotized me. When my husband died I knew I had cheated him, though I am sure he was happy with me. That Argus-eyed Islander mother of his, Madam Shaw-Ruskin, knew it too. Even to this day I wince when she looks at me. Added to that is the fact that John left his half of the large Shaw fortune and his Grandmother Shaw's jewels unconditionally to me. She would give those sensational emeralds of hers if she could secure both for her other son, Phil. To return to our muttons. Never accept a substitute for real love, Pat. It is unfair to both man and woman."

Was she warning her niece to watch her step with Phil? As if she had sensed the thought Sally Shaw announced:—

"I met my charming brother-in-law coming out of the Fashion Show with Maida Parsons. She has changed, and not for the better, since she came here with her husband two years ago. He was ordered to Europe last spring and left her here. I remember now, you were maid of honor at her wedding. Something tells me her marriage is on the way out. Too bad. Jim Parsons is the salt of the earth."

Pat thought of Maida's provocative glances at Cam Fulton during the wedding festivities. Apparently then they had made as little impression as drops of water on lava rock and she thought of how the girl's fickleness had increased her own doubts of marriage with a man she had known for a week only. Perhaps Cam had not been so indifferent as he had appeared, perhaps he had known of Maida's presence here, perhaps that had lured him.

"You are staring at my silver boxes as if you had gone into

a trance. Snap out of it, Pat. You are getting the habit and it is a bad one."

"Sorry, Sally. I was thinking back to Maida's wedding. Colonel Fulton, a lieutenant then, was best man."

"Then you had seen him before this afternoon? I suspected it. I felt an electric vibration in the atmosphere. I invited Phil and Maida to dine with us tonight. The General said he would have time for a few hands of contract. I thought the glamorous Maida would be good for the Colonel's morale."

"Why does that need boosting, Madam Fixit?"

"He had a tough break. Having fallen deeply in love with an English girl he was ordered to the Invasion hell before they became engaged, officially at least. He didn't go back to England. Maybe she turned him down. Maida will be plenty good medicine for his bruised ego. She's dynamite. She's danger—to hear her tell it—and Jim is far away."

Pat blinked back stinging tears. While she had spent hours in aching longing for Cam Fulton he had been in love with another girl. Why care? That canceled the harm she thought she had done him, didn't it? Doubtless he was glad now that she had changed her mind. There had been moments when he had slipped into the background, after Monty Dane had joined the outfit with which she was working, she reminded herself honestly. She managed a laugh.

"How should one treat a downhearted fiancé, Sally? As an invalid, or should one pretend ignorance of the *status quo* and give him the come-on?"

"Good heavens, Pat, don't mention it to him. Sam told me of the love affair and swore me to secrecy."

"Hush-hush stuff. For the good of the service I hope the General doesn't impart military secrets to you."

"Of course he doesn't. And equally of course I wouldn't blab them if he did. I can keep a secret, you'd be surprised." Her mouth took on a self-conscious smirk. The sound of a car stopping drifted through the open window. "Here they come."

2

CAMERON FULTON neither looked nor acted like a cast-off swain as in white dress uniform with the D.S.C. and four other multicolor stripes with battle stars on his tunic he entered the living room looming a head taller than the General who preceded him. His gray eyes widened as they met Pat's.

"Private Carey, as I'm alive. I'm not mistaken, the name is Carey?"

"Pat wasn't a real WAC, she was modeling the uniform." Sally Shaw included the two officers in her explanation. "She has been working herself to skin and bones in the military hospital since her return from Red Cross service in the European theater. There's a certain corporal to whom she is devoting hours of time and oceans of sympathy, almost as if she were doing penance for past sins. I persuaded her to take time off for the Fashion Show. You frightened her out of a year's growth, Sam."

"Sorry," the General's grin was infectious, "but she was in uniform and discipline must be maintained."

"I feel honored to be counted in with the military, Sal," interrupted a suave voice from the threshold.

Cameron Fulton turned to look at the man who was urbanely greeting his hostess. Phil was worth looking at, Pat thought, he was positively imposing in white dinner clothes, with a deep red carnation in his coat lapel. Maida Parson's blond coloring, set off by a shimmery, pale blue frock, was an effective foil for his brownness.

"Cam!" she exclaimed and tucked her hand under his arm. "When did you arrive? Why are you here?"

"Orders, Maida. Where is Jim?"

"As usual working his head off somewhere for an ungrateful superior."

"My luck was on the upbeat when I captured you and Phil for the evening, Maida," Sally Shaw declared. "In my brother-in-law and Mrs. Parsons, I have provided two of the best contract players on the Island for you, Sam."

"And one of the prettiest, I'll bet." The General's smile had plenty on the ball. "Didn't the appearance of that kimonoed Chinese maid mean dinner, Sally? I'm starving."

"It did. Maida—"

"Please let me sit beside Cam, Mrs. Sally, we have so much to talk about." She tightened the hand still resting on his arm and looked up at him adoringly. "He was best man at my wedding and I *mean* best. It will be fun having you here, soldier. Good heavens, I've taken it for granted you are neither engaged nor married; say I'm right, Cam."

"There is a *kapu* sign on my heart, Maida. I learned today that the word means 'No admittance,' or, if you like it better, 'Keep out.'"

For an instant she pressed her pale gold hair against his sleeve, looked up at him and laughed.

"I accept the challenge, Colonel."

Dinner was served on the *lanai* on a level with the emerald velvet lawn sown with double violets whose fragrance scented the air. The afterglow had turned the rolling sea to crimson crisped with fluffy white ruffles where it laved the sandy beach. A plane with rose-tipped silver wings hummed overhead and vanished.

With coffee the moon poked a golden rim above a purple mountain. Slowly it rose, sailing like a spirit freed of hampering restraints, till it laid a path of light across the water to the sea wall at the foot of the garden where myna birds were chattering.

Later, by maneuvers at which she was expert, Sally Shaw seated Maida Parsons and sulky Phil Ruskin at a card table within the sliding window wall of the living room.

"Now that the moon is really up to make the world almost as light as day, Colonel Fulton must see our view," she declared as she took the fourth chair. "Not you, Maida. I know your sense of duty to the armed forces but I want you here as an opponent to the General. You are an ace player and he is too cocky about his game. That goes for you too, Phil. Pat will sell our view."

Now what, Pat wondered, as with a white lace scarf glittering with silver sequins across her shoulders she stood beside Cam Fulton in the palm enclosed *lanai*. Before them the full sweep of the bay faded into a faint glow on the horizon. Far out sentinel battleships were silhouetted against the pink, their red and green lights reflected in the water. The dots and dashes of light they flashed, which had seemed pale at first, brightened as the sky darkened. Below, on the beach, a string of lights gleamed like silver balls. From a dark green setting a tower loomed ethereal violet in the moonlight. Palm fronds rustled and clashed like castanets in the flower-scented breeze.

"This is your chance, say you are sorry you welshed, but don't grovel," Patricia mentally advised Pat.

"Must be a gorgeous view in daylight. What's the red light in the sky?" Cameron Fulton inquired.

She relaxed the fingers she had clenched into fists in preparation for her little speech of repentance.

"That is Madam Pele, the Fire Goddess, domiciled in the pit of Mauna Loa, going temperamental. During the war she flung smoke and cinders miles into the sky and hung out a rosy light which drove the authorities responsible for maintaining the blackout almost out of their minds. Miraculously it was kept a military secret and no comments appeared in the papers."

"I'd say that the fact that Japs didn't take advantage of the beacon and blow the Island to pieces was one of the minor marvels of the war. Smoke?" She shook her head.

"Thought you might have acquired the habit in the last two years." He snapped the case shut and thrust it into the pocket of his tunic.

"Then you do remember that we have met before? This afternoon when you asked my name with all the fire and interest of a robot I decided you had forgotten."

"Sure, I remember. You were in WAC uniform. How could I know you weren't in the service? You haven't told your aunt of our little fling at romance, have you? I knew the moment I met her you hadn't. Why? Ashamed of it?"

"No. I didn't return here from the Post as I expected, I was ordered abroad at once. I thought it better to wait until I could talk with her. It is hard to explain in a letter."

"Some letters get a point across with a wallop. The right time hasn't come to tell her yet, I take it?"

"No. When I returned from overseas she was so worn and weary after four years of war work and emotional strain that I hadn't the heart to add my problems. She is beginning to be like her onetime gay self again."

"And still you haven't told her. I arrived in New York two weeks ago, stopped to pick up warm weather uniforms, flew to Montana to see my father, then across the Pacific and here I am. Did you think I wouldn't find you? You and I have some mopping up to do. I don't like being ditched without a chance to answer back. Don't worry, that doesn't mean that I intend to make love to you. You said it when you compared me to a robot. I haven't the slightest interest in you as a woman. Cam Fulton signed off. Your aunt is right. You are thin. What have you done to yourself since you hit and ran?"

"Cam, what a cruel thing to say."

"What a cruel thing to do. You raised me to the peak of

happiness, then dashed me to the pit of heartbreak because you were afraid to face life with me. However, that's water under the bridge. I take it the guy inside with the Little Jack Horner complex is your current special. Who is he?"

"My aunt's brother-in-law."

"Planning to marry him?" The report of a big gun rattled the windows behind him.

"Night practice on a battleship," Pat announced in a nervous attempt to gain time.

"I have heard guns before and not at practice. You haven't answered my question about Ruskin. Do you want to marry him?"

"Could be, though at present I don't want to marry anyone. I don't like your expression, 'current special,' or the 'What-a-big-boy-am-I' slap. Philip Ruskin is an outstanding success in his work—he is so important that he wasn't allowed to enlist. Believe me, it takes brains to be a sugar technician. Phil has them, plus. He's been talked of as a future governor of the Territory."

"What a man! I gathered all that from his grand manner and autobiographical conversation, also that he is lousy with money. Glad you haven't forgotten your *Mother Goose*, Miss Carey. I'd like to make a further test of your memory. Keep that scarf over your shoulders. The breeze has sharpened." He drew the lace higher—quickly withdrew the hand which had touched her hair.

What had he meant by a "further test of memory," Pat had time to wonder before Phil Ruskin slid open the long window behind them.

"Being dummy, I have been sent to relieve the guard," he announced. "Maida demands you for a partner, Colonel."

"Don't tell me you had to be sent, Phil." If the fervor of Pat's reproach was noted by Cam Fulton there was no hint of it in his amused response.

"I'll go at once, but Mrs. Parsons will find she has the wrong slant when she changes, quote, one of the best contract players in the city, unquote, for me. I'm not so hot. Cards do not interest me particularly." The light from the room made him seem impressively tall and military as he paused in the window opening.

"*Aloha*, Pat, in case I'm gone before you come in. Don't stay out too long, that green frock looks thin. Can't have you taking cold."

The possessive note in his voice set Pat's pulses quickstepping. Would he care if she took cold or had he said it to annoy Phil? It was abundantly evident he didn't like him.

"I'll be darned," Philip Ruskin exploded as the window slid into place. "He calls you Pat the first time he meets you and tells you what to do as if you were his girl. Apparently he hasn't found out that you are a touch-not person. What's the big idea?"

"That's just the army way, Phil, you ought to recognize it by this time. Forget him."

"I'll forget him—definitely. For the nth time I'm asking you to marry me. Mother has set her heart on our marriage. It was my idea first, though. We could have a wonderful life together. I can give you everything you want."

Eyes on big tropic stars slowly being put out of business by the moon, she listened to his lengthy and expertly briefed exposition of what he could give her. Luxuries, distinction, the political heights he intended to reach in the Islands and Washington.

"Napoleon and his star," she commented softly. "I believe all you predict about your future, Phil."

She liked him. Suppose she married him? "Rebound, you've heard of it," Sally had said. There wouldn't be much laughter and gaiety. No romance. No high adventure, but wealth, security and distinction, plenty of the last. Like. What a word to use in connection with marriage. Perhaps, though, liking lasted longer than the aching love she had experienced.

"You will marry me, sweet?"

"Pat, our guests are leaving."

Light from the room behind Sally Shaw revealed the change from assurance to anger in his eyes, the tightening of his narrow mouth.

"Okay, okay, Sal. Let 'em leave. We'll be in later."

"We are going in now," Pat corrected. "Come, Phil."

She didn't wait to hear the whole of his muttered protest. Perhaps Cam hadn't left yet, perhaps there would be a chance to say she was sorry; now that she had seen him she couldn't go through another night without his forgiveness. General Carrington stood in front of the low fire in the living room.

"At her suggestion Fulton has taken the attractive Mrs. Parsons to a dance at which she is overdue," he announced. "They should have rationed charm, while they were about it—not fair for one young woman to have so much. That goes for you too, Miss Carey." He smiled his charming smile and confided in a whisper, "I knew who you were in the *lanai*. The Colonel didn't know I knew, though."

"I have promised to look in at a reception, Sally. The Colonel will join me there, we are on the program. Come on, Ruskin, unless you are staying?"

"He is not, Sally Shaw speaking. I'm dead to the world. I would like you both to depart and no delaying action, either."

"That has all the earmarks of an order, Ruskin. Come on."

As the sound of cars started in the drive drifted into the room Sally Shaw dropped to the couch and pulled off her silver sandals.

"Ooch! They hurt. What a day! Even my shoes are tired, to say nothing of my feet. You weren't very polite to my guests, Pat, staying on the balcony for hours with Phil."

"Don't exaggerate, Sally. Not hours, minutes, and not so many of those."

"I assume he proposed again."

"That's right. Sometimes I wonder if he is Opportunity—with a capital O—knocking at my door."

"Opportunity may be a great pal but as personified by Phil Ruskin not so hot as a husband. His mouth tells the story. I'll bet he would be a nagger, the type who would insist upon shopping with you for clothes, and you'd have a constant fight to run your own life free from the domination of his mother. Watch your step, Patricia."

"I've watched it so carefully for two years that I'm all set to break loose and do something crazy."

"Don't do it by marrying unless you are sure you love the man. Already the record of divorces is rocketing. Parents, the clergy, the courts did their best to stop the hasty war marriages. They were beating their heads against bars. The youngsters wouldn't listen."

"Then you don't believe that instantaneous attraction, love at first sight, lasts?"

"Certainly, I believe it lasts in some cases, but if it is the real thing it will survive separation."

"Perhaps some of the seeds of wisdom sprouted. Would you think it justifiable if a girl who had promised to marry a man, at the last moment stopped, looked, listened and broke it off?"

"I would, it's a pity more of them didn't do it. Better then than after marriage. After that, unless there is something criminally wrong, the woman or man of character sticks to the bargain."

"I hear all you say—and I still wonder. The General is in love with you, isn't he?"

"Do you think so?" Sally Shaw's question was hopefully eager. "I'm forty-four and he is ten years older. If he would ask me to marry him I'd pack a bag with a speed that would make a buzz-bomb hide its head in shame and go to the end of the earth with him. Don't look so shocked, honey—of course I mean after having gone through the formality of a marriage service. Good old convention still at the controls."

"I wasn't shocked. I was thinking that was the way a woman should feel about the man she loves. No doubts. No questions. Just faith in him."

"He won't ask me. I was the quitter. Besides, there is my money, he doesn't like that. He'll wait for me to say, 'I love you.' Discipline. That's the army. I can't make myself do that, yet. Suppose he doesn't really care, suppose I just imagine tenderness in his voice. I've got to be sure." She flinched as she drew on a silver sandal. "These things have shrunk since I took them off. That's an admission of advancing years. I'm dead for sleep." She snapped her lips on a yawn.

"Who's phoning at this time of night—not late, though, is it? Our guests left early. Answer, Pat. If it's someone wanting me on another committee say I'm off to the Mainland— or any other old place—tomorrow."

"Yes. Yes." Pat spoke into the receiver of the telephone in the hall. On the threshold of the living room her aunt listened. "Who? *Who? Monty!* For heavens' sake, what brought you to this part of the world? You are? Of course I'll be glad to see you." She put her hand over the transmitter.

"It is Captain Montgomery Dane, Sally, an officer I met in Germany. He's at the Moana."

"I remember. Your letters were full of him. Ask him to dine with us tomorrow."

"He wants to drop in and say 'Hello' tonight. He is practically next door."

"Tonight. He is the eager swain. Let him come. I'll try to stay awake long enough to say *aloha.*"

Pat spoke into the transmitter, rang off and laughed. "Because I said 'we' would love to see him, he asked if I were married," she explained as she followed her aunt into the living room.

"What did you say?"

"What *would* I say?"

"Hold everything, honey. Your voice when you answered him gave the impression that you didn't care particularly to see him; telling him you were married might detour him. A harmless white lie. You wrote a lot about him. To be honest I was a little worried. Many nights I have lain awake praying not only for your bodily safety but for—" The sentence ended in a long, unsteady breath.

"I know what you mean. You were praying for my moral and spiritual safety as well, weren't you?" Arm on the mantel, Patricia looked down at the fire. Her face reflected the glow of rosy coals. "It had considerable shoving round but my invincible New England conscience held fast in the face of temptation." That and my love for Cam, she added to herself.

"Then there was temptation?"

"Right. I wasn't immune. After the horror of days and nights of ceaseless thunder of guns, searing blasts of exploding shells, of fear that, valiant as you tried to be, made you want to run like crazy, which kept the throat dry, nerves taut to the snapping point, seeing girls with whom you had shared quarters bloody and lifeless, men whom you liked fly away and not return, made the arms of a man you thought loved you, the feel of his shoulder against your cheek, heaven, just heaven. When I reached that stage my conscience flashed a warning and I asked for an exchange to the Belgian front and got it. After that I didn't see Monty again."

Sally Shaw regarded her niece from above the mirror of a compact from which she was powdering her nose.

"Couldn't you have married the man?"

"I couldn't. For one reason he wasn't free. He told me he had a wife after I had refused to week-end with him in a villa on the Riviera he had borrowed."

"Perhaps Captain Dane's wife has freed him and he has come to ask you to marry him."

"I doubt it. I haven't money enough to lure him. His wife is spectacularly rich and holds onto her money with a grip of steel, I was told. What he professed for me wasn't the sort of love for which a man deserts wealth. Looking back, I realize now that I never really trusted him. A car is stopping."

She forgot her anger, remembered only the pleasant part of their friendship, the dangers they had shared, and ran to open the door.

"Monty! It's wonderful to see you!"

The tall, dark-haired, dark-eyed man in the infantry uniform of the United States Army, with two silver bars on the shoulder of his khaki tunic, dropped a brief case to grasp her hands.

She drew him into the living room.

"Aunt Sally, this is Captain Dane. He—" Had another car stopped outside?

"We are happy to welcome you here, Captain. I feel that I know you through Patricia's letters."

"The same here, Mrs. Shaw, Pat used to talk by the hour about you and this home—"

"Sorry to interrupt this tender reunion." Cam Fulton entered from the foyer. "General Carrington sent me back for the address you promised him, Mrs. Shaw. How are you, Captain?"

Monty Dane nodded curtly. Sally Shaw swallowed an obstruction in her throat.

"Sam is so forgetful," she deplored. "Pat, you and the Captain must have a lot to talk over. Show him the view from the *lanai* while I rummage in my desk for the address. And I mean rummage; order may be heaven's first law, but it isn't mine."

Before the glass wall slid shut, Pat heard her say:—

"Now, Cam, what is this all about?"

3

"BEHOLD the prize view of the Island, if you believe Sally Shaw," Pat announced gaily even while she was asking herself why Cam had returned. Had he regretted his sternness to her? Had he come to tell her he loved her? Sally had said that real love survived separation. Crazy thought. As if his could after she had broken her word to him. "Hit and run" he had branded her change of mind at the Post. Sally had called him "Cam." Apparently she had gone all out for him as quickly as her niece had.

"I don't give a hang for the prize view, lovely." Monty Dane's voice recalled her to the present. "I came to see you."

"Take your arm from my shoulders quick, Monty, or you will be left to enjoy the scenery alone."

"Okay, okay." He lighted a cigarette. "Afraid of me, Pat?"

His self-confident laugh infuriated her. How could she have thought she loved him?

"Your mistake. I'm not afraid of you—or of anything any more. I'm a big girl now. I just don't care to have you touch me, that's all."

"Is that so? Unless my memory has been blacked out —it hasn't—you've changed mightily since the night—"

Her heart broke into quickstep as memory flashed the picture with sound effects of a wrecked ambulance in the midst of flames and stifling smoke, of shouts and screams of agony, of a voice calling, "Pat! Pat!" In answer she had flung herself into this man's arms. As they closed protectingly about her she had thought for a frantic second that she loved him.

"Remembering?" he observed complacently.

"It's not necessary to remind me of that moment of horror, Monty. It is burned into my brain. You, if anyone, should realize there is no account for one's reactions in the midst of war."

"What do you mean by that 'you, if anyone'?" His hand was tight on her arm.

"Now you sound frightened. I meant that you were no more really in love with me than I with you. Here at home, my sense of values is swinging steady as a clock pendulum."

"Is Fulton responsible for that?"

"You mean *Colonel* Fulton? Hardly, as I saw him on the Island for the first time this afternoon." Which was quite true; never before had she seen him on the Island. "He knew you. Where did you two meet?"

"He was attached to our outfit in Germany after V-E Day and was responsible for a group of U.S. scientists who were on the trail of the reports that would reveal the secret of how Germany kept the war rolling five years with only a limited supply of natural gas. This country, any country, could use that knowledge—and how. Did he speak of his assignment?"

"No. Did the scientists find the reports?"

"I wouldn't know. Whatever they discovered would be hush-hush if Fulton had the say. Why waste time on him? You haven't asked why I have followed you across two oceans and a continent."

"Sure you came just to see me, Monty?"

"What do you mean?"

"There you go again, snapping off my head when I ask a simple question. I imagined you had been sent to Schofield Barracks for duty. How did you get here?"

"I was in luck. Got a priority on a Clipper—the ships are still being used for transport. I'm on terminal leave. My number one reason for coming was to tell you that I have asked my wife for a divorce, so that I can marry you."

"Sorry you went to all that trouble before you consulted me. Thanks a lot, but I'll never marry you."

"Still sore because I asked you to go on leave with me?"

"No." The sound of a ship's bell drifted across the water. Six slow, resonant strokes. "Eleven o'clock. Aunt Sally has had a long, hard day. I suggest that you say good-night and depart, Monty."

"And this is the Island hospitality I've heard so much about. It's a 'here's your hat, what's your hurry' hand-out you're giving me." As he pushed back the glass wall for her to enter he whispered, "Never is a long time, Pat."

Cam Fulton was holding a light to Sally Shaw's cigarette when they entered the living room.

"I waited to ask if I could drive you into town, Captain," he announced. "Your taxi was leaving just as I drove in. Evidently the driver misunderstood."

"That was swell of you, Colonel. You won't have to take me far, just to the Moana. I covered that guy's palm with gold—figuratively speaking—for bringing me here and told him to wait. Being a Filipino he didn't understand my English, apparently. Good night, Mrs. Shaw. I'll be here to-morrow with a car as planned, Pat, and we'll go dining and stepping somewhere. Ready when you are Colonel."

Pat didn't hear what Cam Fulton said in reply or farewell, her thoughts had been busy framing a flaming denial of a plan to drive with Monty Dane. Before she had a sufficiently devastating one ready the two men were out of the house.

"That's that." Sally Shaw's words came more as a relieved sigh than a voice. "Far be it from me to probe the secrets of your love life, honey, but if you've never really trusted the man why did you promise to drive with him tomorrow?"

"I didn't. I won't—" Pat thought of Cam's cynical eyes as for an instant they met hers while Monty was making his explanation. After all, why not go? Monty could be entertaining and good fun. Even in the horror of war he had proved that. She thought of Maida's hand on Cam's arm, of her provocative glance up into his eyes, of her laughing, "I accept the challenge, Colonel."

"On second thought I will go with Captain Dane," she declared. "Why did Colonel Fulton return? There was something ersatz about his excuse that the General sent him for an address."

"It was straight goods. I had told Sam Carrington that Mother Shaw-Ruskin was giving a high tea tomorrow and invited him to meet us there with the Colonel. It is the first time she has entertained since December 7, 1941. Having heard of it as one of the show places on the Island, his acceptance was prompt. Before I could give him directions for finding it we were interrupted. I like Cam Fulton. He has force, integrity and imagination. He will have ideals about living that he'll achieve."

The sadness in her voice reminded Pat that her husband had been easy-going and too convivial; if he had a pattern of life it had been to indulge his reckless desires to the limit.

"You have made quite a study of the Colonel in two meetings, Sally. I had forgotten the Queen Mother's tea. All right if I take Monty?"

"You could do nothing that would please her more. She adores men, endures women. This time I'm really off to bed. If another of your stag line appears you'll have to entertain him yourself. Here's a black brief case in the foyer. Your Captain must have left it."

"I'll take it to my room, then I will remember to give it to him when he comes tomorrow." As they went up the stairs she protested, "Don't call him my Captain, Sally. He is married. He told me tonight that he has asked his wife to divorce him."

"I don't like that. I don't like it at all." Sally Shaw entered her softly lighted, amethyst-color bedroom in a little whirl of indignation.

"Take it easy, Sally, why get in a rage about persons you don't know?"

"All right for you to laugh, Pat, can't you see what harm it could do you? Suppose she won't consent? Suppose she really loves him, is determined to hold onto him and knows that you and he were in the same outfit overseas? Now he is here. What's to prevent her from dragging you into a mess as a corespondent? She may have nothing else to hang on him."

Pat's heart stopped and thudded on. Her laugh did her credit.

"That's a lovely possibility to dream on. Good night, Sally Shaw."

Darn Monty Dane, she thought, as she slipped out of the lime-color frock. Why had he come? Sally's suggestion that his wife might drag her into a divorce court was absurd. Seated before the mirror of her dressing table she brushed furiously her short waved hair till gleams of gold shone in the chestnut.

Suppose the woman did drag her in? It would be horribly unpleasant but there would be no truth in whatever charges she might make. The night the ambulance had been wrecked, for perhaps five minutes she had clung to him, he had kissed her hard and fast, then had whispered that they would take their leaves together. The suggestion had brought her out of the tailspin of fright, had been like a bucket of ice water splashed on her mind, and she remembered that she had answered with a scornful fury that had set his mouth agape. After that she had seen him but once before she left for the Belgian front. Let his wife make anything out of that if she could. Now he was barging into her life again. Why?

In turquoise blue crepe pajamas she sat up in bed, her bare arms tanned to golden brown, hugging her knees, and looked about the big lovely room which had been hers for years as if seeing it for the first time. Turquoise and cream color curtains beside the long windows open on a balcony; painted blue bed and dressing table laden with crystal and silver appointments; soft cream rugs on the polished floor; a slim crystal vase with one perfect pink rose beside the telephone on the desk, its fragrance spilled by the soft wind that stole through the open window; framed pictures of friends on table and mantel. Not one of Cam.

The gold clock on the table beside the bed ticked rhythmically, the night light threw soft shadows in the corners as she tried to recapture the magic mood of that marvelous week with him. She tightened her arms around her knees and stared at the sea and sky visible between the curtains, not seeing the ship lights flashing at each other or the long wands of light from the forts crossing and wheeling till the stars were mere pricks of gold in the blueblack canopy of sky.

She was seeing Cam's eyes as they had looked deep into hers. He had seemed so young, so gay, so fearless of the horrors of the war he was so soon to face, so passionately in love with her. Now he was stern, uncompromising. His laugh, which had been boyish, held no hint of gaiety. As to love, she might as well have been a dummy in a shop window for all the feeling he had shown when he saw her in the hotel *lanai*. Had the English girl done that to him? Had the war worked the change or had her flight without seeing him again been responsible? The truth was she had been afraid to see him, afraid that the mere touch of his hand would change her mind.

Of course she had been a coward. Equally of course she had paid for it in aching longing for him and the smarting awareness that she had been the worst kind of quitter as day after day passed without the letter for which she hoped. In her work overseas she had tried to square it by marching straight up to the firing line no matter how terrified she was, hoping in some measure to ease the constant hurt of living with a self of whom she was ashamed. Then, as the days and months passed the week at the Post receded. It began to seem like a radiant dream from which she had wakened to the reality of blood, destruction and sudden death.

A scream shocked her back to the present and out of bed in a ballerina leap. She pulled on her blue satin house coat, thrust her feet into matching scuffs and ran to the balcony. The sound had come from the servants' cottage. Mrs. Wong Chun, the cook, and her sister, Sib Lou, the second maid, were there alone tonight. Wong Chun, who was gardener and general man, had gone to evening school in the city. He would spend the night at the house of his mother.

She ran lightly down the stairs, through the living room, across the *lanai* and the lawn to the small house half buried in climbing roses and vines. A light burned beside the door. The excited chatter inside stopped after her knock.

"Who's there?" a girl's shaky voice inquired.

"Miss Patricia, Sib Lou. I heard a scream. Let me in."

The door was opened just enough for her to squeeze through, closed again with a resounding bang. Mrs. Wong Chun's cheeks, usually as rosy as the red cherries on her kimono, were colorless. Sib Lou's lips were white as her pajamas, her dark eyes between their slightly slanting lids were brilliant with excitement. The two women jabbered in excited unison. Pat put her fingers over her ears.

"Wait a minute," she protested. "Speak English, I can't understand a word you are saying. Sib Lou did you scream?"

"Yes, miss, it was a man." The little maid's voice stuck in her throat. She began again. "He knocked at my window. First I hid under the bedclothes. Then I peeked. I could see his face. It was all lighted up, like—like that awful man in the movies. I'll never forget it."

"Was it anyone you had seen before?"

"I couldn't be sure, Miss Pat. He—he—was an officer. Something silver shone on his shoulder when he moved."

4

"IN that pale green frock with the pink flower in your hair you look like the original dream walking," Monty Dane approved as Patricia came down the stairs the next afternoon. "Eureka, you have my black brief case. I had been in a business conference before I came here last evening. I've had a bad attack of jitters trying to remember where I had it last."

"Now that can be off your mind."

"Charge my memory lapse to the dumb driver who walked out on me. I was so mad I forgot the brief case, mad to think I had been left and madder that I had to accept a favor from Colonel Fulton, who never liked me. Did you open it?"

"Certainly not, so relax, Monty. I don't pry into another person's affairs."

"No insult intended, lovely." The lightness of his voice didn't quite disguise his evident relief. "You might have looked inside to find out to whom it belonged, without being accused of prying, mightn't you? You had other guests last evening." He threw in the clutch and the open maroon roadster shot ahead. "Corking day for our together-again celebration, what?"

As he sent the car smoothly along the paved highway bordered by hedges of hibiscus in all colors and shapes, he kept up a running fire of amusing comment and conversation. From the corners of her eyes Pat regarded him. He appeared not to have a care on his mind, and not in the least like a person who would tap on a maid's window at midnight. Why think it was he? She glanced at his captain's bars. "Something silver shone on his shoulder," Sib Lou had said. Cam Fulton wore a silver eagle. If it had been he—of course it hadn't. There were hundreds of men in army uniform on the Island. Sib Lou had been half awake probably and the face had been the fragment of a dream.

"How come? Does that long-drawn breath mean you have solved the problem you've been working on since we started?" Monty Dane's annoyed question smashed head-on into her train of thought. "I'll bet you haven't a sliver of knowledge of what I've said."

"Wrong. I'll prove it." She straightened in her seat and settled the blush pink camellia more firmly in her hair. "First, you said that as you saw Honolulu from the ship—by the way, Hon like *hone*—you thought it was the loveliest city you had seen and waxed slightly poetical as to the way it fitted itself to the curve of the land from Diamond Head to Pearl Harbor. Right?"

"Right so far. Go on."

"You remarked on the way the mountain thrust its bulk out into the iridescent open sea—just there I suspected you had memorized the blurbs of a travel folder. You had started on the loveliness of Hawaiian women, their glowing smiles, sleek hair and soft voices when you suddenly broke into your peroration to question my attention. Right?"

"Right again. I'll bet you have a double-track mind for in spite of your glib transcription I know you were thinking of something else. How clearly the battleships stand out against the blue mountains."

"Aren't they grand? The mere sight of them sets my heart glowing, gives me a feeling of security."

"Chalk up one for a battleship if it can set your heart aglow. I've heard that your New England once was buried in a thousand feet of ice. I'll say that it hasn't thawed in you yet."

Pat met his eyes in the windshield mirror and wrinkled her nose in laughing derision.

"Cheerio, Monty. It will melt—in time. I like it slightly iced. It is a lot more comfortable to live with. Here's where I go into my Island-guide act. We are now passing a sugar plantation. At the first outbreak of war the equipment of this and all other plantations was at once put at the disposal of the armed forces."

"I heard on the Clipper coming over that large areas of productive land were sacrificed to military necessity. That goes for each community in its own way the country over, I'll bet. No wonder we are having the hell of a time getting reconverted. What was the idea dragging me to this party? I wanted you alone. I have a lot to tell you."

"I had to come or Aunt Sally would have been the target of her mother-in-law's wrath. Her invitation is like a command performance, you have to appear—or else. Mrs. Shaw-Ruskin—she had two husbands and keeps both names—was the mother of my aunt's husband, John Shaw. Phil Ruskin, whom you will meet this afternoon, a typical Islander in his psychology and character, is the son by the second marriage."

"Sounds like *Who's Who*."

"It does, but the party will be a lot more interesting if you know something about your hostess. Madam Shaw-Ruskin is *kamaaina,* old-timer to you. Her family goes back to the first missionaries who settled on the Island, and was a power in the court when there was a court here. She speaks several languages, is majoring in Spanish at present. To ignore her invitation is to become a social outcast, from her point of view. She never questions her power to rule her small universe. She uses charm, money, brains to get her way. If those weapons fail she still has her vitriolic tongue which can shrivel a person's reputation or confidence in herself."

"Golly, she sounds like the wicked Queen in *Snow White*. Why expose me to her evil machinations?"

"Because you'll love the party, it will be right up your street. The F.F.'s of Hawaiian society and every member of what Sally calls the 'aristocracy of talent' on the Island—writers, artists, sculptors, musicians and composers—will be among those present."

"Sounds deadly to me. Will there be hula girls?"

"Sorry to black out that note of hope in your voice, Captain, but dollars to dimes there won't. There will be delicious eats, Mainland type—our hostess doesn't lean toward native dishes for tea—and drinks of every known variety and a number known only to the Chinese butler. She believes she is psychic, that she can read a person's mind. Watch your step, Monty, she may feel an urge to take a hand in your destiny."

The road ran past long furrows of rich brown earth, patches of pale green spears pushing upward; taller, larger spears; then waving tassels of cane so high that a worker standing beside them shrank to pigmy proportions. Trucks loaded with cane passed. The air was sweet with the smell of sugar from burning piles of trash. Bamboo fences enclosed small gardens, bamboo awnings shaded windows.

While he drove he told of his plan to go to South America, explained that he had been assured there would be gilt-edged opportunities for an architect.

"South America! Why go there when thousands and thousands of houses need to be built on the Mainland? The lack of housing here is getting to be tragic. People are living in cellars. Madam Shaw-Ruskin and her son are planning to build on land they own."

"Not the type I want to design. I'll make a lot of money and I can't leave Velma till I do. How come you know so much about the housing shortage?"

"I read papers, magazines, and occasionally a book. You'd be surprised how up-to-the-minute Hawaiians are on world affairs, Captain." He laughed.

"No crack at your intelligence intended, lovely."

The maroon roadster rounded a sharp curve in the road designed to preserve a mammoth banyan tree whose roots clutched at the earth like prehistoric claws.

"Here we are. My word, what a lot of cars. The World and his Wife, the Social world, capital S, have come to this party. That Chinese chauffeur is wigwagging to you, Monty.

Better move *wikiwiki*, which means 'quick' in case you don't know. Li Chang is a czar in his domain."

"I don't know anything about this island," Dane growled as they left the car parked under a monkey tree. "I speak but one language, American, so stick close this afternoon, lovely, and steer me clear of social quicksands. What a house! I'll forgive you for dragging me here. That's something to write home about."

It was, Pat agreed. A large, low, sprawling house of cream-color plaster old enough to be mellow, that had turned a golden claret in the light of the slanting sun, where it wasn't obscured by pale yellow climbing roses and long-leaved vines. In a distant haze behind it loomed the sheer cliffs of the *Pali*. In front, lawns smooth as emerald plush sloped to a flower border against a lava wall. Far away stretched a vast expanse of indigo ocean. Swelling rollers broke into milky green, thinned to many colored shallows before they ruffled whitely against a sandy beach. Beyond the rollers battleships and destroyers tugged and swung at anchor. Above a mountain a little cloud blushed rosily in the steam from a volcano crater.

"This is so extravagantly beautiful it sends shivers along my veins," Pat confided. "Heavenly sounds. Those ukuleles and guitars are Hawaiian music at its best."

"I've told every little star," she hummed to the accompaniment of strings. Something, perhaps it was the music, released her imprisoned spirit from the fog of self-condemnation in which she had lived for two years, set her free in a sunshiny present. This must be the way a flier felt when he had won his wings.

"I'd like to see every inch of this house." Monty Dane's enthusiastic voice brought her back to earth. "How'll I go about making myself solid with—what did you call her?"

"Madam Shaw-Ruskin with a hyphen."

"Had I better begin by kissing her hand? I do it the French way. Got to be rather good at it in what was once gay Paree."

"She will love that. Straighten up. Look your most military. She likes the army. She will give me the once-over through her jeweled lorgnon and observe disapprovingly:—

" 'You are still losing flesh, *Pat*—ricia.' She accents the first syllable of my name till it sounds like that of a contender for the heavyweight championship of the world."

Was it really she speaking so gaily? Was it possible that her lighthearted self, the girl Cam Fulton had loved, was on the way back? Why not? Why spend the rest of her life repenting a mistake? After all, had it been a mistake to welsh on her promise to Cam? The way it had been done had been cowardly of course, but when he fell for the English girl that canceled it, didn't it?

"No." The word sounded as clearly in her mind as if a voice had spoken. "You never have been honest with yourself. Never have dragged into the glaring light of memory the bleak cruelty of your act, never have faced squarely what you did."

"Snap out of it, Pat!" Monty Dane's grip on her arm emphasized his words. "Every little while your spirit slips into another world. Concentrate on me. Give my introduction the works. I want the entree here. Already I have a line on adapting this entrance and room to a house plan I have in mind. What a lot of loot from everywhere."

It had more the look of a museum than a home. The glass doors of the foyer had been folded back to make it part of the long drawing room whose walls were mostly floor-to-ceiling windows, each one revealing a view of surpassing beauty. The few spaces walled in native mahogany were hung with rare, colorful Chinese or Polynesian embroideries or shelved to hold choice porcelains and ivories. Chairs and tables had been removed to make room for the guests—lovely women in trailing princess-style *holokus* in soft pastel shades with *leis* to complement them, and a flower in their smooth hair, and army and navy officers and Islanders in white, and men with a gold discharge button in the coat lapel.

A dark-haired woman in a deep red frock caught Pat in her arms, pressed her lips to one cheek and then the other.

"*Bon jour, Chérie, vous me semblez heureuse, vous paraissez élégante, tout à fait charmante,*" she declared breathlessly. "*Je reviendrai! Je reviendrai,*" she added before she dashed away.

"For crying out loud, where did that buzz-bomb come from?" Monty Dane demanded. "What did it say?"

"That was Madam Shaw-Ruskin's companion, Suzette. She has lived here for years. She manages the house from kitchen to flower arrangements. She speaks English perfectly. In moments of exuberance she breaks into her native language. I love her. In case you are interested she said that I looked smart and altogether charming."

"As if I didn't know. Is that our hostess in the thronelike chair on the dais at the end of the room? What a gall! She has a royalty complex and how. What's the yellow thing hanging from her neck?"

"A feather *lei*. They are rare now. Her emerald and dia-

mond collar would finance the production of a B-29, her
white frock with glints of gold is Adrian at his best, and
most costly, the up-to-the-minute hair-do—no silver threads
among that black—and the perfect make-up are by Suzette.
Any more questions, Captain?"

"Like the M-G-M newsreel, you have covered the subject. Handsome creature. I bet those dark eyes 'looked love
to eyes which spake again.' Byron is the only poet I can
quote. How old is she?"

"*Captain,* I am surprised. You, a man of the world, snooping as to a lady's age."

"Right on the crest of the wave with your kidding this
afternoon, aren't you, lovely? It wouldn't be because we are
together again, would it? Our hostess smiled. Gosh, what perfect teeth. The real McCoy?"

"Every pearl her own."

"What a crowd. If one may judge from the 'Hi, Pats,'
you know everyone here. We are slowly but surely being
propelled throneward."

When they reached their hostess Pat's heart zoomed to
her throat and dropped with a dull thud. Cam Fulton, in
white uniform, standing with one foot on the dais, hands
clasped about his raised knee, was smiling and talking with
Madam Shaw-Ruskin. He straightened as if to leave.

"Don't go, Colonel," she protested before she glanced at
the girl who had paused to speak to her. "Oh, it's you, *Pat—*
ricia. At last. Phil has been almost out of his mind since
he discovered that you did not come with Sally. Got your
color back, I see, and the laughter that was in your eyes before you left the Island." She swept Monty Dane from head
to foot with a quick, jealous glance. "Are you responsible for
the renascence, Captain?"

"Your majesty." He rose to the question with a lot more
speed than a hungry trout to a fly, bent his head and raised
her extended hand to his lips with an easy grace that would
have put any one of the romantic lads in Hollywood to shame.
"Rather good at it," he had said. "Good" was an understatement, he was an ace.

"Are you a psychic, majesty, that you see into a situation
so quickly? Divine that my presence has restored our Patricia's
lovely gaiety?"

Pat was uncomfortably aware of the tide of color which
swept to her hair, of Cam Fulton's slightly raised brows as
he regarded her in cool appraisal.

"What is your name, Captain?" There were hints of acid
in Madam Shaw-Ruskin's smooth voice, like the occasional

steely glint of a bayonet in a distant company of marching men. "Unnecessary to inquire whence. Hollywood indubitably."

"Cancel that out, your majesty. Never have been in the town. Name, Montgomery Dane. Profession, architect, until Uncle Sam needed help; now, I am about to become a private citizen once more looking for a job."

"Hmp. I presume *Pat*—ricia brought you, not the hope of commissions? I am planning to build houses on my land. You may be useful. Sit here." She indicated the chair at her left. "I am almost through greeting the late arrivals, then I will talk to you. Colonel, escort Miss Carey to the *lanai* for refreshments. You met at my daughter-in-law's last evening, I understand. Phil will be there to relieve you. Be here at four tomorrow, I have an important matter to discuss with you."

"Yes, your majesty." The perfect imitation of the nuances of Monty Dane's voice and his manner turned the Captain's face a dark and indignant red.

"Forcible feeding for you, Pat," Cam Fulton commiserated as they crossed the wide hall together. "Where does the lady get that 'Come here, go there' complex? I don't like her outrageous manners or her corrosive smile. Apparently she has just acquired a court jester suited to her taste. Was she right? Has Dane restored your 'lovely gaiety'?"

She ignored the question. It might contain a hidden mine or two and she couldn't handle an explosion of temperament here.

"Madam Shaw-Ruskin is a power and knows it. Monty used the perfect approach when he called her psychic. She thinks she is. When she isn't busy ferreting out secrets in the lives of friends and acquaintances, she is giving advice. She reminds me of the gods and goddesses who were everlastingly running up and down Olympus barging into the private lives of mortals."

"You speak feelingly! Has she been probing your life for secrets? Have you a few?"

"Fifty-seven varieties, what girl hasn't?"

"The Phil to whom she referred was the man at dinner last night, I gathered. Sounded to me as if she coveted you for a daughter."

"Could be. Nothing official about it yet, though. We seem to be the first in the *lanai*. Either we are early for refreshments or the guests are all in the lower *lanai* from which rise sounds of revelry. Aren't the tables lovely? No tea. Make mine that pineapple juice Maida is serving from the enormous crystal punch bowl. I'll wait here and enjoy the charm of the setting. Sometimes I think I'm a little mad about color."

"Safe thing to be mad about. I'll go for your drink."

She sat on the arm of a Chinese peel and reed chair with sailcloth cushions of turquoise blue and whistled to a parrot, a stab of brilliant green in a gilded cage. Orchids were growing in the verticals, palm fronds rattled on three sides. To avoid seeing Cam greet the lovely woman in a frock as gold as her hair, who had eagerly stepped forward to meet him, she looked off to sea. It was a blue day. Sky, mountains, ocean were pale blue, even the distant battleships were slightly tinged with navy.

Her glance returned to the *lanai*. Two large round tables with exquisite covers of Filipino lace and centerpieces of golden bowls filled with yellow and blue snapdragon offered a tempting array of sandwiches, canapés and cakes. Four handsome women in white with matching gardenias in their sleek black hair and *leis* of yellow jasmine presided at the massive silver tea and coffee urns. Men's voices and laughter, the lighter laughter of women, and the clink of glass rose from below. Pat could see Chinese boys in dark blue linen coats and wide loose trousers passing trays and glasses.

"Here you are." Cam Fulton presented a small green lacquer tray. "Pineapple juice as ordered. Maida selected the sandwiches and canapés. They look eatable."

"They are. If you don't believe me, try one of these toasted mushroom rolls. They are heavenly."

"Must be to make you look like that. Why aren't you wearing a *lei*? You are the only female here without one."

"The beau who brought me isn't up on the customs of the Islands yet. He'll learn. That is an exquisite creation of yellow cypripedium orchids Maida is wearing. I wonder who the current special is—your phrase, not mine—who sent her that lovely thing?"

"I heard you." Maida Parsons sent her voice ahead as she approached. "Why don't you tell her you did, Cam?"

Instinctively Pat raised is-that-true eyes, lowered them quickly as they met his.

"Maida," a woman behind a coffee urn called, "you are needed at the punch bowl." As the girl in the golden frock hurried back to her post to serve a group of guests, Pat laughed.

"Don't look so guilty, Cam. It has been done before."

"What?"

She knew it wasn't true, a voice in her mind warned, "Don't say it," but she went on just the same.

"Making love to another man's wife."

"Does that mean you think I would be justified in betraying my friend? You have changed your standards in these last years."

"Oh," she shrugged. "One has to keep up with an expanding world viewpoint." The voice in her mind spoke sharply. "You know that belief in fidelity in marriage is a basic part of your creed for living."

"I don't like your flippancy. You—"

"For Pete's sake, Pat." Phil Ruskin darted toward her with the speed of an actor late for his cue. "I thought this would fade on me before I found you." He dropped a *lei* of blush pink camellias with tiny violet orchids over her head. Their color lighted her green frock, her face reflected the soft color.

"Glad to see you here, Colonel. Where have you been keeping yourself, Pat? Mother said you arrived half an hour ago. Who's her new boy friend? She's holding him by the power of her eye, putting on the Ancient Mariner act, and he's fidgeting like the Wedding Guest."

"That is Captain Montgomery Dane, Pat's escort," Cam Fulton explained smoothly. "No wonder he is fidgeting, to be kept so long from her. You must be an artist, Ruskin, to have selected such a perfect *lei* to complement her costume; practice makes perfect, perhaps. Now that she has you for company I will investigate the cause of that ribald laughter drifting up from below. I'll be seeing you later, Patricia." His eyes rested on the pink camellias before he turned away.

Phil Ruskin's frown of annoyance accentuated the dark brownness of his face.

"Something about that guy gets under my skin." Pat realized that his petulant voice when matters did not suit him was one of the traits that kept her from deeply liking him. "Is he that way about you?" he demanded with sudden, sharp suspicion.

She laughed; she hoped it would get by as a laugh.

"Take a look at that sensational orchid *lei* Maida is wearing. He sent it to her. That's your answer."

5

SMOKING, thinking, Cam Fulton strolled across the lawn.
He laughingly shook his head in answer to an officer waving to him from the crowded, noisy lower *lanai* and followed the path bordered with soft pinks, blues, yellows and
whites of fragrant perennials to a lava wall. The faint thrum
of steel, ukuleles and guitars was audible above the susur-
rus of the sea on the sandy shore below where a solitary GI
was pacing back and forth swinging a stick.

His glance shifted from the broken foot cliffs at the edges
of a high mountain to the purple shadows in the forge at its
base, but he was seeing Pat's eyes as they questioned him
about the orchid *lei*. Had she cared? To find an answer to
that question was why he had accepted an assignment to
this island on a confidential mission when he was eager to
return to his home to commence to carry out the ambition
which had germinated in his mind and imagination when he
was a boy, to be governor—and a good one—of his state.

The plan had been given tragic impetus one night in officers' mess, almost cheek to cheek with the German front,
when his best friend, Bob Maitland, had slapped a two-
months'-old newspaper violently against his knee and
flared:—

"Why doesn't the President tell himself, 'To hell with
1948! I'll set some things right I know are wrong if I'm
snowed under for it at the next election!' A little of that
spirit in Washington and we'd get a clean-up that would
set the world's eyes bulging even if a new Congress re-
sulted. Boy, feel the walls shake. That fella almost had
our number."

And he recalled that after the din of the exploding shell
had subsided he had heard a man's voice coming from the
phonograph in the other room, singing:—

> O beautiful for spacious skies,
> For amber waves of grain,

And he remembered that he had listened to the heart-
warming voice a second before he answered Maitland.

"To return to the subject so rudely interrupted, I don't
believe that a turnover in Congress would result from an

honest clean-up. The American people want their representatives to have hearts and guts to match those of the men who have given their lives for them. I'll bet they'd burn up the wires prodding senators and representatives, 'Go to it, boys,' or words to that effect."

"If that's the way you feel, Cam, why in God's name when, if or as you reach home don't you get into the fight to establish integrity in high places? There's always a group fighting for it somewhere. You're the type of citizen who ought to be in politics. You have money—you won't be tempted to sell your soul for thirty pieces of silver. You have brains, superb health in spite of the ripped shoulder, legal training, what in earlier days was known as principles and—"

Even here in a world at peace, he clenched his hands till the nails cut, closed eyes and ears as if to shut out sight and sound, but still he could hear the crash that blew in one side of the building, smell and taste the smothering clouds of plaster dust, see little scarlet-yellow flames lick through them, and when the air cleared, his friend in a bloody, huddled heap on the floor, one uninjured hand clutching the newspaper, and he could hear the strong vibrant voice in the next room:—

> America! America!
> God mend thine every flaw,
> Confirm thy soul in self-control,
> Thy liberty in law!

He had taken the survival of the phonograph in that destructive blast as an omen of the certain victory of right over the powers of evil trampling the world under their iron heels.

There had been weeks of desperate fighting after that. Often in the sinister silence which preceded the burst of a shell he would hear Maitland's voice, "Why in God's name when, if or as you reach home don't you barge into the fight to establish integrity in high places?"

After V-E Day had come the order to escort and protect the U.S. scientists who were searching for ersatz gas formulas. He remembered that he had protested when told of the assignment and he remembered that it had proved anything but dull. Caretakers of plants, inventors themselves, would refuse to produce their books and records until threatened with jail. There had been the problem of the plundered cache.

"What do you guess that fella on the beach has on his mind, Colonel?"

Monty Dane's voice brought him back to the present in a record-breaking flight. The world of war, tragedy and perfidy was replaced by a world of fragrant beauty, of bluish-green hills across which sun and clouds were throwing a pageantry of color.

"You mean the GI?" he asked and handed himself a medal for his quick comeback. "Picking up shells, I'd say." His voice was indifferent but his eyes had sharpened. The man was making letters. Was it a message for someone in the house? If so, the person for whom it was intended better make haste for the tide was coming in. Snow-crested waves were breaking nearer and nearer on the sands. The soldier evidently realized that for he lifted a stick in his left hand—Left hand—the words were a sparkplug. What in thunder was—

"Whatever he was drawing or printing, he's scrambled it now," Dane said. "He is scratching it out. The GI diverted me. Her majesty, Madam Shaw-Ruskin, desires your immediate attendance, Colonel."

Cam glanced at his wrist watch. "Sorry, can't make it. I have a conference at the Barracks. Present my compliments—"

"Not I. I have just escaped and was I given a quiz. I'll bet our hostess knows more about my past than I know myself. What was her idea? To find out if I am intelligent enough to plan houses? I'm looking for Miss Carey, she and I are to dine and dance later. Here she comes now, with the Crown Prince. Among other items, Madam Shaw-Ruskin confided that her son and Pat were unofficially engaged. I don't believe it. That guy with them is a smooth proposition. Latin, I'll bet. He is so smooth he's oily. I don't like the way he looks at Pat."

Cam didn't either, then reminded himself that the lovely, gay girl approaching was quite capable of fending off undesirable attentions. Hadn't she turned him down when—better switch to another station and quick. His job on this island needed his entire attention.

"Presenting Señor Miguel Cardena." Philip Ruskin's smooth voice broke the train of thought. "He asked to meet American officers. When he saw you two together Pat suggested that you were excellent specimens."

"I *didn't* call them specimens, Phil."

"Oh, all right. How about proceeding with the introductions?" He named the men to each other and added, "Señor Cardena is from Brazil."

"Where the nuts come from," Cam added to himself and knew from the flash of laughter in Pat's eyes and on her lips that she also was remembering the line from *Charley's Aunt*, the old farce comedy which even in this modern day rolled 'em in the aisles.

From Brazil, a country friendly and in accord with the policies of the United States, his thoughts ran on, as the other men entered into a discussion of the Pan-American Highway. Cardena was good-looking on the massive side, not oily—jealousy had colored Dane's judgment—too upright and military for that; suave, but distinctly not oily. His blue eyes were cold and keen. Each eyebrow reared in a peak; they and a small mustache waxed at the ends were black as his coal black hair. His clothes were immaculate with a hint of flamboyancy.

"You said you had not met my mother, Señor, let's return to the house," Phil Ruskin suggested.

"I have heard much of Madam Shaw-Ruskin and her influence on this Island from friends who gave me letters to her." Cardena's English, if somewhat stilted, was perfect. "I shall dare ask her help in a great plan I wish to put across to tie our two countries in close friendship."

"Pat and I will leave you here. We are off on a binge," Monty Dane announced with a possessive note in his voice that sent a tinge of color under Ruskin's dark skin.

"Ah, I am desolate that we part, the charming Miss Carey and I," Cardena deplored smoothly. "We will meet again and soon, I hope."

"Come along, Señor, or we'll miss Mother. The party is nearly over." With an effort Phil Ruskin cleared the annoyance from his voice. "Will you join us, Colonel?"

"Thanks, no, I am late for a date now."

He waited until the four were well across the lawn before he opened a gate and ran down a long series of steps to the beach. The GI was whistling softly and switching the sand with his stick.

"I'm here, Sergeant. Were you signaling to me?"

"Yes, sir. I have a hunch one of the guys we're looking for is on this Island. I saw your head above the wall. Thought if you knew about it you might watch out for him in case he showed up at the party. I began to make letters trying to attract your attention."

"You did and the attention of Captain Dane, also. He's the passenger we drove to the hotel last night."

"Shure, an' I was hep to him right off, sir. He was with our outfit for a stretch. Swell-looking fella, but in wrong with the C.O. for doing a little fraternizing with a Frau."

McIlvray's square red face was split by a grin. "Cripes, but the Captain was hot under the collar when his driver walked out on him."

"How did the man you think you've spotted come to the Island?"

"By plane. Landed at Rodgers Airport."

"Anyone with him?"

"A man carrying his bags. From a distance he looked like one of them gentlemen's gentlemen you see in the movies. They registered at the Moana. Some class."

"Keep your eye on them, Sergeant. I'll join you at the jeep in less than ten minutes. Great beach, isn't it?"

"It's a beauty. I got fratty with the maid at Mrs. Shaw's, the cute Chinese trick with the dimples, while I was waiting for you on our second trip, last evening. She's promised to teach me to surf-board when her brother-in-law has time to run their boat. He's gardener and all-round man for her boss."

"You're a fast worker, Sergeant."

"You get that way in the army, sir. You have to make friends quick before you're ordered off somewhere else."

"Be sure they are friendly to the United States as well as to you. Remember that other countries are continuing to arm and increase their supplies of munitions, that even in peacetime this Island and mainland are honeycombed with enemies on the alert to pick up information. Don't forget to report to me any happening that is even a trifle out of the ordinary. General Carrington, you and I are running an Intelligence Division of our own. If even a hint of our mission here gets on the air it may be curtains for us."

"Shure, an' I understand. I won't blab. Didn't I take two years of _Kraut_ pressure to make me tell?" His ruddy face lost its color. He shook as if with ague. Cam touched his shoulder.

"Snap out of it, Mac. Those horrors are past. It is up to us men who suffered and saw them to see that they never happen again."

"They're past, sir. I knew that when you led your men into that filthy compound just as I was being tied up for another beating. I wouldn't have traded you for the President himself."

"About these friendships with women." Cam spoke lightly to switch McIlvray from the memory that whitened his face. "Okay, as long as you keep strictly to friendship, but it's tough on a girl when you kiss and ride away. Remember, Sergeant, you and I may be marked men. If we show noticeable interest in a girl or woman she might be seized as hostage, and no one knows better than you what that could mean. That's all. I'll meet you at the parking place."

"Yes, sir."

McIlvray saluted and vanished among the waving palms which bordered the shore. Cam mounted the steps and closed the gate. His own words came back to him. "Kiss and ride away." Easy to warn the other guy to watch his step. That was the proposition he had put up to Pat, only he had asked for more, a whole lot more, when he had begged her to marry him. He had known then that he was to sail for England in ten days; actually the date of departure was moved forward eight, they would have had but two together. He had been so deeply in love he hadn't thought of her side of it.

As he passed the lower *lanai* Chinese boys in dark blue linen were scurrying about piling glasses on lacquer trays under the direction of a jabbering, gesticulating, frowning overlord. The party appeared to be over, the liquids part of it at least. To the accompaniment of the plaintively gay *Aloha,* he skirted the house whose windows had been turned to crimson by the reflected sunset.

There were half a dozen cars in the parking space but the Chinese chauffeur who had been there when he arrived was gone.

"Li Chang! Li Chang!" a woman's voice called. He had just time to step behind the huge trunk of the banyan tree before Maida Parsons dashed into sight. "Li Chang!" she called again. "Have you seen Colonel—?" She stopped and looked about, her frock and hair turned to pink gold by a shaft of light from the setting sun which seeped through a branch above her head. "Darn that Chinaman, he's gone."

She peered into two army cars, lingered an instant as if considering what move to make, then ran toward the house.

Cam drew a relieved breath. Respite. That was a conceited thought. Why assume that he was the colonel she was seeking? There had been others at the tea. After all, common sense reminded, when a woman looks, talks and acts as she had when he had driven her to the dance last evening a man would be dumb not to sense an invitation to flirtation. She had even suggested the *lei* for this afternoon. He had sent it out of friendship for Jim Parsons.

He had no time for a flirtation or any kind of affair with a woman if he wanted one—which he didn't. After the shock of Pat's runaway his heart had remained numb. He had met plenty of charming war workers, had liked them as friends, had enjoyed being with thm, but never had felt the slightest urge to touch them.

The Sergeant materialized beside the army car. He broke his own speed record joining him. He grinned. Maida sure had him dodging her.

"Shure, an' are you in that hurry to get away, sir? I thought you'd be havin' a swell time. You bust from between the trees as if the devil was after you."

"Not the devil, Sergeant, but memory—of a forgotten engagement. Here's a deluxe limousine driving in. I wonder what dignitary is arriving at this late hour?"

"The man at the wheel is the servant who came this morning by plane." The Sergeant's rich Irish voice was lowered to a hushed whisper. "Shall we go, sir?"

"No. Tinker with the engine. I'd like to get a look at him."

McIlvray was right, the man's thin face with its long nose, watchful dark eyes and tight-lipped mouth did remind one of the screen valets. He gave the impression of being sleek and smooth—too sleek, too smooth.

"A slick customer."

"You've said it, Colonel."

"Sure that he is the man who got off the plane carrying bags?"

"If he isn't he's his twin, sir."

"We'll hang round till his passenger comes. Would you know his boss if you saw him?"

"Wouldn't plunk down money on that, sir. Didn't see his full face."

"Was he met at the airport?"

"Yes, sir. A guy rushed up to him—all he needed was a brass band to hang on his welcome. You'd have thought the visitor was Joe Louis or a king, perhaps. Forgot there aren't many of them doing business now. I hear even that Hirohito guy says he isn't divine like what he'd been givin' out he was."

"Did you learn the name of the welcoming committee of one?"

"I inquired after they drove away—I've got a pal at the airport. Am I the sad sack! They went off in that same black car that just drove in. He said it was one of the big shots here named Ruskin, son of a swell dame on the Island. This is her place we're at now, isn't it?"

"Ruskin! Are you sure, Sergeant?"

"Shure an' I'm shure. I got a great memory for names and faces, if I get a look at 'em. What's that you're muttering, sir?"

"I remarked that I had been barking up the wrong tree. The black limousine is starting. Get a look-see at the passenger, Sergeant."

As the large car passed, Cam looked up. Señor Miguel Cardena on the back seat stuck his head through the open window, raised his peaked eyebrows in surprise, smiled and called:—

"I hope we meet again and soon, Colonel."

The car moved on before Cam could answer. He turned to the Sergeant, whose head was behind the raised engine hood.

"Did you get a good look at him, Mac? What in thunder happened to you?" he demanded. The blood had drained from McIlvray's face. He tried to speak. Gulped. Tried again. Put his hand to his throat and shook his head.

"Take your time. Was the man who spoke to me the man you saw get off the plane?"

"L—looked like him, sir. Whether he is or not he is one of the Storm Trooper officers who used to come and check at the—" He put his hands over his eyes and shuddered.

"Mac! You don't mean—"

"I mean the—the concentration hell where I—put in two years, sir. He's dyed his hair and grown a mustache"—his voice was steady now, hatred had iced it—"but he hasn't changed them crooked eyebrows." He drew a long breath and straightened.

"The folks here boast these islands haven't got reptiles. There's another guess coming to 'em. They've got a snake in the grass, now. Shure, an' there ain't a law in the army that prevents a guy from killin' snakes, is there? The engine's okay if you want to go, sir."

6

THE outrigger canoe reached the surf line. The beach boy standing like a bronze statue in the bow called over his shoulder, "*Hoe!*" Cam heard the paddle in the hands of another boy behind him strike the water. Maida Parsons, on the seat in front in a swim suit, pale gold as the hair which escaped from her tight white cap, brief as easy-going convention permitted, called:—

"Here we go, Cam!"

With a shock and lift the giant wave overtook the canoe.

Cam squared his shoulders in preparation for the breath-snatching velocity, the cold spray lashing his bare back, the swift rush toward the curving shore.

"So this is Waikiki, Maida," he shouted.

The speed of the outrigger carried the words back, not forward to the girl. No wonder the fairylike scene ahead was famous the world over. The yellow sands were dotted with gaily dressed swimmers or surfers resting or waiting for another bout with the rollers. Servicemen in wheel chairs were taking their daily sunning. A row of huge colored umbrellas stood out against a background of waving palms. Pink coral towers rose from the dark green of trees and above the trees coconut palms waved featherlike topknots. Behind them mountains loomed in tier after tier of lava rock. On ledges above the beach charming houses built on different levels were set in blurs of color which were gardens. Far to the right the fluted side of a mountain dipped into the sea. Over and above all spread the incomparable cloud-dotted blue of the sky.

Beside the onrushing outrigger rode laughing surf riders, standing with arms outspread like wings, kneeling, lying flat, miraculously keeping on their long, narrow boards.

"Hi, Cam!"

He turned to look at Pat hailing him. Her bare arms, shoulders and legs appeared gold-plated in contrast to her one-piece white swim suit. A gleaming chestnut curl had escaped from her close cap to dangle in the middle of her forehead. She waved and with the gesture lost balance, fell flat on the board and disappeared into the water.

"Cam!" Maida Parsons's protest was a shriek. "Don't dive. Pat's up. See, she's on her board."

She was and laughing as if the plunge were part of the sport; perhaps it was, but it had taken the stiffness from his knees. The canoe took a wave on high and plumped him back into his seat.

"Shall we try it again, Maida?" he asked as the bronzed boys dragged the outrigger to the beach.

"No, once is enough. It's strenuous. Let's sun, then lunch on the hotel terrace."

"No can do." He glanced from under a shading hand at the brassy disc almost overhead. "I'll give myself fifteen minutes here, then I'm off to keep a date. After that, lunch with my boss."

Arms hugging his knees, he sat on the gay beach rug beside her and thought of his appointment with the head of the Intelligence Division on the Island, to whom he had promptly reported McIlvray's reaction to the sight of Señor

Miguel Cardena. The Sergeant had been interviewed and at the close had been given the choice of swearing under oath that he would keep out of the way of the alleged Brazilian or being transferred that very afternoon by plane to a post on the Mainland. He had chosen to swear. That had been four days ago. Had he broken his word that the General in charge of the Division here had sent for him?

"Come out of the silence, Cam." Maida's impatient voice snapped the threat of conjecture. "You've grown ages older since you were Father's aide two years ago. Now, you are about as responsive as that lava ledge. You were heaps of fun then."

"Meaning that I am a killjoy now?"

"Meaning that now this horrible war is over it's time to recover your *joie de vivre*. Why stay in the army? Get your discharge and spend the winter here. We could have loads of fun together. Surely you have fought and suffered enough. That frightful scar from shoulder to hip must have won you the Purple Heart."

"Don't talk about it."

He drew on quickly the cotton beach coat he had left on the rug. Why snap at Maida? She couldn't know that he had hesitated to bare his back because he dreaded comment about it. The surgeon at the hospital had ordered him to get into the sun and sea, saying that nothing else would so quickly reduce the color of the scar.

"I am staying in the army because too many men are coming out," he answered her first question. "Congress is under terrific pressure to get the boys home. Did you read about the women who have been sending baby shoes tagged 'Bring my Daddy home,' to their senators? Many of them with families should come, those without a wife or kids should stay in till we get conditions overseas straightened out. As a nation we have made commitments. We must abide by them."

"My eye, you have gone serious. If you believe the radio analysts, things are in a mess over there. Here comes Pat Carey. She is stopping to speak to the group of men in wheel chairs. She puts in hours at the hospital. I don't see how she can bear to see the tragedy and suffering."

"Someone has to do it. How did you help during the war, Maida?"

"I sold bonds and worked in the Canteen. It was loads of fun. The doctor said I was too sensitive to do anything else. That pink linen beach coat Pat is wearing is a honey. So like her to cover up when the rest of us look like a bunch of potential strip-teasers. Who is the man with her?

What splashy swim trunks. What shoulders. What lean hips, and does the lad know he's good? You bet. 'Waikiki, here I come.' Where does he hail from?"

"Didn't you see him at Madam Shaw-Ruskin's party? He comes from the Mainland, I understand."

"That's not very definite. Perhaps Pat met him overseas, perhaps having to leave him behind is responsible for the change in her. She is gay and friendly with the officers here who swarmed after her when she returned to the Island, but she wouldn't go out with them and they drifted away to warmer welcomes. Remember what a radiant girl she was at my wedding?"

"I remember."

He stretched at length on the beach rug and clasped his hands over his eyes, ostensibly to shut out the glare, really to shut in the picture of Pat as she had pressed her face against his shoulder and nodded assent to his whispered, "Marry me tomorrow, darling?" Curious that the memory should leave him cold. Her letter had killed something vital in him. Maida was right, his heart had turned as rocky as the lava ledge.

"I thought at the time you were that way about Pat." He sensed her sly glance at him. "But Mother wrote that she left the inn quite suddenly, took the night train the evening after the wedding. She was and is my best friend but I can't make her out now. Sometimes when I speak to her she comes back as if she had been miles away, with a look in her eyes as if she had been knifed which gives me the shivers."

Was she in love with Dane? Had she discovered after she fell for him that he had a wife? That would account for the look in her eyes which gave Maida the shivers.

"For two years Pat was in the midst of war, Maida. The horror she lived through can't be gauged by the most vivid imagination which has not been part of it."

"That may explain some, but not all. I believe there is a buried romance. Were it anyone but Pat Carey I would suspect an affair, but not for her. In college she stuck to ideals and ideas which seemed amusingly outdated to the rest of us. If a man took her out she refused more than a handshake at parting. When we ribbed her about it she would come back:—

" 'Can't help it, girls. I don't want to be kissed, I won't be pawed by Tom, Dick and Harry. Something in me squizzles up like cellophane in fire when they try it.' She wouldn't drink, claimed that if she did some one of the younger girls might use it as an excuse to go the limit."

"Sort of my-brother's-keeper idea, wasn't it?"

"Yes, and she was right, that time. The youngsters adored her. They copied her clothes, her manners, even read the books she read. I don't mean that she put on a holier-than-thou act. She respected our ideas and expected us to respect hers. We went for her in a big way. She was voted the gayest, most amusing, most sympathetically understanding, most popular girl in the class."

"That was going some. Any truth in the rumor that—eventually she will marry Ruskin?"

"If his mother can pull it off she will. She is determined to get the money and Shaw jewels for her son, Phil, that were left to Sally. Pat is her aunt's only near relative and heir apparent."

"So, that's the layout. I understand Ruskin was in the deferred class."

"Right. Our troops and the world had to have sugar. He was wild to get into the service and is jealous, crazy jealous, I think, of a man in uniform who speaks to Pat. Better watch your step, Cam. I hope she won't marry him. He's a born dictator like his mother. His wife will have to kowtow to both—or else. Pat could make good as a night-club singer. He's even jealous of her music."

"I didn't know she was musical, but then, I saw her for one week only and we were busy getting you and Jim married."

"She sings in an Episcopal church here. She hasn't a big voice but it's true and strong and sweet. She's tops with the guitar and of course plays the piano."

"Like her, don't you, Maida?"

"I love her. I admire her beyond words but I wouldn't have her ideas if I could. She misses a lot of fun. Hi, Pat," she hailed the girl approaching. "Are your ears burning? We were talking about you."

"Saying something good, I hope. I'm low in my mind. I could stand an orchid or two."

She pulled off her close cap. Her short wavy hair gleamed in the sun. Cam, who had risen, dropped back to the rug as she and Dane squatted cross-legged on the sand.

"Captain Dane, Maida," Pat introduced them. "He has been tugging at the leash since he caught sight of your hair. He's a push-over for pale gold blondes."

"And I fall for dark-haired men." Her eyes lingered on Dane's head, brown and wet and sleek as the coat of a seal. Cam remembered that Jim Parsons's hair was on the danger line of brick red.

"Then we are all set for a be—autiful friendship. Mind if I call you Maida right off quick?" Captain Dane was at his caressing best. "I have admired you from a respectful distance at the hotel."

"Are you staying at the Moana? How exciting. Do you like cards?"

"Only second in my heart to lovely women. Pat won't lunch with me though I have described in my most intriguing style the charm of the terrace. Would you—"

"Lunch with you? I will—just like that. You were about to invite me, weren't you?"

"I have invited you. I—"

"Found at long last, Monty," a voice strident with triumph interrupted.

For an instant Dane stared unbelievingly at the redhaired woman in a brilliant green swim suit and the bronzed beach boy behind her holding a gay bag and sun umbrella, before he sprang to his feet.

"For the love of Mike! Where did you drop from, Carrots?"

"I didn't drop, I flew, Monty. I've been here four days, keeping strictly in my rooms. Apparently you have been too busy—" her insolent eyes swept the two girls looking up at her—"to answer my letters so I trailed you. Don't you intend to introduce your old wife to your new friends? At the same time you might mention the fact that my name is Velma, *not* Carrots.

Cam, standing near, felt her body tense as her tongue lashed. No doubt about her sentiments toward her husband, hate expressed it—or was it thwarted love? She had a rowdy beauty, her gray-green eyes were sultry, the lines of her mouth bitter. Her hair was a rich auburn, not the carroty hue her husband's nickname implied.

"Sure, I want them to know you." Monty Dane had regained his poise. "Mrs. Dane, Mrs. Parsons. Patricia Carey, who isn't a new friend, *Velma*, and Colonel Fulton."

"You're telling me Miss Carey isn't a new friend. You and she were *together* in the same outfit in Germany, I heard. That experience must have made you *very* close friends." She had a way of hunching her plump shoulders when she emphasized a word.

"Friends, but not what you would call close, Mrs. Dane." Pat was on her feet, her chin was tilted at a defiant angle, a tint of red mounted under the tan of her face, but her voice was smooth and unruffled. "I am glad of this chance to report—Monty is too modest to speak of it—that your husband was one of the heroes of his regiment and a brilliant and intrepid leader. Cam, we are intruding on this happy reunion. Let's go. Coming, Maida?"

"I am not." She sieved sand through her fingers. "I haven't finished sunning and I want to see *more* of charming Mrs. Dane." Her mocking eyes swept the figure of the woman attired in an even more revealing costume than her own. "Besides, I have accepted an invitation to lunch with the Captain. I hope he won't throw me over because another gal has barged into his life. Don't let me keep you, Cam. You said you had a date."

"I did. I have. Two. I'm going. Thanks for the outrigger ride, Maida. I feel after that experience that I am no longer a *malihini*. How's my Hawaiian? I learned that from a booklet my sergeant consults on all occasions. Tomorrow I'll join a surf-riding class. Come on, Pat."

What could he say to her, he wondered, as they walked toward the palms side by side. The woman's "you and she were *together* in the same outfit in Germany, I heard," had been drenched with innuendo. Had a man said that in the same tone he would have knocked his block off, then and there, but to sail into a woman, much as she deserved it—

"Difficult to make a dignified exit when one's feet are plowing through sand, isn't it?" Pat inquired gaily.

"We'll be out of it in a minute. I'll change at the Outrigger Club, then may I drive you home? I have an a.c. and r. here—command and reconnaissance car, to you—which is one degree more comfortable than a jeep. You needn't shake your head so vigorously. One shake will be sufficient to discourage me. At least we can walk to our cars together."

"We can. I have a hunch that I shouldn't have introduced Monty to Maida. I love and admire her, but he has a lot of charm and nice Jim Parsons is far away."

"Did you fall a victim to that charm? Did you know he had a wife?"

"We were talking about Maida."

"My mistake. Why worry about her? Dane would have met her." She was avoiding the subject of the lately arrived wife. He followed her lead. "When a man is determined to meet a certain woman he'll put it across. How come that Maida is staying at that sumptuous hotel? It takes chips and many. Jim's pay would hardly seem adequate." Not that he was in the least interested in the Parsons domestic economy but it kept the conversation from drifting against dangerous ledges.

"Since Maida's marriage her mother has inherited a fortune. She pays her daughter's living bills and gives her a spectacular allowance. Maida declares quite frankly—maybe she has told you—that she and Jim fought like bobcats because she wouldn't live on his pay."

"If she really loved him she would give it a try, at least."

"Would she? I wouldn't know."

"Ever thought that there are lots of things you don't know about human nature, living cool and aloof in your ivory tower, Pat? Were you and Dane in the same outfit in Germany?"

"Good heavens, I was trying to forget that poisonous female and her hateful tongue. Why drag her into the conversation? We were for a while, then I was sent to Belgium. I spent Christmas in the Bulge of tragic memory."

"I know where you spent Christmas."

She stopped walking to demand incredulously, "How did you know?"

"Military secret. What I didn't know was that you and Dane were—"

"If you say *together* in the tone that she-tiger used, I'll —I'll slap your face hard—and I mean hard—right here where everyone can see me."

The fury in her voice, the blaze in her eyes sent the blood coursing through his veins with a force that stopped his breath. He laughed as he hadn't laughed for two years.

"*Miss* Carey! I am shocked at such a display of temper. Take it easy. I was about to observe that I did not know you and Dane had been in the same outfit. Nothing about that to send your blood pressure shooting up to boiling point, is there?"

"N—o, it wasn't what you said but the way I thought you were going to say it."

"Slightly complicated, but I get what you mean. Dane has upset my calculations. I had it figured that Ruskin was my successor in your affections. Am I flattering myself when I believe that I was in your affections—for a while?"

"That means you think I was putting on an act that—that week at the Post. Who knows, perhaps I was, but get this —I may be cool and aloof but you are about as warm as an ice machine and as remote as the crater of Mauna Loa. Good-bye."

"Pat!"

He made a futile clutch at her arm but she evaded him, dashed in among the palms and was gone.

7

THE officer with two stars on the collar of his shirt and a deep wrinkle across his brow, seated behind the flat desk, glanced at the clock on the wall beside the Stars and Stripes.

"On the minute, Colonel. Sit down." As Cam dropped into the chair opposite he pushed a paper toward him. "Take a look at this and tell me what you make of it."

Cam ran his eyes over the typewritten page, returned to the first line and read again.

"Either the operator you put on the job has been fooled or Sergeant McIlvray has mistaken his man." He tapped the paper. "If you believe this, Señor Miguel Cardena can trace his family back to the original settlers of Brazil. Your operator has done a good job on paper but I think somebody took him for a ride."

"That means you doubt the truth of that statement?"

"Not the correctness of the family tree but that the man we know as Cardena is the right piece of fruit to dangle from it."

"What's the setup for that conclusion?"

"The word you used was doubt, sir."

"All right, doubt. What's the answer?"

"Sergeant McIlvray."

"I know, he was damned convincing. Before he was through his story he had General Carrington and me ready to order the arrest of Cardena. We decided on a cooling-off period before we acted and now along comes this screed to prove he is the person he claims to be."

"The fact that I believe he is the man the Sergeant recognized doesn't mean that I think he should be arrested as a Nazi. First, find out why he has come here in disguise. Until he has been thoroughly screened he should remain Señor Miguel Cardena of Brazil to be honored and feted in the style called for by his letters of introduction—faked perhaps."

"If that is done we'll have some soreheads among the socialites when or if he turns out to be an impostor. I hear he was at Madam Shaw-Ruskin's blowout. Did he have a letter to her?"

"I doubt if he'd pass that sacred threshold unless he had.

McIlvray, under examination, said that her son Philip met him at the airport."

"He said also that a ground man told him it was Ruskin. He may have mistaken his man."

"Not probable, sir. Ruskin is well known. He's a big shot here."

"All right, we'll let it go at that. Even after reading that genealogical brain-child of our operator's, General Carrington agrees with you that Señor Miguel Cardena should proceed unmolested to make his social contacts. It's up to you, Colonel, to find out what else he is here for, always supposing you are right in your suspicion. I think the Brazilian is straight goods. You and Carrington are against me. The majority has it. Trot out the fatted calf and strike up the band." He leaned forward.

"Anything new about the other matter?" His voice was little more than a whisper.

"No, sir."

"Carry on, you'll get 'em or him. Now a word to you personally. General Carrington tells me you are planning to leave the service as soon as your work here is finished. Don't. The shooting is over but this country needs men like you to keep up its prestige in conquered territory. We must have soldiers of peace to finish the job. We are in for a long occupation of Germany. We must not forget, we must *not* forget, the horrors of the war years which may be timed to become a scourge the minute we soften up." He drew his hand across his damp forehead.

"I break out in a sweat when I think of the damn complacency of the U.S., daring to let down the efficiency of the different branches of the service instead of keeping them mobile and ready. Think it over. That's all," he grinned, "and enough, isn't it? Good luck to you, Colonel."

Cam drove slowly along a broad boulevard humming with traffic, past white buildings, past the shaft of Aloha Tower rising above tropical palms, past East Indian bazaars and restaurants with Chinese signs. The sidewalks were crowded with men, women, children, GI's, sailors and marines with faces of every tint, color and shade that human skin takes on. They passed back and forth between trees and glistening shop windows in which Polynesian and Oriental objects of art, treasures from all over the world, were spread in tempting array. "The Bells of St. Mary's," relayed by a juke box, drifted from an open door. The air was fragrant with scent from many flower shops.

He thought of the genealogy of Cardena the Intelligence

operator had sent from Brazil as straight goods, and he visualized McIlvray's face after the Señor had passed. That was straighter goods. "Kill the fatted calf," the Intelligence chief had said. That would be easy in this land where life on the surface seemed one prolonged holiday—life as he had seen it, he qualified.

"Don't leave the service," he had advised also. That plea was not so easy to follow. He wanted to go home, wanted to begin to work out the design for living he had made so many years ago. So did a lot of others who were sticking to the task of finishing the job the Allies had fought and died to carry on. That decision could wait until he had completed the assignment which had brought him to the "Crossreads of the Pacific."

He filled his lungs with the flower-scented air. Great climate. Continual June. Fine if one liked it. He'd take a few Montana blizzards in his. Apparently Pat was sold on the Island. How little he had learned of her likes and dislikes that week at the Post. Maida had said she was musical. That meant, probably, that she knew and loved the best, the greatest compositions. He didn't know one symphony from another, they rather bored him. Maida had said also that she wouldn't be kissed. She hadn't resented his kiss. If only he had known some of these things at the Post; he hadn't.

From the first moment he had seen her he had wanted her for his wife, he hadn't thought whether their tastes were similar, if they would be congenial in the wear and tear of daily life, if she cared for children. He wanted not one, but several. As an only child he had suffered moments of aching loneliness. He had loved her wholly, completely, he wanted her as he never had wanted anything before; she had been the one to consider the future. Now, was she eating out her heart for Dane?

Neither had he known that she could fly into a rage. During that week at the Post she had been laughing, gay, tender. Her anger today had been like an electric shock which had revitalized his heart and emotions, made him tinglingly alive once more. Her eyes had blazed, her cheeks had flown battle flags of red. She was even more lovely than he remembered. He hadn't known she could look like that. There was apparently much to learn about her, she was a person of infinite variety. And could she get mad!

The smile the memory of her anger brought to his eyes and lips lingered when he entered his quarters at the Barracks. Sergeant McIlvray was busy in the workroom with its large flat desk and wall maps. His face split in a grin of welcome.

"Shure, an' you look happy as if you'd had the C.M. pinned on you, sir. Did you get a good swim?"

"A swim first, then a lashing of water keen as a needle spray and cold as a Montana sleet storm as the outrigger canoe forged up and through and over rollers. Any calls?"

"General Carrington's office, sir. They've gone nuts about you. Phoned twice to ask if you were back. You're later than you said you'd be."

"Did they leave a message?"

"No, sir."

"While I'm changing give them a buzz, tell them I am here and will call back if the General wants to speak to me." He stopped on the threshold. "You have kept your promise, Sergeant?"

"Saint Patrick, are you worried for fear his nibs has got something on me? You don't have to be. Didn't I swear I'd sidestep getting even with the lousy—you don't have to hold up your hand to stop me, either. I won't name the party. I swore on the Bible I'd cut out the payoff on you-know-who, not that I wanted to, but it was either that or being redeployed to the Mainland. That meant losing you. Shure, an' I'm not sticking my neck out for that trouble. You're my family now, sir. You brought me back from the dead and you got your shoulder ripped by the devils in the fight."

"You squared that, Mac, when you took care of me till I could get back into action."

"An' were you the sick guy. There were days when you didn't speak that scared me stiff, then days when you jabbered all the time that scared me stiffer. Why live that over?" He cleared his voice of gruffness and grinned.

"Didn't you say when we got our discharges we'd be heading stateside—that's what they say here—to your home and the ranch? I bet I'll make the world's No. 1 cowhand."

"I bet you will. Meanwhile how about getting busy with that call to the General?"

As he dressed, the notes of a bugle drifted in through the open window, the sound of a car stopping and starting, a stentorian command. He had had four years of this regimented life. There would be more if he were convinced that he was needed overseas in an administrative capacity. Why think of it now? When his present job was finished there would be time enough. No progress on that, which fact didn't mean that it might not wind up with a speed which would make him dizzy.

"Did you get in touch with the General's office, Sergeant?" he asked when he returned to his workroom.

"Yes, sir. You are to give him a ring as soon as possible. Unless you're needing me to advise you what to say, I'll be going." He grinned in appreciation of his own joke, pushed his field cap at a jauntier angle on his red head and departed.

Seated on a corner of the flat desk Cam clicked the key of the interoffice system. Curious that the General should call him when they were to meet at luncheon. He answered a voice.

"Yes, sir." . . . He listened, laughed. "Sure, it's all right with me, General, if you take a lady to lunch, it's a popular Hawaiian custom. . . . Tea! This afternoon at Mrs. Shaw's . . . Even if it isn't a large party it strikes me we are getting in deep socially for men who have a . . . I'm not criticizing my superior officer, sir. I'll be on hand. 'Mine not to reason why, mine but to do or die'—with my hat off to Lord Tennyson. . . . No, I haven't been drinking, sir. Charge up what you call my unusual burst of high spirits to sea air and water. I have spent most of the morning in both. . . . Five o'clock? *Hiki no,* which means 'can do,' in American. I'll be there."

He couldn't believe his eyes when promptly at five he stepped into the *lanai* at Mrs. Shaw's and saw Monty Dane's wife. Fast work. Who had brought her here? She was beautiful. A gardenia was tucked into her piled-up auburn hair and a huge sunburst of diamonds was at the shoulder of her thin black frock matched by earrings large as hazelnuts. Her single string of lustrous pearls was the real thing if he knew pearls—and he did—and on the purple-nailed third finger of each hand—large, bony hands—she wore knuckle rings, studded with emeralds and diamonds. A lady of wealth, who spent it, undoubtedly.

She was listening to General Carrington seated beside her but her malicious green eyes were watching her husband, who was bending over the tea table. Pat was pouring. Was her face pale or did it seem white in contrast to her coral jacket over a white blouse? Had the arrival of Monty Dane's wife hurt her? Maida Parsons in honey-color slacks and matching cardigan belted with gold kid was assisting Phil Ruskin at the buffet. Mrs. Shaw on the lawn was pointing out Diamond Head to Señor Miguel Cardena. So that was what this party meant, the beginning of the fatted-calf program in honor of the *caballero* from Brazil.

"Cam!" With the delighted exclamation and the clink of broad gold bracelets, Maida's hand slipped under his arm, Maida's fingers pressed his sleeve. "You sneaked in like a ghost or somebody's conscience."

"Come here, Colonel." At the General's hail, he released his arm and joined him. "Mrs. Dane says she met you this morning but that you ran away before she had a chance to become acquainted. Sit here and make your peace with her."

"Running away is a serious charge to make to a man in this uniform, Mrs. Dane," Cam reproached as he took the chair the General had vacated. Her heady perfume must be in the thirty-dollars-an-ounce class, he decided.

"I wasn't so elegant, Colonel, I said you beat it. Say," she lowered her strident voice, "I can't make this party out. Perhaps you can tell me why I was invited to this swell house by someone I never heard of? Not that I don't think I am as good as anybody. Sure, I'm rich, thanks to a gold-digging grandpa, but money doesn't get you far with folks like these, I've discovered. It's different, that Brazilian Señor being here. He was on the Clipper with me. You could tell he was class. Snooty as—ahem, snubbed nice Alec Stanhope, another passenger. You didn't say much on the beach this morning but I felt quick, that you are a right guy. What's the answer to me being here?"

Cam liked her, sensed under her crude frankness a hurt of long standing.

"That's an easy one, Mrs. Dane, nothing mysterious about it. You are the wife of a friend of Mrs. Shaw's niece. Your husband was invited here this afternoon, so of course you would be."

"Oh, yeah? It doesn't always work that way."

"You will find that it does in this house. What may I get you to drink?"

"Tea. It poisons me, but I have a hunch I'd better stick to it this afternoon and remain a perfect lady." She was attractive. When she laughed little sparks of gold like fireflies twinkled in her hair and her green eyes softened. Her teeth were beautiful. "Isn't the Chinese maid cute in that pink kimono?"

"Yes, she's a conversation piece."

"What does that mean?"

"Something to talk about."

"Monty told me before we came not to talk—to listen and I'd learn. Looks like he said something. Think I could get a maid like her to take home? And see what she's serving. Luscious little fried cheese balls on toothpicks, tiny puff paste shells filled with shrimp Newburg, anchovy eggs, o-o-oh. I have had nothing but black coffee today. I'm famished. I don't care if I do put on flesh, Colonel, I intend to eat. Monty, you've hung over that table long enough. Bring me a plate of those hors d'oeuvres."

Her sharp order was like an electric shock which set a lot of wax figures in motion. Dane jerked up his head. Sib Lou clutched the large crystal plate with both hands and stared at him. Pat set down the silver teapot with a little crash. Ruskin glared at Velma Dane. Maida giggled. Sally Shaw and Señor Cardena stepped to the *lanai* from the lawn.

"But not as lovely as it was, Señor." She was evidently replying to a remark of his. "War caught the Island in a stranglehold. As a result it is bursting at the seams from the pressure of three times the normal number of people. How queer you all look. Sib Lou, what's the matter? Are you faint?"

The Chinese maid straightened and shook her head.

"I'm all okay now, Madam." She pointed a shaky finger at Monty Dane. "Why did you tap on my window the other night, Mister?"

In the stunned silence which followed, the only sound was the drip, drip of the little fountain at one side of the *lanai*. Mrs. Dane leaned forward as if crouched for a spring. Cam, standing beside her, watched the Captain between narrowed lids, as he bent his head to speak to Pat. Sally, with a breathless "Oh," laid her hand on the shoulder of the girl leaning against the vine-covered vertical, Maida and Phil Ruskin whispered, the General scowled and settled his tie, Señor Miguel Cardena looked as if he were wondering what it was all about.

"Now it can be told." Monty Dane's jaunty announcement focused all eyes on his slightly reddened face. "When I reached the hotel after making my first call on Mrs. Shaw and Pat the other evening, I missed my brief case. It held important papers which had been entrusted to me to deliver. For a minute heart failure threatened. Then I began to think back. I remembered that I had it when I left the conference, recalled that I dropped it to seize Pat's hands when she held them out in welcome at the door. Had I taken it when I left? I couldn't remember. I had been hot at the driver who walked out on me. If I had left it in Colonel Fulton's jeep, getting it before morning was out. I couldn't go prowling round the Barracks at that time of night. It was too late."

"But not too late to tap at a girl's window."

Dane ignored his wife's acid reminder.

"If I had left the brief case at Mrs. Shaw's, it wouldn't take me long to return there, I figured. I hired a car. The house was dark when I reached it, but there was an outside light beside a door in what I decided was the servants' quarters. My best bet was to go there, rout one of them out, and ask him, or her, to find the brief case without disturbing the family and bring it to me. I had a piece of folding money in my hand to make the trip worth while when I tapped on a window. So that it might be seen how harmless I was, I snapped on my cigarette lighter and held it against my face. A woman screamed—and how. With hysteria about the crime wave what it is, I didn't wait to explain. The guardhouse loomed large in my immediate future. I beat it. That's the story."

"And what a story. You'd be a find for the legitimate if you can ad lib like that, Monty."

"It is quite true, Mrs. Dane, the part about leaving the brief case." Pat rushed to his defense. "Sally discovered it in the hall. I carried it to my room and delivered it to Monty the next afternoon. Remember, Sally?"

"Of course I remember. I'm not yet in my dotage, Patricia. I quite understand your predicament, Captain Dane. But let the experience be a warning, young men in uniform shouldn't tap at strange windows."

"You're telling me. I've never done it before and I never will again. The scream frightened the daylights out of me. I'm really a harmless guy, Sib Lou, will you forgive me?" His ingratiating smile restored the girl's color. She looked at him shyly and dimpled:

"Yes, sir."

"Now that that complication is nicely washed up, let's get on with the party," Phil Ruskin suggested impatiently. "Will you have sherry, Señor Cardena? That is all I can offer you here."

"Sherry will be all right with me, as you say in the States. Are you joining us, Colonel Fulton? A very careless young man, Captain Dane, to have the care of important papers. I would not trust him with mine; how about you, Colonel?"

"I don't carry important papers, Señor. My few reports are turned in as soon as written. None for me, Ruskin. I became a confirmed tea drinker in England."

"I referred to reports written when in occupied Germany," Señor Cardena persisted. "You were in charge of the scientists who searched the ruins of the wrecked plants for oil industry secrets, I understand."

"Is that the only one of my assignments remembered after two years of hard fighting? Such is fame. My reports to which you refer are stored in the Archives of the United

States Library of Congress with all the material the scientists recovered. I hope your plan to tie up our two countries in close friendship may be as successful as their mission proved to be, Señor Cardena."

8

PAT studied the three men as they stood together, three such different types. Phil Ruskin, nervous, frowning; the Brazilian, urbane, with a hint of superciliousness; Cam Fulton, controlled, imperturbable, even as he smilingly replied to something Cardena had said. Was he as cold and remote with everyone as he was with her? This morning when she had felt a furious urge to sting him out of his indifference by threatening to slap his face, he had laughed, had been for a few seconds the lighthearted man she had loved. Lucky he couldn't know that after they parted she had come home and sobbed her heart out. As if he felt her eyes on him he turned and after a word to the two men came to the table.

"How about a cup of tea? I like it strong enough to stand alone with plenty of lemon."

Because his nearness set her heart thumping in her throat she said the last thing she should have said:—

"You know what you want, don't you, Colonel?"

"And go straight for it. Remember?" As if he regretted the admission he added quickly, "Quite a yarn the Captain improvised about the brief case. Watch out, you'll have the cup too full," he warned as her indignant eyes flew to his. She set down the silver teapot quickly.

"It wasn't a yarn. He did leave it here. I did carry it upstairs. Sib Lou did scream. I ought to know that last. I rushed to her rescue in nothing flat."

"You were crazy. Suppose it hadn't been Dane but a baddie from the Barracks? Sib Lou was safe within walls. You were not. Don't do a thing like that again."

"I probably will. I'm determined to conquer fear. *Fear*. You've heard of it?"

"I have. I've known it. While you are licking fear cultivate caution and common sense. The three make good traveling mates. Don't run around alone again at night. Was it heavy?"

"Really, Colonel, how you jump from subject to subject.

Eliza leaping from ice cake to ice cake has nothing on you. Was what heavy?"

"Am I difficult to follow? Charge it up to the sudden plunge into social life after years in camp. I meant, was the brief case heavy?"

Elbow on the table, chin in the palm of her left hand, Pat looked up, her forehead creased in a line of perplexity.

"Heavy? Not especially that I remember. Why?"

"Break it up! Break it up!" Phil Ruskin interrupted jealously. "The peppy Dane says to tell you she is still waiting for the cup of tea you promised her, Colonel."

"The hand grenade the little Chinese maid flung into the party blew us all off the track of what we were doing or thinking. Fill another cup, Miss Carey, and I'll take it along with mine. Let me do it." He lifted the teapot she had raised and set down quickly. "Good Lord, I don't wonder you dropped it. The handle is red-hot."

It wasn't. She had set the teapot down because her hand was unsteady and she didn't want Phil to notice it. Had Cam seen it?

"Tea coming up, Mrs. Dane," he announced as he left the table with a cup and saucer in each hand.

"Boy, he filled that order neatly and quickly. I'll bet he was a waiter in a club or hotel before he entered the army."

"That's absurd, Phil. Of course he wasn't," Pat flared and promptly wished she had held her tongue.

"How come you know so much about him?"

"I resent that suspicious tone, but just for the record I've heard tell he was a lawyer. Where are we dining and dancing tonight? Is your face red! We have a date, haven't we, or am I speaking out of turn?"

"We have, at a night spot with a *lanai* for dancing, where they make a specialty of barbecued steaks, but to tell the truth I've been let in for a party. Maida was stepping out with Dane. Now that his wife has arrived the date is off."

"Didn't she lunch with him today?"

"I wouldn't know. She said she missed her husband so frightfully that she hated to be alone—that listens well—that if I would let her come along with us she would bring a man."

"If she can get one why not go out with him? Why barge in on our evening?"

"This is the first time you have made me feel that you give a hang to go out alone with me, Pat." Triumph gave way to petulance. "I said okay to Maida. It's too late to change. There will be others—Sally wants to bring—"

"Sally, you are having a party and I was not invited," Madam Shaw-Ruskin reproached in an aggrieved voice as she stood in the opening between living room and *lanai*. She was wearing white even to the gardenia which accentuated the sleek black of her hair.

"This isn't a party, Mother Ruskin, just a few friends here for tea," Sally Shaw explained. "I am so glad you dropped in."

Madam Shaw-Ruskin ignored the rattan chair with violet and pink cushions Cam Fulton drew toward her. Aided by a jeweled lorgnon she leisurely inspected each person in the *lanai*. her eyes returned to Velma Dane and lingered.

"Who is the redheaded guest, Sally? I can smell her perfume from here. Her jewels indicate a wife of the Shah of Persia or any other Oriental harem keeper." Her insolence shut off Sally Shaw's breath but not Velma Dane's. She laughed.

"Every minute I spend on this island I see something new," she drawled. Her eyes swept the figure of the woman regarding her through the lorgnon. "Say, you must be what the Colonel calls a conversation piece, a walking ad for the Fountain of Youth. Eighty reduced to sixty. How's it done, Madam, or is it Miss?"

"A fight to the finish and no holds barred," Cam Fulton said in Pat's ear. She disciplined a laugh. Madam Shaw-Ruskin had for once met her match in arrogant insolence. Her black eyes snapped rage, the hand which held the lorgnon shook. She opened her lips to speak but no sound came. Velma Dane laughed.

"Why don't you speak up like a little man, Monty, and tell the old lady I'm your lovin' wife?"

The question brought him out of the spell of dismay. He pushed the chair a little nearer.

"Do sit down, your majesty." As, still speechless, Madam Shaw-Ruskin sank among the cushions he tucked a low stool under her feet. "Comfortable? Come here, Carrots, and be presented to the First Lady of the Pacific."

"You're doing fine, Monty," his wife encouraged satirically, "but the dame will have to take back that harem crack before I'll speak to her. Colonel Fulton, show me that lovely garden."

Cam joined her with the alacrity of a man making his escape from a room on fire behind him. As side by side they stepped to the lawn her voice, warm with enthusiasm, drifted back.

"There is nothing I love quite so much as flowers, Colonel."

"*Auwe*, Captain." Madam Shaw-Ruskin had regained her

voice. "You certainly picked a shrew for better or for worse. You have my heartfelt sympathy. Ill blows the wind that profits nobody. She will, spike your pursuit of *Pat*—ricia and—"

"What will you have to drink, Mother?" Phil Ruskin's question stalled the flaming denial forming on Sally Shaw's lips.

"What a question to ask in *this* house. As if I could have what I wanted. I loathe sherry. Bring me tea. Come here, Señor Cardena, and tell me that my Spanish has improved." She added a mellifluous phrase. "Am I not good?" Her voice was arch, her smile revealed her beautiful teeth.

Sally Shaw's eyes in a face flushed with anger met Pat's. "Armistice," they wirelessed.

Armistice for the duration of her call, Pat determined as she filled a cup with strong tea. Velma Dane must be kept out of the *lanai* till after the departure of the "First Lady of the Pacific." She beckoned to Monty Dane, whose usually cocksure manner was as deflated as a grounded parachute.

"Take this tea to her majesty," she said and succeeded in keeping her voice free of sarcasm. "And by the way, your wife was wrong about her age, she is in the early sixties. See that she gets some of the cheese balls, she loves 'em. Don't look so crushed. Jack up the old charm, Captain, if you want to copy that house of hers. The Señor from Brazil is getting the inside track."

"Why pick on me? I want to talk with you. I haven't had a chance to tell you I was mad as fury at Velma's crack this morning about our friendship overseas."

"She did say something about it, didn't she? What was it? Couldn't have been very important or I would have remembered. Here's the tea. Now do your stuff."

"Where are you going?"

"To order Colonel Fulton to prevent your wife from leaving the garden if it has to be over his dead body. Otherwise there may be a hair-pulling contest that will go down in history as the female battle of all time. Your wife is beautiful, Monty, but she's a glutton for a fight."

"You're telling me," Dane growled and picked up cup and saucer.

Hawaiian evenings are divinely designed for dancing, Pat thought, as several hours later she waltzed with Phil Ruskin in the *lanai* of the night spot to the orchestral accompaniment of "Moon over Waikiki." The Milky Way made a path of silver across the dark sky that dimmed the brilliance of the big stars Pollux and Castor near its border.

"There will be others," Phil had said before he was interrupted by the entrance of his mother this afternoon. Others, was right. A table on the edge of the dance floor had been reserved for his party. Pedro, the Filipino maître d'hôtel, had led them to it with the manner of one escorting royalty.

Only General Carrington and Cam Fulton, in white uniforms, were seated there at the moment. Sally, in her favorite silver gray, was dancing with Señor Cardena. Maida, in diaphanous blue, was floating about with Monty Dane, one white arm around his neck. His wife, wearing an exquisite silver mesh frock with a green orchid in her auburn hair and at her sequin belt, a necklace of diamond roses with flexible petals blazing round her lovely throat, was dancing with a man whom she had met on the Clipper, Alec Stanhope.

His thin, serious face had broken into a resplendent smile when they met in the lounge. He had greeted her with the enthusiastic warmth of a man from Mars welcoming a gal from home to this strange planet, Earth. His, "Boy it's good to see a familiar face," had been from the heart. He was in black dinner clothes, the only male civilian dancing not in white.

The music died away. The dancers returned to their tables. Lights changed from amber to soft pink. The floor show was on. A troop of hula girls in halters, ti-leaf skirts, and *leis* of varicolored hibiscus, with flowers in their hair, moved with slow grace to the center of the *lanai*. To the music of steel guitars and ukuleles they waved their slender arms, swayed their hips, swished their skirts, revealed shapely brown legs and chanted in harmony with the music.

Instead of watching the show she had seen countless times, Pat studied the response to the dancers in the faces about the table. Phil Ruskin was frankly bored. Velma Dane's green eyes glittered with excitement, color which was not rouge dyed her cheeks. Alec Stanhope, beside her, sat with lips slightly parted. Monty Dane, seated at her left, leaned forward, eyes half closed, a satisfied smile on his sensual mouth. Maida, beside him, frowned as if resenting his absorption; Sally was glancing from table to table to locate friends. The General appeared tepidly interested. Cam Fulton, beside Alec Stanhope, was watching Señor Cardena, who was figuratively licking his lips with delight as the hula girls waved, swayed and switched.

The *lanai* went dark. Only the rhythmic beat of the tide and distant hum of a plane broke the uncanny stillness. Pitch blackness. A woman screamed.

Lights flashed on. Diners rose in their seats. Cries of "What happened? What was it?" ran from table to table with the swiftness of hungry flames in dry grass. The dancers in shimmering, revealing skirts of colored cellophane huddled in the center of the *lanai*, staring at Velma Dane, who stood with one hand at her throat, her eyes wide with fright, her lips open as if preparing to scream again. Her husband gripped her shoulder.

"Sit down, Carrots. Quick. Don't talk."

She gulped as if swallowing her heart as he pushed her back into the chair. Pedro motioned to the musicians. Guitars and ukuleles climbed on the air. The dancers swayed. Their glittering fringes swished. Guests settled back in their seats to watch the show. The maître d'hôtel leaned over Velma Dane.

"What was the trouble, Madam?" he had adopted the tone one might use to a child frightened by a nightmare.

The woman's color had returned. Her hand dropped to her lap. She managed a laugh.

"Sorry I made a scene. Something touched my foot. I thought it was a mouse. They terrify me."

"We have no mice here, Madam." Pedro swelled with just resentment. "You might have created a panic with that scream. You should have more self-control."

"You're telling me." She drew something from her silver bag and pressed it into his hand. "Suppose you forget my attack of jitters?" He bowed with slim grace.

"Already the jitters are forgotten, Madam."

He walked to the musicians' stage and held up his hand. The music stopped. The dancers formed a half circle. The spotlight shifted and illumined his dark face, his clothes no whiter than his teeth when he smiled.

"Ladies and gentlemen, Madam thought she felt a mouse on her foot." Dramatically he clasped his hands over his heart. "I swear by this we have no mouses here." He bowed from the waist in response to riotous applause. Steel, guitars and ukuleles sounded off with "On the Shores of Honolulu" and the dancers went into their routine.

"*Toujours la politesse.* Pedro gets away with murder," Phil Ruskin growled to Pat. "Mouse! That was eyewash. It wasn't a mouse that made the peppy Dane clutch that necklace as if she thought it was being snitched. She ought to have sense enough not to wear jewels like that at a night spot. I'll bet someone tried to get it. With the sides of the *lanai* open a guy who had spotted the diamonds could step in and try to snitch them. Boy, where's the man she picked up on the Clipper who was sitting beside her? He was in black clothes. To make him less conspicuous? Maybe it was he. He's gone."

"I remember now that when the lights flashed on after her scream, his chair was empty, but I was so excited I forgot about it. He probably left for a drink. I don't believe he tried to snitch the necklace. I thought him rather attractive with his long thin face and nice brown eyes. If this is his first visit to the Island and this club he wouldn't know enough about the program to plan a robbery."

"How do you know it is his first visit?" She laughed.

"Under cross-examination, your honor. I'll have to admit that I don't."

"The floor show is over. I'll ask Mrs. Dane to dance and apologize for Mother's nasty cracks this afternoon, also quiz her about that bloodcurdling yell. Sally and the General are on the floor, Dane and Maida, Señor Cardena has departed —when did he go? That leaves Fulton for you, Pat."

As Velma Dane rose eagerly in response to his invitation he flung over his shoulder:—

"Take care of my girl for me, will you, Colonel?"

Pat's face burned as with ash tray in hand Cam moved to a chair beside her.

"Sorry I don't dance," he said as he tamped out a cigarette which burned bright for a minute and died down.

"Why not add 'with you'? I saw you rumba with Mrs. Dane shortly after we came in. I was forced on you. Perhaps you'd rather not talk to me. I can go—"

"Sit down." He quickly removed his restraining hand from her bare arm. "What did you make of the Dane lady's fright?"

Apparently he didn't intend to explain why he could dance with Velma Dane and not with Patricia Carey.

"The mouse story left me unconvinced. Phil suspects that someone tried to snitch that sensational necklace she was clutching when the lights went up. Mebbe so, but why not proclaim, 'There's a thief in the house' and try to catch him?"

"Might be that she suspects it was someone she doesn't want caught."

"Do you mean Alec Stanhope, the Clipper acquaintance who was sitting beside her when the lights went out? He was gone when they went up."

"So he was. Now what do you make of that?"

"Well done, Colonel, but you haven't fooled me. You were seated next him. You must have known when he rose?"

"You're not trying to make me accessory after the fact, are you?" His nice grin faded as he leaned forward to replace a glass on the table and brought his head nearer hers. "Pat, please do not make that observation to anyone else—that I was sitting next to him when he left, I mean."

The heavy thud of her heart at his nearness made her think of "Old Ben" pounding out the hour. Could he hear it?

"Will you promise, Pat?"

"I broke one promise to you. Would you trust me or suspect always that I would renege?"

"Please, Pat, please, let's not go into that here. Suppose we begin again? Let's pretend we met for the first time that afternoon in the hotel *lanai* when you were a WAC and I was a visiting officer."

"It won't be difficult. You are not the man with whom I danced and laughed at the Post. I promise. Period. What an attractive couple Mrs. Dane and Phil make. She is so fair and his skin is so dark, so very dark."

"Dark!"

"Why the stunned surprise? You wouldn't call him on the blond side, would you?"

"Certainly not. That word 'dark' flashed a picture of the moment when Mrs. Dane screamed and set me wondering as to what really happened."

"Something tells me we'll never know. What a stunning woman she is. Her clothes give me the gasps."

"Nothing grubby about yours. That white frock brings out the gold lights in your hair."

"Glad you approve. It is what is known in the trade as an 'exclusive little number.' I stopped in New York on my way home for clothes. Went a little crazy over them, I had worn a uniform for so long."

"What sort of a leaf is the diamond clip you are wearing? Native?"

"Yes. Papaya. Aunt Sally gave it to me with the matching earrings as a reward of merit for coming home from overseas whole."

"Even with your heart whole?"

"Not a crack in it."

"Good. I remember that you wore a smashing star sapphire and diamond ring at the Post. More and more I realize how little I really knew about you that week, Pat."

"*What* week? At *what* Post, Colonel?" Her eyes deepened with amazement. "Have you mistaken me for someone else? Have you forgotten that we met for the first time the day of the style show?"

"Right on the nose. You win," he said and laughed. "I'll promise not to forget again. If you—"

"Come on, Pat, this is the last dance and *mine*," Phil Ruskin interrupted jealously. "Sally wants us to go to the house for a bite." As she rose Velma Dane tucked her hand under Cam Fulton's arm.

"Take me along with you, Colonel. That Parsons woman has kidnaped Monty." Her whisper carried. "I have something to tell you. Someone tried to snitch my necklace."

9

THE GI looking up at Kamehameha I before the Judiciary Building appeared so small and somehow lonely in contrast to the heroic bronze that Pat stopped on the step beside him. Her sympathy was for all the men in uniform in strange places, far from home.

"Grand person, isn't he, soldier?"

When he turned to answer his sleeve chevrons proclaimed him a staff sergeant. He touched his field cap with its light blue piping and readjusted it at a slightly more cocky angle on his red hair.

"Shure, an' he is, Miss. What'd the guy ever do to get himself embalmed like that?"

"He was a just and a great king of these islands. This is the only place in the United States where kings and queens have reigned."

"An' I never heard of him. 'Join the U.S. Army and see the world' is right. What's he wearing besides his first birthday suit—there's lots of that on exhibition, Miss."

She liked his grin, the Irish richness of his "shure," and she liked the respectful tone of his "Miss."

"It is a long story. Think you can bear it?"

"If you have time. From your light blue and white uniform, guess you're one of the Nurses' Aides that help in the hospital at the Barracks. I see 'em crossing the parade ground. Can I bear a long story? I can take it and like it. Ever know how it feels to be lonesome as hell? Excuse me, Miss. The word just slipped out. Sorry."

"That's all right, Sergeant. I've been with the army. I know what it is to be lonesome. I served two years with the Red Cross overseas and there were times—Good heavens, why live it over?"

"You've got something there, Miss. About this bronze guy. He's dressed like a chorus boy in a musical comedy movie. You know the kind. He comes marching in giving hot licks on a trumpet. Boom! Boom! Boom!"

He moved his hands back and forth in front of his face as if manipulating the keys of a brass instrument. Pat laughed and applauded softly.

"Something tells me I am talking to the leader of a band."

"Not me. I ran a gas station in Oklahoma before I signed up four years ago. The only music I heard was the grind of tires on gravel—it was music that set the cash register jingling—and the toot of auto horns, except Saturday nights when I made with a flute at the picture house with a lot of guys who gave with the fiddle. Shure, an' we had good shows in Oklahoma."

The hint of nostalgia in his voice tightened Pat's throat.

"We have good shows here, Sergeant. Now that the war is over you will be getting back to your gas station, your flute and your people soon, I hope."

"You got me wrong, Miss, no more gas station for me. I have no family back there, just folks I used to know. I have a boss who is a grand fella. I'm going home to help run his ranch. You said you'd tell me what King Whosis is wearing." He pulled a notebook from his trousers pocket. "I'll take it down. Since Cap. Butcher got his diary about Gen. Ike published—read it, it's great stuff—I've been writing up everything I do and see while I'm trekking with my boss. He isn't a general but give him time and I bet he'll be President of the U.S. You said it was a long story. Why not sit?" He dropped to the step beside her. "All set. Let's go."

"The helmet, made of feathers, is called a *makiole*, the girdle a *malo*. Got that? Stop me if I talk too fast. The cape, *mamo*, six feet long and eight feet wide, is a symbol of kingship. It was made from the feathers of 80,000 birds and took nine generations of skilled cloak makers to complete it."

"What do you know about that! What kind of feathers?"

"From the mamo; that's why the cape is called a mamo. A tiny tuft was plucked from above and below the tail. The quill of each feather was bent and firmly tied to a net of fine fiber so that each smoothly overlapped to make an unbroken yellow surface, a golden cape."

"Must have been some guy to rate all that work."

"He was. A great guy in what is a great part of our country, yours and mine, Sergeant. He had courage and the vision to realize that these islands would become of world importance and fought rival leaders who did not think as he did."

"A go-through guy, what?"

"A go-through guy is right. Look up at the tower behind us. See the words chiseled in the stone? It is the motto of the Territory of Hawaii, which many believe will be the gateway for a new world trade in the Pacific islands formerly controlled by Japan, and soon will take its place as the forty-ninth state in the Union. Seven rows of seven stars instead of six rows of eight on the flag. '*Ua mau ke ea o ka aina i ka pono*. The life of the land is preserved in righteousness.'"

"I liked the foreign sounding words best, they were so smooth the way you said 'em. Thanks for the story of the king. I got it down. It will be something to write about to the fiddlers back home—they are doughs like me—if any get home," he added somberly.

"I'll send you the story about him and the later kings, if you will give me your address." She rose and glanced over her shoulder. "Here come sight-seers out of the building to look at Kamehameha the Great. I'm going before I'm mistaken for a professional guide." His eyes had followed hers.

"Shure, an' I'm obliged to you, Miss," he said hurriedly. "I liked it fine, the story I mean. Here's the address." He scribbled on a page, tore it from the book, twisted it and thrust it into her hand. "Don't lose it, I'd be terrible disappointed not to get the book. I better beat it or I'll land in the doghouse."

He touched his cap and ran down to the street with the speed of a master skier on a snowy hill. All that was needed to complete the effect was widespread arms. Did he belong at the Barracks? She would check on him and if he were as nice as he seemed would invite him to bring his flute and play with her. She started to untwist the paper.

"Señorita Carey, meeting you is an unexpected happiness."

She thrust the address into the pocket of her apron before she turned to answer the suave greeting. Señor Miguel Cardena in white, which made his ruddy skin appear even ruddier and his black hair blacker, a broad-brim Panama hat under his left arm, stood on the step above her. His smile didn't reach his cold blue eyes under their curiously peaked brows. Behind him stood a dark-skinned, dark-haired man with a long nose, thin mouth and the obsequious air of a movie valet.

"I hope I did not interrupt what, in the States, you call 'a talk-fest' with a friend?"

"Not—an interruption, Señor." She had started to say, not a friend, just a lonely soldier, but for an unaccountable reason changed. "I am surprised to see you. We heard you left our Island the day after the night club party." He walked beside her to the street. The man whom she had thought was with him lingered to look up at the statue.

"I flew to Maui to see the House of the Sun, which, I was

informed, is the world's largest crater. I would not leave finally without first paying my respects to your aunt who has made me so welcome, and to Madam Shaw-Ruskin with whom I am dining tonight. You are all so kind to me, is it surprising that I like this beautiful island?"

"You would have loved it if you could have seen it before Pearl Harbor on December 7, 1941. Life here, which had been so colorful and gay, changed overnight to the tragic business of war."

"It may be on its way back to gaiety before I leave. I find that my business here will take more time than I figured. May I walk to your car with you?"

"It is around the corner. It is difficult to get through the street crowd at the noon hour. People queue in front of the shop windows."

"It is not strange. They are such remarkable shops. Before I leave maybe you will be so kind as to advise me in the selection of gifts which will carry the atmosphere of the Islands, for my wife and daughter?"

"I'd love it. You'll have to tell me about them, so that I will have an idea what to choose."

"I would prefer something like that beautiful clip you wore at the night club."

"It will be fun to buy diamonds. The shops aren't what they were before Pearl Harbor, but even so I have reveled in their color, glitter and extravagance since I returned from the drabness of the shambles overseas."

"You must cherish that service as a privilege, Señorita. Auwe—I have picked up that expression since I landed here —my country sent troops but I was kept at home on government affairs. Colonel Fulton and Captain Dane served in the German sector, I have been informed. Perhaps you were with them?"

She didn't like the inflection in his voice, she didn't like the boring keenness of his blue eyes as he asked the question.

"Captain Dane and I served in the same outfit for a while, then I was sent to Belgium."

"Indeed. You must share many memories. Were you with Colonel Fulton, also?"

"No, Señor."

"He has interested me greatly. A typical high-class American, I judge. He is so calm, so much the master of himself. Before I came here I met one of the United States scientists whom he—shall I say—had the care of, while they were poking among German ruins. Of course he has told you about that?"

"No."

"He is not a communicative person. I tried to get him to talk about his experiences to me the other evening at the night club—That reminds me. Did Mrs. Dane recover her necklace? When the lights went down I left for the foyer to smoke. I do not like a dark room with many persons in it, it is unsafe. I heard a scream. Later, in the bar, there was a rumor that her necklace had been stolen. It would be a costly loss. The diamond centers in those roses were superb."

"She didn't lose it. She screamed because she felt a mouse run over her foot and she is afraid of mice. There was a sprightly minute till we knew what had happened, though."

She thought of Velma Dane's whispered words to Cam, "Someone tried to snitch my necklace," and for one hectic instant she remembered that Señor Cardena said he had not been in the dark room. Why make a point of telling her that? How come that he knew the stones in the necklace were superb from a casual glance? He had just commented on her own diamond clip. He was a mysterious sort of person, maybe he was an international jewel thief. Stranger things had happened. Maybe he was—

"I am glad to hear that it was not stolen." The suave voice brought her out of her absurd imaginings. Of course he wasn't a jewel thief. Hadn't he presented a letter to Madam Shaw-Ruskin from the American Minister to Brazil, and to Sally from her friend the Consul in Rio?

"When I heard of the attempt at robbery, which you now tell me fortunately is untrue, I wondered about the man who danced with Mrs. Dane. He sat at table between her and Colonel Fulton. He was on the Clipper and was most attentive to her during the crossing. Also, he was on the plane to Maui. I didn't see him after we reached the House of the Sun. I had a hunch, as you call it in the States, that he was a friend of Colonel Fulton's."

He was quizzing her. Why? Was Alec Stanhope Cam's friend? He had asked her to promise not to mention the fact that he was seated next to him before he left the *lanai* at the night club. Had he tried to steal the necklace? Was Cam shielding him?

"I really wouldn't know, Señor Cardena, about Colonel Fulton's friends. He and I met on the Island for the first time a few days ago." That evasion was becoming a habit.

"What's going on here?" He stopped to look up at Aloha Tower. "They are hauling down flags."

"They have flown over the station four years. The Tower is being reinstated as a harbor entrance and returned to the territorial Board of Harbor Commissioners. During the war it was an important part of Hawaii's defense. I read in the morning paper that the ceremony was scheduled for today. Here is my car. Sorry I can't take you whither you are bound but I mustn't be late for hospital duty."

"You are most kind to think of it, Señorita, but my man is following with the car I have managed to secure for the duration of my stay."

"Glad you haven't said farewell to the Island as we feared. *Aloha.*" She was in the gray sedan and had it in motion before he could answer.

What is it all about, she wondered as she sent the car smoothly forward along the black highway, past white buildings from many of which the brilliant colors of the Stars and Stripes fluttered in the hibiscus-scented breeze. Was the smoothie who had followed Cardena out of the Judiciary Building his man? Something about him had started prickles along her nerves.

The Señor had appeared only faintly interested in the attempted theft of the necklace. Unless intuition had failed her, what he really wanted was information about Alec Stanhope, the man Velma Dane had introduced into the party. He had remembered that Stanhope sat next to Cam, a fact upon which Cam had asked her not to comment. Her flash that the Brazilian might be a jewel thief was crazy—or was it? He had referred to his "business." What was it?

Did anyone know? Since the afternoon she had seen Cam approaching across the hotel *lanai* she had felt a curious awareness of undercurrents. Perhaps there was no reason for it, perhaps her imagination was keyed to melodrama by her experiences overseas, or maybe she was caught in a net of plots and counterplots. That was a gruesome thought to have on a heavenly day like this when the sky was a clear blue and the few clouds piled up in grotesque patterns were edged with rainbows where the sun touched them.

As she ran up the steps of the hospital she met Cam coming down.

"Where's the fire?" He caught her blue sleeve and held it.

"Don't detain me, please, I'm late. You are the third man who has held me up on my way to duty."

"Not very serious lateness if you can smile about it. Who were the other two?"

"The first was a snappy staff sergeant. I fall hard for sergeants. They have a way with them. I think I'll take out a license as an Island guide. I gave—and how—about the bronze statue of Kamehameha I in front of the Judiciary Building."

"A go-through guy, what?" the Sergeant had said. Her conscience administered its familiar pinch. Ooch, as if she needed to be reminded that a go-through guy was what she had *not* been.

"Who was the second?"

"Second? Oh, the second man? Señor Miguel Cardena. I was surprised to see him, we thought he had left the Islands. He flew to Maui to see the House of the Sun. He expects to stay here till his mission is accomplished; it will take longer than he thought. He had heard there was an attempt to snitch Mrs. Dane's necklace at the night club the other evening."

"Didn't you tell him it wasn't stolen? That she was frightened by a mouse?"

"I told him she *said* that. It seems he had been suspicious of Stanhope—by the way, he flew to Maui also—and was much interested to know if he were your friend. He remembered that he was seated beside you at table. Don't glare at me so sharply."

"I was not glaring. What did you tell him?"

"That I knew nothing of your friends, having met you on the Island for the first time a few days ago. Right? Believe it or not, Señor Cardena asked me to select take-home presents for his wife and daughter."

"Wife? Daughter? Did you say you would?"

"You sound as if you didn't believe the man had a wife and daughter. Of course I said yes. Think of the fun of being turned loose in a jeweler's shop with oodles of money to spend—even if it were not for oneself."

"How do you know the man has oodles? Why so sure he would buy jewels?"

"He talks and appears as if he had a Brazilian gold mine or two behind him. There is an adorable gold ring and bracelet, set with olivines, rare greenish crystals found in lava which are called Madam Pele's Tears, I have been mad to own, but I'll be noble and recommend them for the Señor's daughter."

"Don't shop with him, Pat."

"Why not? I like him"—that's a lie—"He builds me up with his eyes and voice, makes me feel I'm the only girl he ever lov—" She choked on the word. Her heart went into a crash dive. Cam had said that to her. Was he remembering? Did he hate her more than ever for her flippancy? She said with an attempt at gaiety that didn't come off, "Good heavens, I had forgotten his wife and daughter."

"Apparently that isn't all you have forgotten. Go ahead and shop with him, but keep your fingers crossed. I don't like the picking up of that sergeant, either. Good morning." He ran down the steps before she could answer.

Her eyes smarted with unshed tears as she watched him. He would never forgive her. Nothing she did interested him. She had chattered about the olivine jewelry to cover her hurt at his indifference. He might have something in his objection to Señor Miguel Cardena, she didn't trust him herself, but there could be nothing wrong about that nice sergeant. Would he have given her his address if he hadn't been on the level? By the way, she had better look at it. She drew the twisted paper from the pocket of her apron. Read the scribbled words. Read them again.

Don't speak to the guy coming this way. He's poison.

She closed her eyes and visualized the man coming toward her as he scribbled. Señor Cardena? Or had he meant the smooth person behind him? She tore the paper into bits and dropped them into her pocket. Pulled open the heavy door of the hospital.

"Sergeant, whichever person you meant, you've got something," she said under her breath. "You don't know it yet, but you and I are to become pals."

10

"CORPORAL Skinner has been asking for you, Miss Carey," announced the white-frocked nurse in attendance at the desk when she reported for duty. An overworked woman if one were to judge by the two deep lines across her forehead, the tired droop of her mouth and the nervous twitch of her eyes.

"The boy has something on his mind. Encourage him to tell it. If he starts let him talk, don't stop him. He may not be with us tomorrow. Nothing we can do will keep him in this world."

"Is he failing fast? I'm sorry. Sorry seems such a futile word, doesn't it? I like him. He has so much courage. I hoped we could pull him through."

"You've put a lot of your vitality into the job, but why try to hold him, smashed up as he is? The smashing happened after he was sent here for redeployment. A crazy driver with too much liquor aboard got off scot-free and the passenger paid the bill. They're still doing it. That's all, Miss Carey," she dismissed curtly.

Pat smiled and nodded to the men in the white beds as she passed through the sunny ward, which shone with cleanliness and smelled of disinfectants. Usually she stopped and spoke to them, but not today. Skinner had asked for her and the nurse had warned that he had not much time left in which to talk. What did he want? When she had first given him special attention he had asked her never to mention his name outside the hospital. Did that mean that he was afraid of someone?

His bed was next to the wall at the end of the long room. The eyes that looked up in response to her greeting were brilliant with fever, the thin, good-looking face was flushed, the breathing difficult.

"I heard you were inquiring for me, Corporal, and did it make me feel important." She sat in a low chair between the wall and bed and took the hand which was picking at the coverlet warmly in hers. "How can I help you?"

"You help by just being you." The faint smile on his lips gave way to gravity. "I've got to—tell you something. When I've passed out—you needn't say I'm not going—I—know—do what you think best with what I tell you." He tried to turn his head toward the next bed. "Can that guy hear?"

"No. He is wearing earphones. Probably listening to a football game somewhere on the Mainland; he is keeping score. The men across the room can't hear. Go on."

"There is a flat black leather bag in the hospital safety vault. This will unlock it." He indicated a small key fastened to the dog tag which hung about his neck. "Take it."

"But, Corporal—"

"You said you wanted to help, didn't you? Then take it—quick. I haven't got time to—argue." His urgent voice was thick with tears of weakness. She unfastened the key.

"I have it. Now what?"

"Hold onto it. Get the bag."

"Will they give it to me?"

"I talked with the Post Commander this morning. Told him it contained family papers which you would take over and send to my people with letters I had dictated to you." He closed his eyes for a moment as if to gather strength.

"I thought at first I couldn't put it across but the P.C. said he knew you—that you would do things right. He showed me how to word and sign an order." He drew an envelope from under his pillow. "Here it is. Go for the bag now. Bring it here. I must be sure you have it."

She nodded and walked quickly between the two long rows of beds with the envelope clutched in one hand and the fingers of the other tight about the key in her pocket, wondering what it was all about, questioning if the bag would be delivered to her.

It was, a black brief case, with a minimum amount of comment about her errand and a maximum amount of conversation about the help she was in the hospital by the lieutenant in charge of the vault, and how much he would like a date with her.

It was rather heavy, must be quite a lot of "family papers" in it, she decided as she returned through the ward. Skinner was dozing when she reached his bed. She seated herself in the low chair next the wall with the brief case in her lap. It might be a twin of the one Monty Dane had left in the foyer at Silver Ledges. The Corporal's eyes opened slowly as if the lids were heavy.

"Get it?"

She leaned nearer to answer his whisper.

"Yes. Is this the one?"

"Put it on the bed where I can feel it." His fingers closed about the corner as if testing the thickness. "That's it. Is the GI still listening on the radio?" She nodded. "Okay, take it home with you. Don't let anyone know you have it until—you haven't mentioned my name outside, have you?" Anxiety hoarsened his weak voice. She shook her head.

"Keep all this q.t. till after I've passed out. Hide the bag. Get it? *Hide* the bag. Keep it safe. There's a guy who wouldn't stop at—at mur—der to get it."

"But *Corporal*—"

"I know I'm putting a lot on you—" he acknowledged, as if the horror in her exclamation had gotten through to him. "But, I've watched you helping here—you—you can take any —thing." He closed his eyes. Was he slipping into a coma? Pat rose to touch the bell. He lifted his lids.

"Don't go. I can finish. I—I must finish. Lean nearer. I stole the stuff in this bag—under pressure from a higher-up." She could feel the effort to rally his strength. "He threatened to have me court-martialed for a little black-market deal I'd put across—if—if I didn't pull it—off."

"Rest a few minutes, Corporal, before you go on."

"I can't, I tell you, I *can't*." Tears of weakness shook his voice. "I've got to finish. The higher-up said we'd get our rake-off, a big one, if it was delivered to a party who'd contact us, on this island. It—took—time to get the stuff and before I could hand it over to him the outfit was scattered. I've had a hell of a time—hiding it—to get it this far. I'll bet the heel—has been raking the list of returned—doughs with a finetooth comb to find me. He hasn't yet." In his excitement he tried to raise himself on an elbow. Sank back. "Give me a drink—of that stuff—it will help me finish."

Pat gently raised his shoulders on her arm and held a glass to his lips, wondering if this were partly delirium, if she should call the nurse, remembering she had been told to let him talk. She lowered his head against the pillow.

"That's better," the words came in an exhausted whisper. "Now I can go on."

"Tell me what I am to do with the black bag, Corporal? You don't want me to hunt for the heel who blackmailed you into stealing the 'stuff' and deliver it to him, do you?"

"That's what I don't want. Two months ago I wrote to my buddy, a noncom, where I was, told him there was something he must do for me. No answer. Perhaps he's dead—too. He didn't know I'd stole the—the papers—he'd have shot me on sight if he had." His voice was weaker. "I'm sorry I did. Better if I'd taken the court-martial, I hadn't any folks living to be shamed. I wouldn't have had to live with this damn knowledge I'd been—a thief. The black market was only gray." He pulled himself up on his elbow.

"Hold tight to that bag till—I'm gone," he whispered. "Watch out for the heel who'll try to get the—the stuff. His name is—" He dropped back heavily. His eyes closed. Pat leaned over him.

"Corporal! Corporal! His name? Quick," she prompted. "Please, please, don't go—to sleep." His eyes opened weakly as if he caught the break in her voice. "It may save murder. Remember? You said murder." Would the horrible word rouse him?

"Murder?" His voice was so faint she had to lean close to hear it. "Sure—he might—try it—on you." As if realizing for the first time what it could mean to her, he whispered thickly, "I'm sorry—I let—you in for—it, but there's no one else." He closed his eyes as if to pull himself together, caught her hand. "Don't go. That guy—I told you about—my buddy who could help—he may be dead—you'll have to take over—it means a lot to—take your time—be sure you have a regular guy before—you tell about—" His lids drooped wearily.

"The name of the heel? Quick, Skinner, quick," Pat urged.

"The heel," he repeated without opening his eyes. "Sure, his name is—" His head rolled on the pillow. "I'm so tired—I'm so doggone tired—hiding—hiding—counting—I'll tell you—tomorrow—" He drew a hoarse, quick breath, and was still.

Pat laid her fingers on his pulse. Gone. Tomorrow wouldn't come for him.

She brushed her hand across her eyes to clean them of blinding tears, and touched the bell at the head of the bed. Had she called for help earlier could he have been saved? No. The nurse had said, "If he starts, let him talk. Don't stop him."

"This is enough for you today, Miss Carey," the matron declared sternly as she drew a screen around the bed. "You're white as a sheet. Get a cup of hot, strong coffee, and I mean strong, and go home. That's an order," she added as Pat hesitated. "What's that brief case you're clutching?"

"The Corporal's papers I am to send to his family. He talked with the Post Commander this morning and told him that I was to take care of them."

"Then it's okay. Go along. Don't stop to speak to the patients. I'm too busy to pick you up in a dead faint. Scram."

Outside the ward Pat removed her white apron and threw it over her left arm to hide the brief case she carried. She wouldn't stop for coffee. Better get home. Was she faint or had the power of suggestion made her dizzy?

"Well, see who's here!"

She turned from the gray sedan to answer Monty Dane's hail. Had he seen her place the brief case that was like his on the seat before she dropped her apron over it?

"You are the last person I would expect to see around a hospital, Monty. How come?" She had her hand on the wheel when she asked the question. He stooped to pick up something on the ground before he answered.

"I heard there was a doughfoot here who was in my company in Germany who got smashed in an auto accident. He sent for me. I'm not much good at holding the hands of the sick, but I couldn't refuse."

Smashed up in an accident. Could he mean the boy who had just died? Skinner had said he had written to a guy he knew in the army, had told him there was something he could do. Perhaps Monty was the person? Perhaps she could turn the brief case over to him this minute and shift the load of responsibility which had been dropped on her shoulders to his.

She laid her hand on the apron which covered the brief case. Withdrew it as if she had touched something hot. No, Skinner had spoken of a noncom buddy. Monty was a captain. He had said, "Take your time. Be sure you have a regular guy—before—you tell about—" It wouldn't be taking her time if she turned it over to Monty now.

"You look all in, Pat. What the dickens have you been doing?" It seemed to her as if she had been debating mentally for hours. Apparently he hadn't noticed a gap between sentences.

"If you tell me I look white I shall faint away, then what will you do with a limp female on your hands? If you must know I saw something in the hospital which knocked the bottom out of my stomach and gave my knees the jitters."

"After what you took in action, don't tell me you are getting soft, gal."

"I'll harden up. I'll jolly well have to. I am to help in the surgical ward next week. I hope your wife is enjoying the Island."

"Is that a crack?"

"What do you mean, a *crack?* Of course it isn't."

"Sure, she likes it—does a cat like cream? Why wouldn't she with Mrs. Shaw taking her up as if she were a crowned head? Just why?" His eyes were hard with suspicion. "Anyone with half an eye can see that Carrots isn't in her class."

"My aunt admires her. Admires the way she shot back at Madam Shaw-Ruskin. The indispensable woman has been found. Sally has principles about putting her mother-in-law in her place herself, she thinks rowing in-laws are the lowest form of animal life. Mrs. Dane made her a friend for keeps. You don't half appreciate your wife, Monty. She's a grand person."

"So you think. Wait till you see what she intends to do to you. I'll be seeing you."

"Monty!"

He strode on without turning at her call. What had he meant by that cryptic, "Wait till you see what she intends to do to you"?

Sally Shaw, in a violet and white print frock, was having luncheon at a small table in the *lanai* when she reached home.

"Pat! What has happened, you—"

"Don't tell me I look white. If I do, it isn't a patch on the commotion inside. My corporal died while he was talking with me." She drew up a chair to the small table. "Pour me a cup of coffee. Can you spare part of the omelette? Perhaps if I eat I'll stop feeling shaky. I'll go for a plate."

"Sit still. I'll get it. With the blackout lifted and the curfew silenced, and the new workers coming from the Philippines to harvest the sugar—ten thousand acres of mature cane had to be left standing for want of man power last year—far be it from me to be ungrateful for minor blessings, but having a schoolgirl for part-time help has its drawbacks."

As she waited for her aunt's return Pat rested her head against the cushions of the rattan chair. To keep from visualizing Skinner's waxen face as she had seen it last, she thought back to the encounter with Monty Dane. What had the Captain meant by, "Wait till you see what she intends to do to you"?

Why get panicky? What could Velma Dane do? Nothing which had a foundation of fact. He had tried to frighten her because she had championed his wife. Sally Shaw returned with a tray.

"Your color is better; you had me scared stiff, what with the flu epidemic at high. Behold, hot coffee and popovers. Mrs. Wong Chun was holding out on me, she had made them for herself. Said she knew I wouldn't eat them for fear I would get fat. Who appointed her my official streamliner?" She set the small silver pot and the plate of crisp, puffy popovers on the table and returned to the chair opposite Pat.

"Don't talk, honey. Drink the coffee' while it is hot." She lifted a silver cover and served a portion of golden omelette which gave out the spicy aroma of herbs. "Eat, then I'll hear all about it."

As she obeyed orders Pat wondered how much she had better tell of the morning's encounters. Nothing of the Sergeant or she might inadvertently refer to that twisted note. Señor Cardena as a subject would bear touching upon. Not a word more of Skinner's passing, it was so tied up with the brief case he had left in her care. She could bring Monty Dane and his warning out into the open to get an opinion on it.

"Your prescription worked to a charm, Sally," she attested. She set the table with its trays within the living room. "Did you know that Señor Cardena is to dine with the Queen Mother tonight?" She stretched out on a chaise longue. "Hasn't she taken him up rather violently—for her?"

"He had letters to her, among others, from brass hats stationed in Rio. He is paying her very special attention; sometimes I wonder if it's the spell that makes the world go round. The General and I are invited to the dinner."

"Do you like him—the Brazilian, I mean—I know your sentiments about the General."

"I did let my hair down about him, didn't I? Auwe, you are a safe confidante. As to Cardena—yes and no. That's always such an intelligent answer. Whom else did you contact this morning?"

"I met Colonel Fulton for a minute as I was going into the hospital and Captain Dane for several minutes as I was leaving. He was curious to know why you are taking up his wife as if she were a crowned head. Those are his words, not mine. I told him you admired the way she went to bat—

in the Shaw-Ruskin-Dane showdown. When I reminded him that he didn't half appreciate his wife, he came back, 'Wait till you see what she intends to do to you.' What do you make of that, Sally?"

"What I have been horribly afraid of, that she would drag you into court."

"How can she?" Pat swung her feet to the floor and sat up. "She hasn't a sliver of fact upon which to base an accusation."

"A woman like her doesn't need fact, she wants to smear out of revenge. Dane told you he had asked her to divorce him, didn't he? Doubtless he named you as the 'other woman.' Anyone can see she's a fool about him. She won't let him go, if she has to raise the proverbial Cain to keep him. That's why I'm going all out to be nice to her, to draw her fangs. That's one reason, the other is I like her. She is refreshing."

"Rough-diamond-but-heart-of-gold type. Another reason couldn't be that she might give you a nice fat check for that Disabled Vet Club of yours, could it?"

"She has given me one, smarty." Sally's funny little grimace of disdain made her seem about fifteen. "I didn't ask for it either. I repeat, I like her. She worked every day her husband was away in a hospital and nights at a canteen. She waves Old Glory at every opportunity. I have a feeling that it isn't all talk, that she would sacrifice a lot to help. Whom else did you see? Usually you bring home more news about people I know than I can find in the personal column of the morning paper."

"They were changing the flags of Aloha Tower. Its war job is finished."

"Finished? Hmp, the toughest fighting is ahead of us in the United States. On the Mainland industries and labor are battling, two million workers out on strike, war wives are pestering Ike Eisenhower to bring their husbands back, and the GI's want out. He knows they are needed in this tense time of domestic and international tension when the UN is still an infant on the bottle. Peace, ain't it wonderful. That isn't original so don't quote it later as being a *bon mot* of mine, honey. We've got our chance to make over the world into a collector's item and so far what a botch we're making of the job. People have forgotten the horror, the tragedy of the last four years."

"Cheerio, Sally, there are a lot who have not forgotten, who are determined that the make-over job shall not be botched, to have a world that will be a worthy memorial to the countless men and women who gave their lives to better it."

"You are arguing as if you were forty years old instead of twenty-four."

"One can't see what I saw of our fighters, Sally, see them die with a smile and wave of a weak hand, without having an immense belief in the American way. If we could win against those powers of evil which threatened the world, we can lick the threat to the world of peace. Having regaled you with my words of wisdom I'll shower and change, in the hope of reducing my present forty to at least thirty. What are you wearing to the tennis tea this afternoon, in honor of the stop-over celebrities on their way to advisory assignments in Japan? Flats or heels? In other words, sport clothes, or a dress?"

"Wear the flamingo linen, the color does a lot for you, it may even reduce the thirty years to twenty-five. Run along, rest a little before you change. You crowd too much into your days, honey. You have me worried."

What would she think if she knew that she crowded her days so that she would be too dead tired to lie awake at night and think of the botch she had made of her life, Pat asked herself. She picked up the brief case from the table in the foyer and went slowly up the stairs.

In her room she removed the white apron wrapped around the worn leather brief case. Had she better examine its contents and begin to work out a plan for its disposal? She had the time now, she might not have it tomorrow. She reached into her apron pocket for the key. Her heart stopped. Gone? Not really? Where could she have dropped it?

Her thoughts traveled back to the moment when she had thrust it into the apron pocket. Careless thing to do. You don't have to remind me of that, she flared at herself. She had dropped the apron over the brief case when she had put it on the seat of the car. Had the key fallen out then? Monty had stooped to pick up something. Had it been the key? If so, why hadn't he thought it might be hers? Why hadn't he spoken of it? Why would he want to conceal it? Suppose that were all true? The question was how could she get it?

11

AS Cam Fulton entered his workroom Sergeant McIlvray
quickly dropped the newspaper he had been about to cut
with a pocket knife, snapped the blade and saluted.

"Shure, an' it's a rough time they're having back in the
U.S., sir." Cam knew from his flushed face and slow way of
speaking that he had thought up the remark hurriedly.

"You are in the United States now, remember, Sergeant.
Mainland, with the capital M, is the term in use here. Any
calls?"

"On the desk pad, sir. Mrs. Montgomery Dane sounded as
if she'd go nuts if you didn't call her right back, sir. Then,
you-know-who would like you to join the party he is throwing
at the Officers' Club at Haleiwa Bay, later in the week."

"Did you answer him, Sergeant?"

"Shure, an' why not? Who else was here, to do it? You
wouldn't have known my voice, though. I'll bet he thought it
was a dame saying, 'Colonel Fulton's office.'" The words
were in the dulcet conversational tones of a mezzo-soprano.
"I started to wisecrack, 'Spill it to me, I'm his trouble-
shooter,' stopped just in time. It didn't sound like what a
femme secretary would say."

"Right. When did you acquire that vocal accomplishment?"

"I found I could do it when I was—was boardin' with the
Nazis. Got a laugh out of the P.W.'s every time so I kept it
up. God knows they needed a laugh." He tipped his field
cap at a jaunty angle and swaggered. "Shure, an' I got a lot
of good points you never discovered, sir."

Cam liked his swagger, liked his grin; it had been a tonic
to him during the dragging days when he was recovering
from his wound, beefing because he couldn't get back into
the fight.

"Name some of them, Mac."

"I give with the flute when a lotta doughs get together
and I'm pretty near primed to be a tourist guide on this
island. I've got old Kameham—you know the guy I mean—
down fine."

"Who is teaching you?" Had it been Pat? A week ago when
he had spoken to her on the hospital steps, she had said she
had met a snappy sergeant. Mac filled that bill.

"Remember the maid at Mrs. Shaw's, the cute Chinese

trick I told you about, sir? I met her near the, what do they
call it, Judiciary Building. She's no lallygagger, sir, she's an
all-right kid, she was there to deliver a note from her boss
to some guy inside."

"I remember her, I remember also that I advised you to
keep strictly to friendship."

"I've done that, sir. She's been teaching me to surf-ride.
You don't get much time for love-makin' when you're on one
of them boards; your mind is on keeping your balance, not
on a dame."

"You've got something there. You get around, don't you,
Sergeant?"

"Shure, an' I get around." He grinned. "About that party
at Haleiwa Bay, you wouldn't let me go along to look after
you, would you, sir?"

"I would not. Keep out of the way of Señor Cardena and
his man. That's an order, get it?"

"Yes, sir. I figure the man—'slick customer,' you sized him
up—is sort of a bodyguard as well as a chauffeur. I hear his
boss has hired a convertible, one of those with a white canvas top. I'll beat it to the jeweler's now and call for that
package you told me to get."

"Wait a minute. Did you phone for the shorts we saw
advertised?"

"I did. No soap. Shorts—plural, that's a joke. 'Only one to
a customer' is getting to be the national slogan. I'm off, sir."

The Sergeant was in a tearing hurry to go, Cam thought,
as he put in a call for Mrs. Montgomery Dane. What could
she want of him? She must have been sitting in the lap of
the phone, figuratively speaking, for it seemed but a minute
before she answered.

"Ohmigosh, Colonel, I've been walking the floor while I
waited to hear from you. Will you lunch with me today? I
must talk with you. It's very important. It isn't only for myself."

What in thunder did she mean by that? Trouble for Pat or
someone else?

"Colonel? Colonel? Are you still on the line?"

"Yes. I was mentally juggling my appointments. What time
lunch and where?"

"At one, here on the terrace. The coast will be clear," she
whispered and rang off.

What is it all about, Cam asked himself as he cradled the
phone. I don't like that conspirational, "The coast is clear."
Clear of whom? Her husband? Crude as she was, her manner
with men was one of frank pleasure in their companionship,
with not a trace of Maida's bid for an emotional response to

her caressing voice and eyes, the hand slipped under a man's arm.

He checked his engagements. He must be at the Barracks at four when the command of the Post would be transferred from one general to another. It would be an impressive ceremony and ought to draw a crowd. Had the papers featured it?

He picked up the newspaper on the desk and glanced through the military news. Directly beneath it, the word PERSONAL in outstanding black type caught his eye.

PERSONAL

Flute player. GI. Meet me at same place. Any noon. Hear something to your advantage. Island Guide.

Cam stared at the bluish haze of the Waianae Range that loomed in the distance. His eyes came back to the paper. Had Mac been about to cut out the ad? Looked like it. He had had a knife in his hand and there was a small break in the paper where the point had entered. He backtracked on a trail of thought. Pat had met a "snappy sergeant" to whom she had told the story of King Kamehameha I. "And was I good? I think I will take out a license as an Island Guide," she had said and a few moments ago Mac had admitted he played the flute.

If she wanted to contact the Sergeant why take this round-about way of doing it? What was behind it? McIlvray was engaged in a task where even a shadow must be investigated. If she were seen with him, and by chance Cardena recognized him as a onetime P.W. who might reveal that he was a Nazi in disguise, he or his henchman would make short shrift of man or woman whom they thought suspected their identity.

He reread the Personal. "Any noon." He glanced at the wall clock. Mac had left in plenty of time to make the Judiciary Building at that hour, if that was where the rendezvous was to be. Was that why he had been in such an all-fired hurry?

He slapped on his cap. At the risk of being accused of spying he must ease his mind about Pat. It was unsafe for her to be with Sergeant McIlvray. Suppose someone else had seen that Personal and was on the watch to discover what it meant?

Perhaps there was a menace in it and perhaps he was just plain nutty, he reasoned as he drove through the broad, palm-bordered street slowly. Doubtless there were dozens of flute-playing GI's at the Barracks and as many women who worked at being Island Guides. Women? Perhaps a man had inserted the Personal. Nothing in it had a distinctive femme touch.

The Judiciary Building was just ahead. The sudden reduction of speed of the jeep brought a frantic toot of indignation from a car behind. Now he was opposite the statue. Good Lord, he had forgotten that his war-hardened nerves could give such a jump. He would know the tilt of the field cap on that red head if he were to see it in the midst of the thousands of troops at the Barracks. Notebook in hand, Sergeant McIlvray stood looking up at Kamehameha I.

If he stopped the Sergeant would see him and forever after suspect him of spying. Better drive on—and fast. He was sure that the Personal had been directed to Mac. Pat—if it were she who had had it inserted—might not come today. What was cooking? McIlvray had taken an eager step forward and as suddenly returned to scribbling in the notebook. Cam's taut nerves relaxed with a suddenness that left him limp. So that was it? Mrs. Shaw's Chinese maid, Sib Lou, in a school-girlish bright plaid skirt and navy cardigan, was running eagerly toward him.

The mystery was solved. He shot the car ahead. Frowned. Was it? How come if the Sergeant had appeared in response to the ad that he had resumed scribbling in his notebook after he looked up and saw the Chinese girl? Was there something behind that meeting that was part of his job to know?

Velma Dane was waiting in the lounge for him when he reached the hotel. The bright green she was wearing undoubtedly was what the stylists dubbed a resort costume. A gardenia was tucked in a wave of her auburn hair, which hung to her shoulders without being lumped into one of the hideous mesh bags girls were affecting. It was evident that she was the current subject of speculation among the hotel guests. The face of every person present was turned their way as she and he followed the maître d'hôtel the length of the terrace to a table for two partially screened by a spreading palm. Crisp rolls and crystal cups of jellied green turtle consommé with slices of lemon already were on the table.

"I ordered the lunch, Colonel. What will you have to drink?"

"Coffee."

"I ordered that." An armful of silver bracelets clashed as she waved away a hovering Filipino waiter.

"Why the SOS?" he inquired as he selected a cigarette from the gold case she offered. He held a lighter to one between her lips before he added, "It sounded like that on the phone. What is on your mind?"

She leaned a little toward him. Her green eyes were clouded with anxiety.

"I told you the other day I know you are a right guy. *Believe me*," her shrugged shoulders emphasized the words, "I've seen plenty of the other kind, okay on the outside, rotten inside—who have been attracted to my money like wasps to a lobster bake on Mount Desert."

"You are not fair to yourself, Mrs. Dane."

"Can the old oil and let's get down to Velma and Cam. How about it?"

"Suits me fine—Velma. Now let's proceed to the reason you sent for me. Spill it."

"Later."

A waiter served breasts of chicken garnished with huge broiled mushrooms, flanked with new potato balls in Hollandaise sauce and corn fritters that looked like puff balls; a green salad with Roquefort cheese dressing.

"Anything else you would like?" she asked while the waiter filled cups with steaming, dark-amber coffee.

"We have again for the first time since the war the delicious Sultana Roll for dessert, Madam," the Filipino tempted.

"That luscious stuff? Here's where I fall from my diet with a crash. Bring it when I ring, waiter, and keep away from this table till I do. Understand."

"Yes, Madam. I go. *Wikiwiki*."

"It's about Monty," she explained without preamble. Her eyes were the hard green he had noticed the first time he had seen her. "I'm crazy about him but not such a fool that I can't see when he's walking straight into trouble."

He stiffened. Was she about to confide her suspicion of her husband's relations with Pat in Germany? It would be a break to have her bring it into the open. Let her try it. This would be his chance to set her straight with a speed that would make her head swim.

"Not woman trouble," she explained as if she divined his thoughts. "He wrote me from abroad he had seen a girl he wanted to marry, would I divorce him? I guess he isn't the only officer who had that sort of a brainstorm while in service. He had the nerve to name the girl and I followed him here, loaded to make it hot for her."

"*Don't* speak her name."

"Ohmigosh, why glare like that? Think I haven't sense enough to know you'd send my head rolling into a basket if I mentioned her? That I wasn't keen enough to get hep the first time I saw her that she would never fall seriously for a wolf like Monty?"

"All right, all *right*—that being settled, what's on your mind?"

"Relax. You're so jumpy I can't think straight."

"I'm relaxed as a deflated balloon. Go on."

"Monty is heading for trouble. I've admitted I'm crazy about him, but I'm just as crazy about something else and that's the good old U.S.A."

He had been right, there was fine stuff in her, the stuff of her pioneer forebears. Monty heading for trouble. Crazy about the U.S.A. The words shuttled into meaning like the pieces of a picture puzzle. His pulses broke into quick-step.

"Just what do you mean, Velma? Why are you telling me this?"

She leaned forward.

"Because I'm scared stiff for fear my husband is getting into a serious jam. I must save him. I've known he wasn't honest about women—about my money—that he gambles, recklessly—now I suspect—"

"Go on," Cam's voice was as low as hers.

"Now I suspect he is doing a little subversive stuff on the side."

12

THE trade wind seemed to grow colder. It sent little prickles along his nerves. The scent of the gardenia in Velma Dane's hair became sickening, the Byzantine blue of the sky at which he was frowning, hazy. As long as he lived when he heard an orchestra playing "Till the End of Time" he would remember this moment.

The woman across the table had confided in him merely because she believed him to be a "right guy," and he was in the employ of Intelligence bound by oath to get and pass on to the proper quarters any hint of subversive activities. When the news of his mission here in the Island broke she would accuse him of double-crossing her. On the other hand if he could learn what had aroused her suspicion and act on the information quickly he might save her husband from long years in prison. The government was not indulging in sentimental softness toward proved traitors.

"You look as if I'd knocked the breath out of you, Colonel. I can't believe it of Monty, either."

No use to admit that he could believe anything that was crooked about Dane, that from their first meeting in Germany he had distrusted him, that he had kept a close check on him since his arrival on the Island. She would bristle to his defense and set out to convince him that Captain Montgomery Dane was in the Sir Galahad class, circa 1946. Once before, to his chagrin, he had come up against such a turnabout.

"There is still some breath left in me, Velma, though I confess you had me cockeyed for a minute. Sure that your resentment at your husband's request for a divorce hasn't set you to imagining trouble?"

"I'd give all the jewels I own if I weren't so sure. About once a day since I became suspicious I've told myself, 'You've been reading too many whodunit stories'—they are the only kind I can read without falling asleep—'of course Monty is straight as a string with the government, didn't Miss Carey say he was a great leader'—but wham, back comes the conviction that he isn't.'"

"What reason would he have for turning from a 'great leader' to a traitor? That is an almost unbelievable jump. Have you figured it out?"

"Money. I may be partly responsible. When he wrote from Germany that he wanted a divorce, I cut off the big allowance I had given him since our marriage—and cut it quick. I wouldn't put it past him to be frightfully in debt—he plays for high stakes—in desperation he may have taken any way to get the dough to cover up. Haven't you read in the papers about brave fighters who, out of the service, have returned to a life of crime?"

"Yes, but what started the suspicion of your husband? Have you seen him palling with a person whom you think might be subversive?"

She waited till the man and girl who had risen from the next table had departed before she leaned forward:—

"Monty was very friendly with Alec Stanhope while he was here."

"Stanhope!" Cam coughed in the hope of covering up the incredulous exclamation. "He subversive? You introduced him to your husband, didn't you?"

"Yes, but now I'm wondering. They became pals too quick. Stanhope is away from the Island. That's why I dared ask you to come. I had a hunch he was shadowing me. Monty said he was booked to fly on the same plane with Señor Cardena."

"Is your husband friendly with the Brazilian?"

"I thought at first he was the man Monty came here to meet who had promised him gilt-edge house-planning jobs if he will go to South America."

"But Dane is just back from Germany. Could he have made arrangements there to contact a South American?"

"I guess that part is imagination. Monty detests him, is everlastingly warning me to watch my step *and* my diamonds when I am with him. He thinks the smoothie who drives for him is a tough guy, though he looks as if he wouldn't swat a fly that lighted on his nose."

"That warning about your diamonds is ridiculous. Cardena belongs to one of the top-drawer families in Brazil."

"Then Monty has got his trolley off. I wouldn't put it past my cagey husband to say that about the Señor because he is Madam Shaw-Ruskin's white-haired boy at present when he wants to be ace with her. He is crazy about her house. Declares he will design one on the same plan, plus improvements. That's Monty, he must top the other guy. He is honestly in love with his profession. I'll hand him that."

"You suspect he is trading with an enemy—any idea what he would have to trade?"

"Wait till the boy has served the dessert."

Cam smoked and thought while the Filipino removed plates and substituted others of glass holding slices of pistachio ice cream, looking like pale green islands with snowy centers entirely surrounded by a claret-red sea. He hadn't seen Stanhope since the evening at the night spot two weeks ago. Cardena had told Pat that he was on the plane to Maui. Had he remained on that island?

"Luscious. Better than I dreamed." Velma Dane drew a long sigh of satisfaction. "Since we went to war Sultana Roll has been the forgotten dessert. The check, waiter." She signed the slip and returned it with a dollar bill. "That's all. Don't come back," she ordered imperiously. Cam laughed.

"Don't worry. He won't. You have him scared stiff. The power of gold," he added lightly.

"It will do a lot but often it won't buy the thing you want most." She shrugged. "Velma Dane, the hard-boiled, going sob sister. That's a laugh. Must be this eighty degrees climate. What shall I do about it? My suspicion of Monty, I mean?"

"*Nothing.* After all, it is only a suspicion and even though the war is technically over, the world is heavy with suspicion, one government of another, man of his fellow man, with intelligence operatives planted in every country. Sit tight and keep your eyes and ears open. You distrust your husband's friendship with a man you met on the Clipper. So what? You liked Stanhope right off, didn't you?"

"I thought he was regular and a lot of fun. His nice brown eyes were full of little gold sparks when he laughed."

"There you are. Why shouldn't your husband fall for him at first sight, also? What soured you on Stanhope?"

"Señor Cardena. He invited me to have a drink with him here on the terrace the day he returned from Maui. I stuck to pineapple juice and to my amazement he drank tea. He said it is getting to be a Brazilian custom."

"It was then that he warned you about Alec Stanhope?"

"Perhaps you wouldn't call it a warning. He said he had heard unpleasant rumors about him and then asked if I had thought he might have tried to steal my necklace at the night club."

"Apparently he had forgotten that you screamed because a mouse ran over your foot."

"I reminded him of that and he laughed. I don't like his laugh. I told you that night when you drove me to Mrs. Shaw's that someone tried to snitch my necklace."

"Later, when I asked you whom you suspected, you came back with, 'No one. I guess I had a brainstorm.'" He watched the slow color steal to her eyes.

"I am glad I hedged. Now I am convinced that Stanhope tried to get it."

"Anything so valuable would have an intricate safety clasp that would take a professional thief, or someone who knew the combination, to loosen it. He didn't look like that kind of a man to me. I've heard all you say and I still don't understand why you suspect a person I won't name of subversive activities."

"I hope you are right, Cam." Her eagerness was pathetic. "I don't want to distrust him."

"Don't, but if the suspicion persists, don't let him know it. If you do the fat will be in the fire and we'll never get the truth. I think you've got the stuff in you to play possum. Right?"

"Sure, I'll carry on. You can put your money on me. Look! Rain is falling like a silver mist and the sun is shining through."

"The Hawaiians have a name for it, 'liquid sunshine.' There's a rainbow. We'll take that as an omen that you and I have made the right decision as to your problem. I must go. Thanks for a delicious luncheon."

"I'll walk to your car. I need exercise after that feed. Speaking of our Señor, I have a hunch he's out to annex one of the Shaw widows and her fortune." They had reached the jeep parked at the side of the palm-bordered drive back of the hotel.

"If all your hunches are as crazy as that, I'm not worried about what you told me at luncheon. The man has a wife and daughter—I have been told."

"*Married!* Ohmigosh! I thought he was one of those bachelor career men who float from country to country leaving a trail of broken hearts behind. Not that he could break my heart. I don't like him. He's too much like those bulky SS Troopers in the newsreels. I like 'em slim and tall and straight. Thanks a million for coming, Cam. I've got a lot off my chest. I guess you're right, I am sore at Monty for wanting a divorce."

"Forget it. You have decided that the girl he said he wanted won't have him, haven't you?"

"I'm sure she won't. I can see why he fell hard for her, though. She's a knockout in looks, has loads of class and the loveliest hands—Monty always notices a woman's hands. Mine are so ugly I hate 'em."

"You have a lot on the ball yourself. *Aloha.*"

When the car reached the end of the drive Cam looked back. Velma was standing where he had left her, talking eagerly with Señor Cardena. Where had he come from? Had he been watching while he and she stood together by the jeep? She was using her hands as if to illustrate her words, and her shoulders to emphasize them. Was she repeating to the Brazilian the gist of what she had confided to him? Cockeyed thought. Hadn't she said she didn't like the man? Was it probable that she would tell him of her suspicion of her husband? Not a chance. She was nobody's fool if she was "crazy" about a no-good guy like Monty Dane.

The approach to the Bowl at the Barracks was olive green with tanks and trucks, the bleachers were colorful with spectators when he reached it. The light rain had laid the dust. The air was crystal clear. Headquarters band was playing, "All-American Soldier." Near the reviewing stand, still as a figure cast in bronze, a soldier held a staff from which rippled the Stars and Stripes; on each side of him a motionless GI gripped a rifle in white gloved hands. Three pairs of eyes were fixed on the ranks made up of thousands of men drawn up for review, their khaki faded by many washings.

Often as he had saluted the Red, White and Blue of the Colors, the sight of them now tightened his throat. He had seen men die, seen them tragically maimed; they had been tortured, in defense of the principles for which that Flag stood. Had it all to be done over again? Were there hidden men, in the country, even in this Paradise of the Pacific, with the intention and the will to help the enemy regain its corrupt and cunning power?

He shook off his depression. Velma Dane's suspicion that a man like her husband, who had fought valiantly for his country, was preparing to double-cross it had given him the heebie-jeebies. It must not be done over again. There must be enough soldiers of peace to circumvent the traitors.

General Carrington had asked him to play host to Mrs. Shaw and her niece while he was engaged in the ceremony of the transfer of Command of the Post. Where were they? He glanced along the rows of seats in the section reserved for officers and their guests, followed a wave of Sally Shaw's hand and slipped into a seat between her and Pat. Hatless, both of them; Pat in tangerine linen wore a white gardenia in her hair, her aunt in an amethyst color frock, had a pale pink japonica in her silvery waves. Pat gave him a tepidly friendly nod and returned to absorbed attention to what Phil Ruskin on the other side of her was saying.

"This is old hat to you. I suppose," Sally Shaw observed. "I have seen the ceremony countless times but it never fails to make my eyes feel as if they were prickly with sand and send little creepy, creepy chills of excitement up my backbone."

"I haven't seen a show like this for two years, it gets me too."

"There goes the bu-gle." Her voice caught. She laughed. "Don't mind me. I'm just an emotional kid at a time like this. That last fanfare snapped the lines to attention."

Unit after unit of straight-bodied, weather-beaten men marched toward the reviewing stand, its band playing it past, with instruments flashing in the sunlight. Drum majors strutted and flourished their batons, the regimental colors fluttered from their standards. Tanks and horses, the terrible paraphernalia of war thundered past.

Eyes on the parade, mind busy with Velma Dane's confidence, Cam reviewed it sentence by sentence. Summed up, to what had it amounted? That a hurt, jealous woman was suspicious of her husband's friendship with Alec Stanhope; that Señor Cardena had warned her against her Clipper acquaintance; that last fact was the most significant of her entire story.

"Come back to the world, Colonel." Pat's voice speaking, Pat's reminding touch on his sleeve. "Here's where we stand in honor of the National Anthem, in case you've forgotten."

He had been miles away in thought. As he stood at attention, he tried to figure out what break Stanhope had made to draw Velma Dane's suspicion.

"Parade dismissed, Colonel." Pat's voice again brought him back to his surroundings. "You are about as responsive to sit beside as one of those bronze men seated on a tank with crossed arms. One might think you were facing the lone payment of our nation's debt. Carry on. It's a mere trifle of three hundred billion. You'll make it."

"Thanks for the expression of confidence. First, I am as remote as Mauna Loa, now I'm a man of bronze. I thought you were being well entertained and didn't need me. Here comes General Carrington looking as if Atlas had dropped the world on his shoulders." He caught Phil Ruskin's quick look at him, then at the white-faced officer approaching. Why in thunder had he called attention to the General?

"What's the matter, Sam? You look pale," Sally Shaw inquired solicitously as Carrington joined them.

"Standing in that hot sun got me. Thought I'd pitch on my head before those marching men and be humiliated for life as a General who couldn't take it." He settled his tie nervously. "Mr. Ruskin, steer the ladies through the crowd to the Officers' Club for tea and drinks. I'll sit here for a minute till the world turns back from red with green pinwheels to its normal color. Fulton, stand by, will you?"

For a man who professed to be all in, the General was doing a lot of talking. Sally Shaw hesitated. Carrington shook his head and impatiently motioned for her to go. When they were quite alone he laid his hand on Cam's arm and pulled himself to his feet with an effort.

"They've found Stanhope," he whispered, "murdered."

13

SOFTLY lighted by rainbow tints, rose, blue, lilac, green and amber, which sifted through the colorful commemorative windows, faintly fragrant of the white lilies between tall tapers burning in massive silver sticks on the pulpit; hushed nave, glowing chancel, dusky transepts of the church echoed to the lovely contralto voice:—

"The Lord is My Shepherd: I shall not want."

Sweet and true the music of a flute accompanied softly.

"He maketh me to rest in green pastures."

A vagrant ray of sunshine strayed in, rested on the hair of the singing girl in the choir gallery and turned her soft beige gown to rosy gold. It set afire a bit of nickel on the flute in the hands of the man in khaki beside her. On through the anthem went voice and instrument in harmonious accord.

"Yes, surely peace and mercy all my life shall follow me:
And I will dwell with God forever more. Amen."

Amen, echoed the flute and waned softly into silence. The church settled into solemn quiet. The crackle of the sheet music as Pat laid it down shattered the spell.

"The flute obbligato was perfect, Sergeant. I could feel tears crowding up behind my eyes. I thought when you came in you seemed nervous but you quickly settled down. If you play like that Sunday morning you will start an epidemic of sniffles."

"Shure, an' for my money, it will be your voice that'll start the waterworks. How'd you come to think of me playing in church?"

"Just one of those hunches, ever have them? The day we met in front of the late Kamehameha I, you said you had played the flute at the movies. Flash! Ask him to accompany you when you sing 'The Lord is My Shepherd,' prompted the lookout monitor in my mind."

"It's a jump from the movies to church."

"But you made it."

"Shure, an' I made it. When Sergeant McIlvray sets out to give, he gives." She loved his swagger. "The words aren't just as I remember them at Sunday School, Miss."

"Often a composer changes words to suit his music but most of the original text is in the anthem and all the beauty and meaning of the Twenty-third Psalm. Your flute added the perfect touch."

"You gave me a workout first at your house before you had the nerve to let me rehearse here, though." His accusing grin brought a responsive laugh.

"Call it an audition, that's more professional. Of course I tried you out. There are flute players and near-flute players. I wanted a flute player. You didn't give me your name the day we met. I thought up the Personal. It worked."

"Shure, an' it did. I saw it just in time to hotfoot to the

bronze guy—I can't get my tongue round his name real good, yet, it's a mouthful. I savvied it was you put the ad in the paper but I wasn't sure till the Chinese eyeful slipped me the note."

"What did you mean by the message you scribbled the first time we met, Sergeant? To find out was another reason I had to see you. 'He's poison,' you warned. Two men were coming toward us. Which one?"

He appeared to be absorbed in fastening the flute case. His voice was so low she had to bend her head to hear.

"I can't tell you any more. You were so kind an' cute and pretty, I couldn't let you go without putting you wise, even if I got cashiered out of the army for—someone moved down there in the church. I've gotta go—"

"Whoever it is can't see us here in the rear of the gallery. Go on, quick, what were you putting me wise about, Sergeant?"

"No soap. Shure, an' I've said too much already. Never let out what I wrote, or you may set off a mine of trouble. I don't care for myself but it might blow my boss into the ash-can. Keep it under your hat and your—" he was halfway down the stairs when the words "eyes peeled" drifted back.

She wasn't in the least wiser than when she had read the word "poison," she realized, as she waited till she heard the cautious closing of the door below.

She ran down the stairs, through a doorway beside the pulpit, sped along the crimson velvet aisle of the nave, feeling as if the trouble of which the Sergeant had warned might tap her on the shoulder at any moment and thunder—

"What's the hurry?" The voice fitting into her imaginings sent her heart rocketing to her throat.

"What was the idea, Colonel, jumping at me like that?" she demanded. Fright gave way to indignation. "You scared me stiff speaking from the shadow as if you were the voice of doom."

"It couldn't have been your own guilty conscience that scared you, could it?"

"Why assume that I have a guilty conscience, and just why should you be here? How long have you been lurking round?"

"I object to that word 'lurking.' I heard the last line of your song. That 'Amen,' followed by the flute echo, did something to my eyes. Couldn't see for a minute. Who was the flute player?"

"The—the flute player?" Better not tell him it was the Sergeant to whose "picking-up" he had objected.

"That's what I said. You weren't doubling with voice and

instrument, were you?" They reached the street before she had an answer ready that would be the truth and not tell too much.

"I—I heard he played and—and tried him out. Good, wasn't he?"

"Better, a whole lot better than the yarn you're telling. This gray sedan is your car, isn't it? I'll drive. Your aunt sent me to bring you home."

"What's—happened to Sally?"

"Nothing to hoarsen your voice. Hop in." He waited until he had shot the car ahead before he answered her frightened question.

"Her house was turned upside down while she was away and the cook was having her afternoon out. What's her name?"

"Mrs. Wong Chun. Good heavens, why stop for names? Was anything stolen? Sally's jewels? The heirloom silver?"

"Not that she had discovered when I left. The visitor gave particular attention to your room. Know any reason why he should?"

"My room? Why mine? Except for my papaya-leaf diamond earrings and clip, my star sapphire ring, which I have on, my jewelry is junk. Slim pick—oh, my goodness!"

"Thought of something?"

She had. Skinner's brief case. He had warned that someone might even commit murder to get it. Had the person tried theft first? Days had passed since she had brought it home, and each day she had hidden it in a different spot trying to figure out what to do with it. Last night she had placed it in the bottom of the clothes hamper in her dressing room, had crumpled two sets of blue crepe pajamas and dropped them over it. It had been there when she left for the hospital this morning.

"The days are lengthening, aren't they?" Cam remarked conversationally. "Going to tell me what's on your mind, Patricia? I'm not saying this to frighten you, but I scent danger."

Should she confide Skinner's secret? He had said there was one guy he could trust, that he had written to him, had not received an answer, thought he might be dead. Anyone would trust Cam.

"You didn't," an officious voice in her mind reminded. No time to pursue that train of thought. Skinner had told her to do what she thought best about the papers. She had not been able to look at them because the key was missing. It had seemed wise to wait before she took the bag to a locksmith. The person who had found the key might be watching for that move. She must tell someone, she needed advice. Cam could be trusted. As if he sensed her decision he prompted:—

"I'm waiting, Pat."

"When you were in Germany did you happen to come in contact with a corporal named Skinner—Cam? I don't wonder you smile. It's like asking if you ever found a needle in a haystack."

"I wasn't smiling at the question, it was at the way you always say Cam, as if you were afraid it might set off a hidden mine. It won't."

"You assured me of that the first evening on the *lanai*."

"With that mistake nicely ironed out, go on with the story. I don't remember a corporal named—hold on a minute. I have a hazy memory that a GI by that name was mixed up in a black market scandal. Take it from there."

She began with the nurse's warning to let the dying man talk. It was *pau-haua*, work hour. They passed trucks filled with dusty, grimy, home-going men; crossed a bridge beneath which gurgled and splashed swift water; skirted a rolling pineapple field and further on drove through air spicy with the scent of ginger. The sea, which shaded from deep jade green to lapis lazuli blue, sprinkled with black dots which were the heads of surfers, thinned to translucent green that broke into white frills when it touched the yellow beach. Pat went on with the story, told of the moment at home when she had discovered that the key was missing, of hiding the brief case in a different place each night, of dropping it into the hamper. Cam waited for the drone of a plane flying low to pass.

"And you don't yet know what is in the black leather bag, as Skinner called it?"

"No. Several times he spoke of the stuff—"

"Stuff!"

"That's the way he expressed it, once or twice he said 'papers.'" She explained why she had not tried to get a key. "Perhaps I should have had one fitted at once but the Corporal made such a point of caution that I waited."

"You might have dropped it after leaving the hospital. Have you inquired there if a key had been found?"

"Yes. None had been turned in." She told of meeting Monty Dane near her car and seeing him pick up something. "If it had been a key wouldn't he have inquired if I had dropped it?"

"Perhaps it wasn't a key he found, may have been a bit of money. Never ask him about it. Never let him know you lost a key. The situation begins to sound like a bad dream, but I am afraid it isn't. I'd give a fortune if Skinner hadn't drawn you into the mess, Pat."

"I'm proud that he did, that he trusted me enough to know I can keep a secret."

"Who knows that better than I? Here we are. Shoot for that clothes hamper. Don't let your aunt suspect what you are looking for."

She was out of the gray sedan and into the house before the car came to a stop. She dashed through the foyer, ignoring Sally Shaw's excited, "Pat! Pat!" Up the stairs. To the door of her room. The impact of what she saw stopped her on the threshold.

"My word!" she whispered. "My *word!*"

She had seen a room in a great house in Belgium which had been ransacked by the retreating enemy which had looked like this, except that there a huge pier mirror had been cracked from top to bottom and punctured by bullet holes, and here the glass in her dressing table was intact. Cushions had been wrenched from deep wicker chairs. The contents of drawers had been dumped on the rug. Blue hangings had been wrenched from their poles. The glass from a large silver photograph frame lay in glistening splinters on the hearth. Logs from the fireplace were scattered on the floor. Bedclothes were in a heap. The mattress was tilted at a crazy angle, half off the box spring. The small crystal and gold clock from the bedside table was face down on the rug. Cam Fulton whistled softly behind her.

"Someone was in a hurry. Have you checked on your diamonds?"

"Too stunned to think of them. The sight of this room paralyzed my motor nerves. They were in the top drawer of the dresser. If they are still here they are buried under that heap of scarfs and dickies."

"Look for the brief case in the hamper first. I told your aunt we would be down in a minute to report as to the diamonds."

It seemed but a second before she was back in the room.

"Gone!" she whispered. "Gone. So are the pajamas. The thief must have taken them to cover the brief case. What shall we do next?"

"Your aunt is calling. Go down. She sent for the police. They may have arrived. She told them where to pick up the cook in the city, she was the last person known to be in the house before the break. If you are asked if you know a reason why your room should be turned topsy-turvy, look dazed, shake your head, then suddenly remember your diamonds. We must cover the loss of the brief case. It may have been dropped over the balcony into the shrubs below. I'll take a look-see. Shoot. I'll be along presently."

When Pat entered the living room Mrs. Wong Chun, in the long, dark blue embroidered jacket and matching trousers she wore when she visited in the city, with a red hibiscus over each ear in her black hair, was on the verge of tears as she stood with hands tucked into her sleeves before Police Captain Parkus, who, seated at a table with a brown-uniformed stenographer at his elbow, was questioning her.

The gray-haired, red-faced officer whom Patricia had met many times in her hospital work looked up, puffed his cheeks in a half smile, and proceeded with his cross-examination. He didn't elicit much information. Mrs. Wong Chun had left the place at about noon for her afternoon off. Yes, sa, it was earlier than usual as Madam was to be away at luncheon time and Miss Pat usually ate at the hospital. No, sa, she had seen no one prowling about the place. Yes, sa, she had locked the back door of the house when she left the kitchen. No, sa, she wouldn't swear it was locked but she thought it was. The Captain stopped to scowl at Cam Fulton when he entered and resumed his questions.

"You said your sister works here, Mrs. Wong Chun. Where was she today?"

Question and answer divulged that Sib Lou had planned to come directly home from school at two o'clock, leave her books and then go surf-riding.

"Going with someone?"

"Yes, sa."

"Man? What's his name? Speak up, don't mumble."

"It might have been annoda fella. Sib Lou have many fellas."

"Who did she expect?"

Mrs. Wong Chun rolled her eyes in the direction of white-faced Sally Shaw seated on the very edge of the divan.

"If you know who it was tell Captain Parkus, Mrs. Wong Chun," she encouraged.

"It was a solda."

"What kind of a soldier? Know his name?"

"Sib Lou called him Mac, sa."

Pat held her breath. She had sent Sib Lou with a note to meet Sergeant McIlvray, she hadn't known his name then. Was he the soldier the girl had been expecting? Was she responsible for starting an acquaintance which might harm Sib Lou? That was silly. If he wasn't honest there wasn't an honest man in the world. Besides, hadn't he been at the church with her this afternoon?

"I think I can help here, Captain." Cam Fulton backed against the mantel and smiled at the officer. "I know that Sergeant McIlvray, who is attached to my quarters, has been surf-riding with Mrs. Shaw's maid."

If he knew that, did he know also that this same Sergeant had been the flute player practicing with her this afternoon? McIlvray had said, "You may start trouble and my boss might land in the ashcan." She hadn't known then that Cam was his boss.

"Hmp. Know where the Sergeant was this afternoon, Colonel?"

"He's a free soul when I don't need him. I never inquire as to his dates. I was busy at the Barracks. No reason, so far as I was concerned, why he couldn't have come here to meet the girl at two o'clock."

"He was—". The crash of fire irons drowned Pat's voice. Sally Shaw jumped to her feet and settled back on the edge of the divan with an unsteady little laugh.

"If this keeps on I shall have a nervous breakdown. Burglary hasn't figured largely in my life to date."

"Sorry, Mrs. Sally." Cam restored the brass shovel and tongs to their stand. "I didn't realize the darn things were so near my foot. I moved it and over they went."

"What were you about to say when the *accident* interrupted, Miss Carey?" The Captain's question was tinctured with acid. "You began, 'He was.' Did you know him?"

The crash had given Pat time to think. Cam had tried and succeeded in railroading her admission that Sergeant McIlvray had been with her at the church.

"I saw him once with Sib Lou. I had started to say, he was very friendly, that I wondered why you were dragging him into this. If you could see him you would know he is absolutely honest."

"I'm dragging him into this, Miss Carey, because so far as I know he was on the premises at two o'clock. This breaking and entering must have occurred between the noon hour when the cook left the place—if she is on the level—and about four-thirty when Mrs. Shaw returned and discovered it. You may go—for the present, Mrs. Wong Chun." The woman scuffed out of the room like a frightened rabbit. Parkus rose.

"Mrs. Shaw, you said that as far as you could discover nothing on this floor had been stolen. Come upstairs, all of you, and I mean all," he emphasized, with a look at Cam Fulton as if he suspected he might be planning to whisk them off the Island.

He and his stenographer filled the doorway of Pat's room. Arm in arm she and Sally Shaw stood behind them; Cam Fulton's head loomed above theirs.

"Quite a mess. Quite a mess," Parkus mumbled. "Don't look like a professional job to me. I understand this is your room, Miss Carey. Any jewels they might have been after?"

"A lovely diamond clip and earrings." For the first time since she had mentioned them to Cam she remembered she had not looked for them. "I—I was so excited when I saw the room like this I forgot to hunt for them."

"Hmp! A woman forgetting her diamonds. This certainly is a changed world. Check on 'em now," Parkus ordered.

On her knees Pat burrowed under a colorful pile of silks and laces on the floor in front of the dresser and withdrew a white velvet case.

"Here they are," she announced jubilantly. She touched a spring. The cover flew up. She frowned down at the satin lining. Dropped the case to her lap.

"They—they've gone," she whispered.

14

PAT looked down at the empty white velvet case on her knees and up at the glowering officer in the doorway.

"I—I adored them," she said with a little-girl break in her voice. Parkus cleared a frog from his throat.

"Drop that case. Don't touch it again," he ordered. "Sparks, pick it up in your handkerchief." After the man in brown had deftly lifted it from her lap Pat sprang to her feet.

"Now that we know they were after the diamonds, we can find them, can't we, Captain?"

"Just like that. When did you wear them last?"

"Let me see—the night we all went dancing at the night club. Remember, Colonel, you asked me what kind of a leaf the clip represented?"

"I remember. You said your aunt had given it to you when you came home from Red Cross work. It was after Mrs. Dane screamed and we thought her necklace had been stolen."

"What's that? What's that?" Parkus's voice ruffled like

the feathers of a cock in the wind. "There was no report to *me* that a necklace had been stolen."

"That's the catch, it hadn't been," Cam Fulton's amused voice corrected. "She had felt a mouse run against her shoe and let out a yell. For a minute we thought her spectacular diamonds had been snitched. They hadn't. The necklace still blazed about her throat when the lights went up, and what a necklace."

"Isn't that like a woman? How can they be such darn fools as to wear stuff like that dancing round among hundreds of people they don't know? The mouse yarn sounds phony to me. Any strangers at the table that night?"

Pat thought of Alec Stanhope and her flash of suspicion that Señor Cardena might be a diamond thief. Stanhope had left the Island, Sally had told her. The Brazilian had been at this house many times. Had she been right? Could it have been he? He had remarked on the beauty of her clip when they had walked from the Judiciary Building together.

"Yes," Cam was answering the Captain's question. "There was a man named Stanhope, who came over on the Clipper—"

"You mean the guy who was found murdered down by the shore? He gets a clean bill on this break," Parkus declared with a touch of sardonic humor.

Stanhope murdered? Pat's brain whirled and steadied. Sally had said he had left the Island. Did she know how he had left?

"Pick up that clock, Sparks. It may give us a clue as to the time this happened. What's it say?" he growled as the man turned it over carefully with his tongs.

"Stopped at just one thirty-five, Captain."

"That doesn't prove anything these days, the hands could have been moved before the clock was dropped."

One thirty-five and the Sergeant was to meet Sib Lou here at two, Pat figured. He would have had time to ransack the place, meet the girl and later keep his date with her. He had been nervous and jerky at the church until he had picked up his flute. She had attributed it to his unaccustomed surroundings and the fact that he was perhaps embarrassed with her. No matter how she reasoned, she couldn't believe he was a thief.

The brief case. She had completely forgotten that in the shock of finding her diamonds missing. Had it been taken for a blind, or had the theft of the jewels been the red herring across the trail? Skinner had said they wouldn't stop at murder to get it.

"Close this room and don't let anyone come in, Mrs. Shaw,"

Parkus ordered. "I'll send a fingerprint man here in an hour. That's all for the present. Come on, Sparks."

Sally Shaw followed the two men down. Pat caught Cam's sleeve. She listened till a car started outside.

"When was Stanhope's body found?" she whispered.

"Forget it, Pat. I can't bear to see you mixed up in this mess."

"When?" she persisted.

"The day before the military show at the Barracks. Pat, if I get a priority for you, will you fly to the Mainland tomorrow?"

"Run away? No. I'll stay until I finish the job for Skinner."

"Okay, then there is only one thing for me to do, go on M.P. duty here. Come on. If we leave your aunt alone she will suspect we have found out something we are concealing from her."

Sally Shaw was in the *lanai* filling a cup with tea from the silver pot Mrs. Wong Chun had brought in. The hot-water kettle sent up a white spout of steam. Hands in her sleeves, the Chinese woman looked at Cam Fulton.

"You t'ink halm come to Sib Lou, sa?" she inquired anxiously.

"No. Where is she?"

"She be back to set table, cook dinna here, my day off, she come now. Sib Lou, *wikiwiki*," she called to the girl who was crossing the lawn between the service cottage and the *lanai,* smiling and humming. Smile and tune died as she saw them watching her approach.

"What's the matter, Lilly Yee Lung?" Her sister answered in Chinese.

"Speak English, Sib Lou." Sally Shaw set her untouched tea back on the table. "What did she say?" she prompted.

"She ask me if Sergeant Mac went surf-boarding with me this afternoon. He did. He was waiting here when I came from school at two."

"What time did he leave you?" Cam inquired.

Sib Lou tipped back her head, closed her eyes and considered. Was it an act?

"Three and a half o'clock. He say he go Honolulu way. I say he take me for ice-cream soda. He hurry. He had a date at four o'clock."

"Did he have anything in his hand when he met you here after school?" Pat asked eagerly.

"His black flute case. I asked him to play for me at Waikiki, he say, 'No, sea air gives the flute the screamies.'" She giggled. "He's a funny soldier."

"Did he—did he seem excited when you came, Sib Lou?"

The Chinese girl lowered her long lashes, twisted her shoulders, and gave her dimples a workout.

"He always seems much glad to see me, Miss Pat." She preened. "So does the Captain who looked in my window."

Touching a live wire wouldn't give her more of a shock than hearing that Monty Dane came to see Sib Lou, but she wouldn't have survived the contact with a live wire, Pat corrected herself. Would the girl answer if she inquired how many times he had been to see her?

"So, Captain Dane is one of your admirers." Cam wasn't afraid to ask the question. "Lots of fun, isn't he? See him often?"

"She do not," Mrs. Wong Chun declared with asperity. "I say she be sent to Momma an' Poppa on Mainland if she don't stop him coming. She geta bad name."

"Keep your shirt on, Lilly Yee Lung," Sib Lou advised contemptuously. "I know he's married, think I play round with him for serious? First he takes me for sodas to pay for scaring me. Think I don't know he comes to ask questions about Miss Pat? He's nuts about her. He pays me money to tell where she goes. I don't know but I tell him just the same."

"Sib Lou, I thought you liked me as much as I like you."

"I do, Miss Pat, I do." There was no mistaking the girl's sincerity. "I don't like the Captain. You like him much. I think he not good for you. I lie to keep you safe."

"If you want to keep Miss Pat safe, Sib Lou, and I am sure you do, tell me what kind of questions Captain Dane asks about her?"

"You won't tell on me, Mister Colonel?"

"No. I want to protect Miss Pat even more than you do. When did you see him last?"

"Yesterday. He met me coming from school. Asked would I like ice-cream soda? Sure, I say. I had two. He asked me would Lilly Yee Lung be home tomorrow noon to take a package he wanted to leave for Miss Pat? I said, No, no one home tomorrow till late afternoon. Lilly Yee Lung's afternoon off, friend take Wong Chun Honolulu in truck to get knife for grasscutter. Mrs. Shaw all day at Vet Club and Miss Pat at hospital in the morning, rehearse at church afternoon, he better wait, come some other time."

"Yesterday you told him that about today?"

"Yes, sir."

"Did you tell anyone that Captain Dane asked the questions?"

"Only Sergeant Mac. He came by last evening to ask if we

go surf-riding today and I told him. He likes to hear who I see and what I do, he says it makes an old man like him feel young." She giggled. "He's plenty young for me."

"What did he say?"

" 'Now what d'you know about that? Suppose the Captain is slipping a few of his wife's diamonds to your boss's niece?' He was laughing all the time he talked."

"Sib Lou, he didn't say that."

"Sure he did, Miss Pat. But he didn't mean it. He's always joking. He forgot about it in a minute and said what time would he meet me here? I said he could come to school. He put his finger in his mouth like he was a kid and said, 'Shure, an' I'm too bashful.' He's a funny fella."

"A very funny fellow, Sib Lou."

Pat looked quickly at Cam Fulton. She didn't like his tone. It argued ill for Sergeant McIlvray. Now that he knew that Mac had been at the church—he couldn't help knowing it after Sib Lou's remarks about the flute case—would the Sergeant be disciplined? Somewhere a clock chimed six. Mrs. Wong Chun started as if she had been stung.

"Now I am here, I get dinna for you, Madam. Sib Lou, you come an' help." She looked at Cam Fulton. "You through questions, sa?"

"Yes. Go ahead, both of you." The woman and girl entered the house, their excited jabbering trailing away in the direction of the kitchen.

"There is something in the air I don't understand," Sally Shaw admitted nervously. "I wish any one of the police captains was on this case but Parkus. He doesn't like army officers. He and the General are bound to clash. I'm not a coward, but after what has happened I don't think Pat and I are safe here without a man, Cam."

"You're not going to be without a man. I'm coming back to stay till this mystery is cleared—"

"Sal, what's this I hear about a robbery?" Phil Ruskin interrupted. He stood in the opening between *lanai* and the living room. His black hair was lacquer smooth, his white clothes as unrumpled as if they had just arrived from the tailor, the dark red carnation in his lapel fresh and fragrant.

"Where did you hear of it?" his sister-in-law inquired.

"As I was driving home from the mill. It was broadcast on the radio. Did they take the Shaw jewels, Sal?"

Oh dear, if the whole world knows it, the thief will be on guard, we will never find Skinner's brief case, Pat thought. Cam looks as calm as if a theft were all in the day's work. Why would he be excited about it? It hadn't been given to him in trust. Phil thought only of the Shaw jewels.

"It doesn't seem to occur to you, Phil, that Pat and I might have been murdered in our beds," Sally Shaw reminded indignantly.

"You weren't in your beds when it happened, were you; why should I worry about that? I heard they messed things up but didn't get anything. Correct?"

"Not entirely," Cam responded. "They tried to open your sister's safe but were in too much of a hurry to finish the job. They turned Pat's room upside down. Her diamonds are missing."

"Boy, those cost money. Anyone on the job of finding them?"

"Only Captain Parkus and a dozen or so of his men, Phil. We're not dumbbells," Sally Shaw flared. "Pat, pour me a cup of tea. The hot water kettle has been steaming like a geyser ever since Mrs. Wong Chun brought in the tray. It will give me a lift. Now that the excitement is wearing thin I'm all in."

"It will give us all a lift," Cam Fulton agreed. "Only one cup here. Tell me where to get more and I'll bring them."

"If you are like most of the men I know you couldn't find them if the course was charted," Pat declared. "I'll get them."

When she returned to the *lanai* with a tray laden with china and a plate of cookies, she almost dropped it in her dismay. Monty Dane was standing behind Sally Shaw's chair, his arms crossed on the high back. He had colossal nerve to come here after pretending to Sib Lou that he wanted to leave a package for her. Why take the Chinese maid into his confidence?

"There you are, Pat," he greeted. "Yesterday I got hep to a fresh lot of chocolates. Met Sib Lou and asked her if there would be anyone here today with whom I could leave them. She said not until after five. So here I am with an offering to the fairest of her sex. See that box on the table? Five pounds of the Mainland's best. Don't I get even a smile for it?"

"You'd look grim if you had lost your diamonds, Captain. Give me that, Pat." Cam Fulton took the tray and set it on the table. "You've waited a long time, Mrs. Shaw, for the lift. Sit down, Pat, and pour the tea."

"What d'you mean, she's lost her diamonds?" Monty Dane demanded. If he wasn't sincere in the shocked question, she wouldn't believe there was an honest man in the world, Pat thought. For the first time she realized that since Sib Lou had said that he knew everyone would be away from Silver Ledges this afternoon, deep in her mind had been suspicion of him.

"Don't you listen to the radio?" Phil Ruskin inquired aggressively. "Don't you know that this house was broken into this afternoon?"

"Is that true, Mrs. Sally?" White-faced from shock Monty Dane looked from Pat to Cam Fulton. He couldn't put on that pallor, he just couldn't, Pat told herself.

"It is true, but don't let's go into the details again, I shall burst into tears if one more person asks me about it—and here he is," Sally Shaw added dryly as General Carrington appeared in the living room entrance. He was puffing a little from haste. He nervously settled his tie.

"All right, Sally? I heard—"

"I'm all right and I know what you heard. Sit down, Sam, and get your breath. I lost nothing. Pat's room—"

"What will you take, tea or sherry, General?" Cam Fulton inquired. "You'll need something when you hear that Patricia's earrings and clip were looted."

Lucky he sidetracked Sally's information that her room had been torn to pieces, Pat thought. Much as it hurt to lose the only jewelry she owned it would hurt more to have the loss of Skinner's brief case made public.

"Were you here when the theft was pulled off, Colonel?" Was Monty Dane being deliberately insulting or just stupid? To Pat's surprise, instead of being furiously indignant, Cam Fulton laughed.

"Tell the Captain, Mrs. Shaw, that far from being an accessory to the crime, I happened in, only in time to save you from hysterics."

"You got me wrong, Colonel. I—"

"Forget it, Dane. I know what you meant. Mrs. Shaw has had about all she can take and—"

"Did they get the Shaw jewels, Sally?" Madam Shaw-Ruskin demanded shrilly from the living room. "I heard about the break over the car radio and came here at once. You are careless. I knew my son John was taking a risk when—"

"Stop and get your breath, Mother." Phil Ruskin gripped her by the shoulder and sat her down hard in a wicker chair. "Boy, why did you bring his nibs?" he asked as Señor Cardena hurried out from the living room. He grasped Sally Shaw's hands.

"Señora. You are not hurt? You are safe? I was driving with Madam. We heard over the car—"

"If you repeat what you heard I shall scream." Sally Shaw freed her hands. "Something tells me this is about to become a party. I'm going upstairs. I have had all I can take."

"Oh, no, you haven't, Sally. Hail! Hail! The gang's all

here!" Pat sang theatrically as Velma Dane swept into the *lanai* like a redheaded tornado.

"I heard that someone had—"

"They have stolen Pat's diamonds," Monty Dane solemnly interrupted his wife's excited voice.

"*Pat*—ricia's diamonds. What do those few stones matter?" Madam Shaw-Ruskin sank back in the chair and regarded Velma Dane through her lorgnon. "Monty, your wife is getting fat."

Sally Shaw put her hands over her face and began to cry, dry, rasping sobs.

"Every one of you get out of here," General Carrington roared, "or I'll have you cleaned out with a machine gun."

For one horrible moment Pat feared hysterics. He looks as if he meant it, she thought, and fought off a combination laugh and sob. Velma Dane seized her husband's arm.

"The General is right, Monty. Come on. We're hovering here like a lot of buzzards over something dead. Take your old lady home, Phil, before she loses her tongue in her excitement." She flung the suggestion over her shoulder from the threshold of the living room.

Madam Shaw-Ruskin started in pursuit with Señor Cardena and her son at her heels. The silence in the *lanai* was broken by the slam of automobile doors, the snort of abused engines and the sound of Sally Shaw's stifled sobs.

"Come here, Sal." The General caught her in his arms. "You've had all you can take, all I'll let you take from that cruel old woman. I'm going back to Germany. Come with me?"

"Sam! Do you mean—"

"I mean that I love you—I've loved you for twenty years, no one else. Will you marry me?"

"Oh, Sam! *Sam*—"

"That's our exit cue, Pat." Cam caught her hand. Together they went softly into the living room and closed the glass wall behind them.

15

"HOW long do you expect to be away, sir?" Sergeant McIlvray stopped on the threshold of Cam's workroom to inquire. "How big a bag shall I pack?"

"Lounge robe, pajamas and a shaving kit. I will report on

the job here, every day. When you finish packing, come back, you and I have a little washing up to do."

"Yes, sir," McIlvray agreed and departed.

Tilted back in the desk chair, eyes on a wall map of the Hawaiian Islands, Cam recalled the events of the afternoon from the moment he had dropped in at Silver Ledges with a message for Mrs. Shaw which General Carrington wouldn't trust to the telephone, and found her dazed and frightened by the evidence of burglary, till an hour ago when he had left the house after hearing the General's proposal to the woman he loved. He hadn't known before that he planned to return to Germany. Had Sally's sobs crystallized inclination to decision?

Who had taken Skinner's brief case? What did it contain? "Papers. Stuff," he had said. That last word had given him a start. Could it be possible that he was the GI who had robbed the cache? He had told Pat that murder might be committed to gain possession of his "black leather bag." Had Alec Stanhope been on the track of it? Stanhope wasn't his name. He was one of the Sword and Dagger men trained for espionage who never would be acclaimed for what he accomplished, who would wear no ribbons or decorations, who would go to his death without even his nearest and dearest knowing what his part in victory had been.

Cardena had told Pat that Stanhope had been on the plane to Maui. General Carrington had it on the best authority that he had not been a passenger. That implicated the Brazilian. Why would he lie about it unless he knew that the man had been put out of the way and by whom? It fitted in with his character as McIlvray had described the Storm Trooper who had visited the concentration camp.

If only Pat had not been drawn into what might end in more tragedy. Too many persons knew she had taken the brief case from the hospital—the Post Commander, the lieutenant in charge of the vault, the matron, Captain Dane, who might have seen her place it on the seat of the sedan. Where was it now? Pat had admitted that the Corporal might have been delirious when telling of its contents.

"Bag is packed, sir."

What and how much did McIlvray know of the events of the afternoon? He would stake his life that the man was honest, he knew also that he could hold his tongue under torture and threat of death.

"Close the door and come in, Sergeant. At ease. Sit down."

"I'd rather stand, sir."

"Suit yourself. You were playing the flute for Miss Carey this afternoon?"

"Shure, an' was it you down there in the church? If I'd known that I wouldn't have gone haywire."

"Did you go haywire? Why?"

"Well, you see it was this way, sir. I went surf-boarding with the cute Chinese trick this afternoon—"

"Let's start back. You went to Mrs. Shaw's for her?"

"Shure, an' I did." Cam felt his lips widen in response to the Sergeant's grin and quickly tightened them. Mac had a lot to explain before they two could resume their friendly footing. "When I take a dame out I don't ask her to meet me at the corner drugstore. I go get her."

"What time did you reach Silver Ledges?"

"Mrs. Shaw's place?" He closed his eyes and screwed his lips in meditation. "The clock was striking two when Sib Lou came running across the lawn."

"I asked you at what time *you* arrived, Sergeant?"

"I'd guess about ten minutes ahead of her, sir. Never like to keep a girl waiting, they get sore."

"Stop fencing. I want the truth. You must have heard, apparently every other person on the Island has, that Mrs. Shaw's house was entered this afternoon, that her niece's diamonds are missing."

Sergeant McIlvray's always prominent eyes gave every indication of being about to pop from his head.

"No," he contradicted in a voice drenched with horror. "*No.* You're kiddin', sir." If the man was acting he shouldn't be wearing a sergeant's chevrons, he should be on the stage.

"I am not kidding. Miss Carey's room looked as if a typhoon had romped through it. When she discovered under a pile of clothing the case which had held her clip and earrings and opened it, the jewels were gone. She was broken up about it."

"Why, the poor kid. Got any idea who broke in, sir?"

"I'm beginning to get warm. I may be off the beam."

"Anything I can do to help, sir?"

"Yes. Come clean. Did you know a corporal named Skinner in our outfit in Germany? The outfit to which we were attached when we were acting as nursemaids to the U.S. scientists who were after the Nazi fuel formulas?"

"Funny you should mention him just now, sir. You mean the guy who the brass hats thought was doing a little black-marketing on the side? Shure, an' I knew him. They didn't pin anything on him, though."

"Did you know that he was in hospital at the Barracks? Stop shifting from one foot to another and answer."

"I'm not shifting 'cause I got a guilty conscience, sir, least-way, not about him—my foot hurts. Slipped on a sharp pebble. Honest to God, I didn't know he was here till I got a letter from him written a month before. It had been following me around."

"How did he know where you would be?"

"He didn't. I used to pal with him a little over there, he seemed so kind of lonely. No one liked him. He said he had no family. Would I give him my registration number so if anything happened to him, I'd get his insurance. I knew that was crazy talk, but I thought, what to hell, why not let the poor lonesome guy have a string on me?"

"What was in the letter?"

McIlvray opened the door, peered into the corridor, closed it and returned to face him across the desk.

"He wrote he had been sent to Schofield Barracks for redeployment—he didn't want to quit the army—and had been in the hospital there a month after being smashed up in an auto accident. That makes it two months ago he landed in hospital. At the top of the sheet of paper he had printed in big letters, 'HUSH. HUSH.'"

"Go on."

"He had a bag, a black leather bag, he wanted to turn over to me; he wrote I would understand when I saw what was in it, why I'd got to find the right party to give it to. He wrote that they had tried to kid him at the hospital but he knew his number was up; he'd give the bag to a nurse who had been kind to him and ask her to find me; he'd got to get it off his conscience before he passed on to wherever guys like him went. When I read the letter I hotfooted it to the hospital. He had died the day before. I had a hunch he might have what we were sent here to find, though I'd have sworn he was honest, and I almost went crazy."

"Did you inquire at the hospital if there had been a black leather bag among his effects?"

"Shure, an' I did, sir. When I asked the lieutenant in charge of GI stuff in storage he bawled me out:—

"'What's all this excitement about Corporal Skinner? Has he left a fortune behind him? You're the second person who's been here snooping.'"

"The second. Did you ask who the first was?"

"I did. Not another word could I get out of that lieut or anyone else."

"Did you ask if there had been inquiries for Skinner, if anyone had come to see him?"

"Shure, an' I didn't think of that, sir, he wrote I was the only person he could trust—me, and that nurse."

"When you went to the hospital did you see anyone you knew?"

"Nary a guy—come to think of it, I did, sir. That Captain Dane we drove back to the Moana from Mrs. Shaw's, the guy who was with our outfit who I told you got in wrong with the C.O. for playing cozy with a *Frau*. Ran into him, once or twice. The dame at the desk told me he was looking for one of his men he had heard was there."

"Now, I suspect he is doing a little subversive stuff on the side. I wouldn't put it past him."

Velma Dane's troubled voice echoed through Cam's memory. Had her husband heard in some underground way of Skinner's anxiety about papers? Had he been the "higher-up" who had threatened to have the Corporal court-martialed if he didn't steal—that was the catch. What did he steal? Had he been searching for him when Pat saw him at the hospital the day Skinner died? She suspected that he had picked up the key to the brief case. Suppose he tied her into it? The possibility brought him to his feet.

"What's cookin', sir? You jumped out of your chair as if that old wound had given you a jab."

"It's a new one, Sergeant, and it hurt like the devil. Have you come across the Brazilian or his man?"

"I've seen 'em once or twice but I faded out of sight quick. You're frightened for Miss Carey, aren't you? Shure, an' you're square in your rights to scowl. 'Tisn't my intention to butt into your affairs. Perhaps you'll remember that I took care of you when you were sick; you didn't know it, but you were woozy most of the time about a party named Pat. First I thought it was a man that had done you dirt, but I got hep it was a girl."

"What did I say?"

"Take it easy, sir—nothing but the name, only 'twas the way you said it put me wise to the fact there'd been trouble. When the Chinese trick told me Miss Carey's name was Patricia I put two and two together—"

"And got six."

"If you say I added up wrong, I guess it's so. When I met her in front of that bronze statue—"

"Was that planned?"

"Gee, no sir, she'd never seen me before. She told me about the king fella just as she'd tell any other doughfoot. I guess she's the kind that wants to help. I'll come clean. I knew who she was, and when the guy whose name I don't mention came out of the door with that slick guy following, I gave her the lowdown on him." He told what he had scribbled on the paper. "In spite of the fact she'd hurt you something fierce, I knew 'twould break your heart if anything happened to her through that snake. She didn't know who I was from a hole in the ground. I didn't let on I knew you."

"I know that or she wouldn't have put the Personal in the paper, and while we are on the subject, she didn't do me dirt, that was just fever muddling my brain. Understand, Sergeant?"

"Yes, sir."

"Since then have you explained to her what you meant by 'poison'?"

"No, sir, honest to God, though she tried to quiz me."

Cam crossed to the window and looked out at the lights of the camp as he put together scraps of evidence. Captain Dane had been checking on one of his men at the hospital here; he had been in the outfit in Germany when a cache of U.S. money, package after package of new bills hidden by the wealthy owner of a laboratory, had been rifled and part of the contents carried away. The man who had buried the cash for his employer, who had disappeared, had sworn to the C.O. of the outfit that he had not touched the money, that he had been friendly with a U.S. officer, admitted that perhaps he had talked too much over their beer. The only persons who knew that the money had been taken were the man who had buried it for his employer, General Carrington, a high official in the occupation forces, the C.O., McIlvray, and himself. The only way Dane could have known of the theft was to have been implicated. Was he the officer who had drunk beer with the caretaker? Was the pattern beginning to shape?

He fitted in another piece. Many of the men in the outfit had been sent to Honolulu for redeployment. Intelligence had received a tip that a GI suspected of having dug up the cash was among them—on his way, maybe, to contact the owner. The Army was mortified that the theft had been possible in the territory that it had been assigned to guard. Because General Carrington, McIlvray and he knew what had been taken they had been put on the job of following up the case, had been sent to the Island under cover of assignment to the Barracks for duty.

Velma Dane had confided that her husband had come because a girl he wanted to marry was here; second because he had agreed to meet a South American who had held out the prospect of gilt-edge house-planning jobs if he could measure up to the requirements.

It didn't look good. Curious that Señor Miguel Cardena, claiming to be a citizen of Brazil, whom McIlvray had recognized as an SS trooper, should arrive at the same time as Captain Dane. Velma declared that her husband hated

Cardena. If the two were in cahoots wouldn't he put up that bluff? Sure he would.

Why the Captain's alleged friendship for the man who had called himself Alec Stanhope? Was it possible that he or the Señor had seen Stanhope slip a paper to him that night at the club? It was such a tiny paper that after he had read the three words on it he had burned it in an ash tray as he tamped out his cigarette. "Watch dark horse," the message had read. Had the "dark horse" discovered that Stanhope was on his trail?

"Think you've got it worked out, sir?"

At McIlvray's question he returned to his desk.

"Not yet. I shall stay at Mrs. Shaw's nights till the mystery of the break there is cleared up. That's off the record, Sergeant."

"Shure an' I get you, sir." He picked up the bag. "I'll put this in the jeep. Shall I drive you over?"

"Yes, and come for me at seven in the morning. I want to get away before breakfast. Let's go."

Sally Shaw was her normal self when he entered the *lanai* at Silver Ledges. Her crepe frock was the deep red in the heart of the amethysts in her filigree gold necklace and earrings, she wore a matching hibiscus in her white hair. If an occasional hint of vibrato in her voice was reminiscent of the recent tear tempest, her radiantly happy eyes, her gay repartee, immediately canceled out the impression.

Patricia, in a frock which matched the sheen of her hair, showed the strain of the afternoon more than her aunt. She waited till Sally and the General began setting out card tables in the living room before she explained:—

"Sally phoned for Phil, Maida, the Danes and Señor Cardena to come for gin rummy tonight. She said she must make up for the General's 'Get out or I'll shoot' order. They would think him a savage when really he is a dear. I was on the verge of hysterics as one after another they arrived this afternoon. I almost succumbed when they scuttled away like a lot of poultry being shooed out of a lettuce bed." Her laugh rippled.

"You are not too steady now. I'm sorry they are coming. I wanted to do a little sleuthing in your room this evening."

"You couldn't, it is off limits. Parkus sent a man here to seal it while you were at the Barracks. He stood by while I removed the clothing I will need and watched like a man-of-war bird on the lookout for a fish-full booby that I didn't touch anything else."

"Where will you sleep?"

"On the couch in Sally's dressing room. She was terribly

frightened. Now she is so radiant she's on top of the world. She adores the General. She wants nothing said about their plans for the present."

"Are you happy about her approaching marriage?"

"Happy! I think it is wonderful when love lasts through twenty years of separation."

"It has happened before. Have you recovered from the shock of finding your room a shambles?"

"I'm as unruffled as the Stars and Stripes on Aloha Tower on a windless day. There are two guest suites for you to choose from but it isn't necessary for you to stay tonight."

"That's what you think." The slam of car doors, laughter and voices drifted from the drive.

Four hours later, standing at the long open window of the bedroom whose balcony was an extension of the one outside Pat's sealed room, Cam Fulton listened. No sound in the house behind him. The scent of damp earth and the fragrance from a potpourri of flowers rose from below. From outside came the distant pound of rollers breaking on the beach, the occasional swish of a meteor streaking across the heavens, miraculously avoiding collision with the brilliant tropical stars. Lights twinkled on distant battleships. Lights in clusters, lights like jeweled necklaces, were strung along the fingerlike ridges. Only an occasional light glowed in the white blurs which were houses.

He snapped on his lighter, as quickly snapped it out and returned the package of cigarettes to the pocket of his long tan lounge robe. The scent of tobacco might betray him while he waited in the hope of confirming his hunch that the person who had taken the brief case had hidden it on the place, fearing to carry it away in daylight, and would return tonight to get it. It would have been a simple matter to drop it from the window into the shrubs below and return for it when the coast was clear.

He stepped to the balcony and leaned against the window frame in the shadow where he could hear the slightest movement. It had been a long evening and a noisy one. It was as if each guest had picked up the germ of the afternoon's excitement, which still lingered. Voices had been pitched high, laughter almost incessant at repartee which ordinarily would have hardly cracked a smile. Pat had prepared a huge crystal bowl full of sparkling, iced fruit juices. Flanked with silver plates of chewy brownies the brew had been so popular that the bowl had been filled and refilled.

Maida Parsons and Velma Dane had received the news that Pat's rifled room was sealed against inspection with indignant protests, after which they had settled down to a cutthroat game of gin rummy. Dane, Cardena and Ruskin had shown no desire to view the scene of the—he had almost thought, "crime." That was too drastic a word—or was it?

A sound? He stiffened against the long shutter. Strained his ears. There it was again. Someone was cautiously reaching into the shrubs below.

He held his breath. Tiptoed forward in moccasined feet. Leaned cautiously over the iron railing. A dark shape moving. He drew an electric torch from his pocket. Too late. A light illumined the shrubs. Illumined a man who sprang erect, shading his face with his hands.

"Lost something, Phil?" Pat Carey inquired.

16

PHILIP RUSKIN!

Cam repeated the name to himself incredulously. He had told the Sergeant that his hunch as to the person who had broken and entered might be off the beam, but this situation was a million light years away from it. Of all the could-be's he was the last he would have picked for that job. Hold on, though. At the night club when Pat had spoken of Ruskin's dark skin, suspicion that he might be Stanhope's "dark horse" had flamed for an instant like the tiny paper in the tray under his cigarette and had died down as quickly. It was too absurd to survive.

"Why are you here, Phil?" Pat's voice, low, implacable, broke into his reflections.

"Couldn't settle down at home. Had your missing diamonds on my mind." There was a hint of bravado in the answer. "Kept figuring what I would have done with them till the hunt was over had I stolen them from your room."

"You would have tossed them into the shrubs, I judge from your presence here. Too bad you took the trouble to come, Phil. They aren't there. I had the same brilliant idea and went through the bushes with a rake before dinner."

Apparently a lot had happened while he was at the Barracks. Had Pat really been looking for the brief case instead of the jewels? He had suggested that it might have been dropped over the balcony. She would have told him had she found it. Too bad if she had. Had it been left there the man who wanted it would try to retrieve it tonight and be caught.

"Go home, Phil." The indignation in her low voice carried. "And I mean go."

"Boy, you don't think I'm getting scratched up in these shrubs for fun, do you? Don't you know that what hurts you hurts me? You loved those diamonds."

"Not so much that I want you prowling under my window at midnight to find them, and what's more I don't believe you came here to hunt for them."

"Perhaps I didn't. So what? I got hep to the fact that Fulton didn't go when the rest of you left. Decided I would find out if he was hanging round. You told me you met him for the first time on the Island the day of the Fashion Show. Now I know you played round with him at Maida Parson's wedding. I don't like it."

"And I don't like your spying. Did you leave your car in our drive?"

"I did not. Think I'm a dumbbell? Left it at the foot of the ledge. Wouldn't risk driving up for fear Sal would hear me and raise the roof."

"That's a break. The case is closed. Go home. I'll play Sister Ann at the living room window till you disappear. Don't come back. I intend to sit there with a gun in my hand till daylight."

A window below closed softly. A dark figure stole around the corner of the house. Not a minute too soon, for a light shone from the doorway of the servants' quarters. A man stepped out, lingered as if listening, went in and closed the door. The lawn returned to silent, fragrant darkness under the glittering canopy of sky.

It was so still he could hear the slam of a car door, the snort of a motor. Phil Ruskin was departing, mad as a hatter, if the distant sounds were an indication. Had Pat meant it when she declared she would sit at the living room window till daylight? The question sent him downstairs on a soundless run.

"Who's there?" demanded a breathless voice.

"Don't shoot, Pat, it's Cam, you crazy kid." Miraculously, without casualty to himself or the furniture, he crossed the dark room and snapped on a lamp.

She was curled in a deep chair by the window. Her brown eyes were enormous as they met his. She tightened the belt of her pale blue satin house coat with one hand and fastened the big rhinestone button at the throat with the other. A large electric torch fell to the rug. He started forward to pick it up.

"Don't," she protested. "I'll get it."

"You're the doctor, but if you intend to spend the night

here it needn't be in the dark." He went around the room lowering the reed blinds. "That's more like it. Cozy shut in like this, isn't it? Let's make a night of it. How about gin rummy? I can't sleep either. Ruskin said he came to look for your diamonds. He had the nerve to admit he had come to check on my whereabouts."

"How do you know what he said?"

"I was on the balcony overhead ready to drop over if needed. You handled the situation so competently I decided I had better not appear. Did you think you were the only person in the house with a sleuth complex? I thought the thief might return to the scene of his crime to get the brief case he could have dropped into the shrubs and laid my plans accordingly. Have you a gun concealed about your person? If so, give it to me. This is where the army takes over."

"I haven't one, foolish. You are not terribly concerned about the loss of my diamonds, are you?"

"I object to the sting in that question. I thought *you* were more concerned about that 'black leather bag' entrusted to you than about your jewelry."

"I am. I *am*. How can we find it?"

"We can't tonight. Your voice keeps getting raggedy with tears, in spite of your claim that you are as unruffled as the flag on Aloha Tower on a still day. On second thought we won't make a night of it. I'll take over the sentinel act. It won't be the first time. Go to bed."

"I'm staying here."

"That's what you think. You are not. You are going upstairs." She curled deeper into the chair. He removed the hands which had been thrust hard into the pockets of his robe and stepped toward her purposefully. "Have I got to pick you up and carry you?"

"You have *not*." She was out of the chair and at the door with a speed that made him laugh. She paused on the threshold.

"I think Parkus suspects who has the diamonds," she whispered and disappeared into the foyer.

What had she meant by that? Parkus didn't appear like an upholder of law and order who would confide his suspicions to a girl. He waited on the threshold till he heard a door above softly open. Came the murmur of a woman's voice. Another answered. A happy laugh. Silence.

In the living room he snapped off the light, rolled up the blinds and let in the soft, fragrant night air. He picked up the torch Pat had dropped in her flight—it had been flight—settled into the chair by the window, tipped back his head against the cushion and thought of the first evening he had come to the house. He had slashed at Pat. The fierce disappointment and pain which had shaken him when he received her letter at the Post, dulled by the excitement and horror of war, had flared up in burning fury. He had wanted to hurt her. He had succeeded. His harshness had proved a boomerang to hurt him. With cigarettes and memory for company he prepared to keep watch until dawn.

Mrs. Wong Chun was standing in the foyer when he stole downstairs silently in the morning. Finger on her lips she beckoned. "Now what?" he wondered as he followed her waddling figure into the blue and white kitchen.

"Madam tole me have coffee fo' you befo' you left, sa." She drew a chair to a table and set down a Chinese plate with two huge crisp popovers and filled a matching cup with clear, dark amber coffee.

"That looks and smells delicious, Mrs. Wong Chun. Sorry to make you so much trouble."

"That not trouble. I got odda. You Mees Pat's fliend, I like tell you."

"Go ahead." By the prickling of my thumbs, mystery this way comes. The silly lines jingled through his mind. Was the woman about to furnish another scrap for his puzzle?

"I did not tell p'lice yestelday. I t'ink all night pl'haps I oughta." She came close to the table and thrust her short stubby hands into the sleeves of her white smock. "I hav' time befo' I go Honolulu way yestelday noon. I tink, Mees Pat, she said would I wash some t'ings. I do it now. W'at you say, sa?"

"Nothing. The coffee was so hot it scalded my throat." His heart had skipped a beat and caused the gurgle. What things had she washed? "Go on, Mrs. Wong Chun, what should you have told the police?"

"I take pajamas, two sets flom clothes hampa in Mees Pat's dlessing loom. Way down unda was black bag like men cally Honolulu. I t'ink p'laps it fall in w'en she put it on cova. She not know that; thlow pajamas into hampa and cova it. I t'ink, she hunt and hunt and not find. I take it out and lay it on bed."

Handed to the thief on a silver platter and no questions asked.

"Was the room torn to pieces when you put the brief—black bag on the bed, Mrs. Wong Chun?"

"No, sa. In orda just Mees Pat always leave it."

"Then what did you do?"

"I close downstai' doo', take pajamas to my house to wash."

"Did you come back to the kitchen after that?"

"No, sa. I go Honolulu. You t'ink I oughta go tell p'lice w'at I do?"

"N-ó-o, Mrs. Wong Chun." He hoped his deliberation was convincing. "They are not interested in the black bag, the missing diamonds are what they are after. In fact, it will help a lot if you don't mention the fact that you went to Miss Pat's room for the pajamas yesterday. Police get queer ideas. Have you told anyone but me?" She shook her head vigorously, her eyes between the slanting lids bulged with fear.

"You t'ink p'lice say me, Lilly Yee Lung Wong Chun, stole Mees Pat's di'monds?"

"I don't say they would, but to make sure they don't, say nothing about going to the room for the pajamas. You were right, perfectly right to get them, but police are queer ducks, they've got to find the person who stole the jewels or they'll lose their jobs, they'll run everyone ragged who stepped into that room. Keep your mouth shut, Mrs. Wong Chun, and they won't think of you."

"I keep mouth shut tight. I see in movie, p'lice how they make thief tell. Bad time he have. You, only one know I go to Mees Pat's loom."

"Forget you went there. Remember, if you don't talk nothing can be pinned on you. One more cup of coffee and I'll finish the popover. Delicious. Never tasted anything so good."

Sergeant McIlvray saluted as he approached the jeep in the drive.

"Great morning, sir," he observed as they drove away.

"You've said something, Mac." It was a great morning. There was no dust from traffic, from soil cultivation, or smoke from cane-field fires which were apt to make the afternoons hazy. The air was sweet and crystal clear. Broken ledges loomed sharp as red-brown cutouts, trails on the mountains showed up like the black lines of railroads on a map. Wounds on mountain slopes, made by the war, stood out with pitiful clarity.

At a turn in the road Pearl Harbor, with its landlocked basins and entrance guarded by coral reefs, lay ahead. With long barracks and ships at anchor on a sea still as a blue mirror, it was like a massive painting of the photographic school, all blue and green, brown and amber. Overlooking it on a mountainside stretched the cemetery where rested the bodies of sailors and marines, officers and men alike, who fell there, under row upon row of white crosses, symbols of their supreme sacrifice. Suppose as a tribute to them each man who had survived the horrors of war years gave of his best? What a world this would be.

Back in quarters, Cam slipped off his tunic, dropped into the chair at the desk and picked up the engagement pad.

"Any messages for me, Sergeant?"

"No, sir. The story of the robbery at Mrs. Shaw's is rolling round the Barracks like dry grass in a gale. They've got three suspects locked up in the guardhouse. Captain Parkus and a stooge called to see you last evening. They came for fingerprints. Two of the guys canned were deserters the M.P.'s picked up."

"Were the police in this room?"

"Yes, sir, the Cap and his fingerprint man. He said he had to make some notes and could they sit at your desk?"

"Were you here all the time they were?"

"Except for a few minutes when I went for a glass of water. The Cap said he had to take an aspirin pill."

"He wouldn't have been after our fingerprints, would he?"

"Saint Patrick! Why should he? They are on record here at the Barracks. He isn't gonna try to put the finger on me for the theft of those diamonds, is he?"

"Hold everything, Sergeant, if you are innocent you have nothing to fear."

"What do you mean, *if*? You don't think I was the guy who broke and entered at Mrs. Shaw's, do you, sir?"

Cam tipped back in the swivel chair and clasped his hands behind his head.

"I do, Sergeant. I don't think you went there for the diamonds. Suppose you come clean? The police will find your fingerprints on about every piece of overturned furniture in Miss Carey's room—unless you had the forethought to provide yourself with gloves. You were after Skinner's bag, weren't you?

"Right about that, sir. I was sure when I got down to hardpan thinking that Miss Carey had the brief case. I found out at the hospital that she was with him when he passed out. You're wrong about the furniture. I didn't touch it." That brought Cam to his feet.

"You mean you didn't smash up that room?"

"I'll swear I didn't, sir. I had a tip—nothing right straight out, just went Sherlock on some information handed me— that someone else would be after Skinner's bag yesterday afternoon. I beat him to it. The kitchen door was unlocked. That stopped me for a minute, 'twas too easy, but I crept up the back stairs expecting I'd be sniped at before I reached the top. Shure, an' I almost died from shock when I went into a bedroom, which I thought from the look of it was Miss Carey's, and saw a black brief case lying on the bed. It scared me. For a minute I didn't dare touch it, it was too much like a booby trap the Nazis used to leave lying round."

Cam walked to the window. Far away the Waianae Range, usually clothed in pale blue haze, stood our redly in contrast to the green of sugar plantations which appeared to roll almost to its back though there must be miles and miles between. The sense of distance helped him think. "I had a tip that someone else would be after it yesterday afternoon," the Sergeant had said. The repetition of the words started a transcription in his memory. The voice was Sib Lou's.

"Yesterday. He met me coming from school. Asked would I like ice-cream soda. Sure, I say. I had two. He asked would Lilly Yee Lung be home tomorrow noon to take package he wanted to leave for Miss Pat? I said, No one home tomorrow, Lilly Yee Lung's afternoon off, friend take Wong Chun Honolulu in truck to get knife for grasscutter, Mrs. Shaw all day at Vet Club, Miss Pat at hospital in morning, rehearse at church afternoon. He better wait, come some other time."

"Had you told anyone that Captain Dane asked the question?" His own voice.

"Only Sergeant Mac. He came by last evening to ask if we go surf-riding today and I told him." That was enough. He returned to the desk, wrote something on a slip of paper and held it out to McIlvray.

"Is that the person you went Sherlock on, Mac?"

"Yes, sir. Jeepers, how'd you guess that—?"

"The name is off the record. What did you do with the bag?"

"Dropped it over the balcony into the shrubs, sir. Planned to pick it up when I brought Sib Lou home."

"Did you?"

"Shure, an' I bet you'll want to kill me, sir, but the Chinese trick wouldn't come home—held me up for a soda, then I had to meet Miss Carey at the church. That's why I didn't shoot the works to you yesterday about what I'd done."

"Good Lord, do you mean you left that brief case you thought important enough to *steal*, lying in those bushes?"

"I went back for it in the evening, sir."

"Find it?"

"No sir. No trace of it."

"My God, do you know what I believe was in it? One million bucks."

"You mean that stuff we're after? Can't believe it of Skinner, sir. Remember, he wrote me he had 'papers'?" McIlvray's voice was hoarse.

"What *papers* did you think were important enough to warrant taking the brief case from Miss Carey's room?"

"I thought Skinner might have snitched the missing formulas for ersatz gas, sir, some of those disappeared. You'd told me that a woman mixed up in the hunt we are in would be in danger. I figured that if the fella who was after the brief case got hep that Miss Carey had it she might be pulled into the fight. I was trying to save her. Saint Patrick! One million bucks chucked into the shrubs! Brother, that's something! 'Tain't possible. What do we do next, sir?"

"That's what I'm asking myself, Sergeant."

Had Ruskin found it? Transcription. Pat's voice:—

"Too bad you took the trouble to come, Phil. They aren't there. I had that same brilliant thought and went through the shrubs with a rake before dinner."

Had she really hunted for the diamonds or was she bluffing Ruskin? Why hadn't he asked her last night when she was curled in the chair by the living room window? The answer to that was easy. When she looked up at him his heart had zoomed to his throat, he had thought that they would have been together like this, happily together, if she hadn't run away that night two years ago.

Why spend a minute on that footless detour? To return to Ruskin. Had the brief case been tucked under his arm when he slipped around the corner? He had been a dark, moving shadow, he might have carried a trunk and got away with it. Who had opened the door of the servants' house at that minute? Wong Chun? Why in thunder would Ruskin want the thing? Had he been tipped off as to its contents? Unbelievable. He was talked of as a delegate to Congress, not likely he would jeopardize his chances by mixing into a criminal situation. His explanation that he was checking on him was plausible. Maida had said he was "crazy jealous." Who really knew what the missing brief case contained? Skinner might have been half delirious when he turned it over to Pat. His warning, "There is a man who wouldn't stop at murder to get it," smacked of a feverish nightmare.

That explanation was out. He had written McIlvray that he had important papers he wanted to turn over to him. Who was knocking at this time in the morning? His muscles tensed. Was all this mystery running him ragged?

"Shall I answer, sir?"

"Snap into it, Sergeant. What are you afraid of?"

"Me? Nothing, sir. You acted so kind of jumpy I thought perhaps you were." He grinned and opened the door. "Special delivery," he flung over his shoulder. "Shure, I can sign for it," he blustered to someone in the corridor. "Ain't I the Colonel's trouble-shooter? Hand it over. Nah, he won't come himself. And don't call me Sarge. Gimme that pencil."

He slammed the door and handed Cam a long white envelope. "I don't know what the U.S. Army's coming to when a pfc. sets out to give orders to a staff sergeant," he griped.

His words made no impression, his voice was like a loose clapboard slapping against Cam's mind as he frowned down at the sheet of carbon he had drawn from the envelope. It bore the typewritten impression of a letter.

17

"MORE trouble, sir?"

"May be, may be not, Sergeant." Cam held the corner of the black carbon paper between the thumb and forefinger of his right hand and thrust the envelope in which it had come into the breast pocket of his khaki shirt. "Bring me the pliers from the desk drawer. Got 'em? Okay. Nip this above my fingers. Now, I'll take it. Bring my portable and the magnifying glass into the bedroom."

"Okay, sir," the Sergeant reported when he returned.

"If there is a phone call, answer that I will be back in an hour, that you can't get in touch with me till then. Whether it is one hour or two, don't interrupt me." He shook the carbon dangling from the pliers. "Something tells me this will require my undivided attention."

"Shure, an' they'll have to lay me out cold to get to you, sir. It wouldn't be anything about the missing diamonds, would it? I won't be certain you don't think I snitched 'em till they're found. You told me to forget about the brief case—'tain't that easy. It's drivin' me nuts to think I lost it."

"Then do your darnedest to round up the thief, Sergeant. I have a feeling that its disappearance is tied up with our million dollar job on the Island. I may be wrong, it may have been just a common or garden variety of theft. I doubt if this communication will give us the dope on it."

In his bedroom he sat at a table by the sunny window on which McIlvray had set the typewriter and carefully laid the sheet of carbon beside it. Later it would be tested for fingerprints. Of more importance now was its contents. Whence, could be ferreted out also. There were two impressions. The later and clearer lines were copy for an ad in a newspaper:—

Want to locate person who will give ukulele lessons. Free at 6 P.M. Mondays. Answer in this column.
                    Malihini, much *Malihini.*

Malihini, much *malihini* meant stranger. That signature didn't cut much ice. A *kamaaina,* old-timer might have used it.

He copied the advertisement, made a note at the bottom of the sheet, "Watch newspaper column for answer."

He rolled a fresh sheet of yellow paper into the machine. Getting at the first impression wouldn't be such a cinch. Line after line he moved the strong magnifying glass down the black paper, line after line he typed it, working slowly, stopping every few moments to hold the carbon nearer the light. The machine on which it had been inscribed had been in perfect condition. Not a broken letter or one that wiggled as there would have been to furnish a clue in a detective story. Perhaps it had been a new machine. That was an idea.

With a sigh of relief at a tedious job accomplished he pulled the paper from under the roller, tipped back in his chair and read the result of his careful work. There was no date.

You had the right dope about the man Stanhope. Super-spy. Last night he slipped something to Silver Eagles at the table. Just then a woman screamed. She may be in his game. Perhaps she yelled to draw attention from him. Watch her. We may have to take care of her. The job will move faster without S. That's up to you, boss. No trace of GI with you know what. Answer cipher ad when you've got the goods. Danger in contact. Those guys you're watching have eyes in the bac— O.K. the Chi—

The carbon had been torn raggedly across the two words, one of which undoubtedly was *back;* was the other the beginning of *Chinaman* or *woman?* Line by line he reread the message, interpreting as he read.

The person to whom the letter had been written had suspected that Stanhope was a "super-spy." Silver Eagles was undoubtedly himself; "last night" meant that the letter had been typed the day after Philip Ruskin's party at the night club; Stanhope's body had been found days later. "The job will move faster without S. That's up to you, boss." Evidently the "job" had not been hurried.

The sinister suggestion started icy shivers crawling through his veins. These people were swift and sure, devilishly sure. The woman who screamed was Velma. "She may be in his game." The writer had his trolley off there, she wasn't in the game he and General Carrington were playing. Good Lord, there wasn't much play to it. Her scream had given Pedro, the maître d'hôtel, a jolt, he had hovered

about the table as if he feared she would yell again. He had
been right when he said she might have started a panic.
Who was the "boss"? No doubt now that the gang which had
removed the man known as Stanhope was after the money.
Was Skinner the GI who had stolen it? Had he drawn Pat
into this hideous mess?

The horror of the thought brought him to his feet.
Thank God, no one knew what she meant to him; should the
"boss" find out he wouldn't hesitate to use her as a hostage.
That reference to Velma shot to pieces his suspicion that
Monty Dane had written the two letters, that his wife had
found the carbon and mailed it. The Captain was untrust-
worthy, ten to one he had cleared the way for the breaking
and entering at Silver Ledges, if he hadn't done it himself;
but that he was a devil who would direct suspicion toward
his wife was unbelievable. He summed up what Velma had
told him: she had cut off his allowance; he gambled; "the
Captain's the guy who got in wrong with the C.O. for doing
a little fraternizing with a *Frau*," McIlvray had said.

For a terrifying instant Cam felt as if his mind were
whirled in an airplane test, then it steadied. Had that
Frau known of the hidden millions, had she prevailed on Dane
to have part of it stolen? In some grapevine way had she
communicated with the owner that it would be sent here—
here! Cardena. The name shot through his mind like
forked lightning on a dark sky. Cardena—the SS trooper.
Had he the pattern at last?

He reread the last lines he had typed on the yellow sheet,
"Answer cipher ad when you've got the goods." Cipher
meant the top impression on the carbon, the ad for ukulele
lessons. "Those guys you're watching have eyes in the bac—"
meant back of their heads, of course. The next broken line,
"O.K. the Chi—" introduced a new menace. Had the gang
bribed a Chinaman or Chinese woman to help in its dirty
work?

He laid the carbon between two sheets of white paper,
placed it with the copies in his clothes locker and returned the keys to his pocket. As he entered the office the
Sergeant wheeled from the window.

"What gives?" he asked eagerly.

"Nothing about the diamonds. I have a job for you. Put
my typewriter out of commission—not too seriously, but
enough so it won't work."

"Saint Patrick! Your typewriter! Your white-haired kid on
which you're thumping out your book? Shure, an' you can't
mean it. You're ready to knock my block off if I so much
as breathe down its neck. You—"

"Hold everything, Sergeant, let me finish."

"Excuse me for shootin' off my mouth like that, sir."

"All right, now listen. This is important and strictly between you and me. Leave the machine to be repaired, not at the Barracks—somewhere in the city. Say you must have one in its place. Dimes to dollars you won't get it. Weep on the salesman's shoulder, ask if a new one has been sold on the Island recently or within the last few months that you could buy or hire."

"I get you, sir. You're out to locate a new typewriter."

"That's right. Any calls while I was busy in the other room?"

"Our General, sir. I told him you were out but he seemed hep to the fact you weren't. He buzzed to remind you that his special detachment of the U.S. Army was expected to report at the concert Madam Shaw-Ruskin is sponsoring this afternoon."

"I'd completely forgotten that concert. Don't the people here do anything but amuse themselves?"

"I guess they've had a pretty raw deal these last four years. The Island was crowded with troops—33,144 Hawaiian men and women served in this damned war."

"Out of a total population of less than half a million. You are right, they are entitled to all the fun and relaxation they can think up. Also, they have taught the world a lesson, that many races can live together in peace and harmony. That reminds me, have you ever seen *Mr.* Wong Chun?"

"Shure, an' I have. He's the cute Chinese trick's brother-in-law. He took us out in his boat when she began to teach me to surf-ride."

"What is he like?"

"Like the rest of 'em. When you see one in Chinese rig you've seen 'em all."

"Would you say he is keen for money?"

"On the make regardless? Jeepers, no sir, that is, so far as I know. When I offered to pay him for the boat he just grinned, shook his head. 'Velly glad. Velly glad take you. No money. No money.' He's an awful fusser, though, Sib Lou says. If anyone touches a thing in his tool house he's fit to tie, and he knows every plant and shrub on the place. She says he goes out every night and counts 'em, but that last is just her little joke. Even Mrs. Shaw doesn't dare take a rake, she has her own when she works in her garden. If that isn't being a slave to labor, I'll eat my hat. She ought to strike."

If Wong Chun didn't care for money he wasn't the other

half or three quarters of that "Chi" on the torn carbon. That explanation was out.

"Any special reason to be interested in him, sir?"

"N—o, I wondered if while raking up the grounds he might have come on that brief case you dropped into the shrubs. That happened at about one-thirty, I take it. The person who scrambled the room, who must have followed you in about an hour, had been put wise to the fact that everyone would be away at that time. The clock on the floor had stopped at one thirty-five."

"But I was in the room after that—'twas neat as a pin."

"Parkus suggested the clock had been doctored. *Forget the brief case for the present.* Your job is to locate a new typewriter. Start demolishing mine. Remember, Mac, lives may depend on the way you handle this. You are on the business of replacing a broken machine. Nothing else. Understand?"

"Yes, sir. When she licked me my mother used to gripe, 'This hurts me, Joey, more than it hurts you.' I guess I'll know she said something when I take a crack at that typewriter I've lugged half round the world, a thing like that gets to be sort of a person. Better stuff cotton in your ears so you won't hear it go, sir." His grin didn't quite disguise the fact that he hated the job he had to do.

"Kamakani Ka Ili Aloha." The beautiful soprano voice rang through the crowded auditorium as Cam slipped into a rear seat. The concert was almost over. Doubtless the General was fuming because he was late, but if only he knew it, he was lucky to be there at all. His jeep had barely escaped a head-on collision. A coolie, driving a heavy truck loaded with young trees, had lunged from a side street just as he was crossing and scraped the forward wheel. Only in a movie had he seen a crowd gather so quickly, and only in the Tower of Babel could there have been such a conglomeration of language sounds. He had assured the traffic cop that he had no charge to make and had escaped as soon as possible, wondering as he went if the episode had been entirely accidental. There was that broken word "Chi—" still to be explained.

He pushed the suspicion into the back of his mind. Mentally he had been at work decoding the meaning of that carbon all day, had conferred with the General about it. His judgment would be better if he could forget it for a while. The singer had a lovely voice. She was slight and dark and was dressed in a pink Mother-Hubbardy sort of dress the Hawaiian women affected.

She was directing her song toward the box at stage right, where Madam Shaw-Ruskin was seated prominently in front. Even at this distance he caught the twinkle of her diamonds. Sally Shaw, in gray, sat a little behind her, Pat, in a sort of flamingo red frock, at her left. That glint of gold braid must be the General. Apparently the autocrat of society had forgiven the "Get out or you'll be shot out" command of his yesterday. There were two blurs which were faces in the background.

He stood at attention and joined in singing "The Star-Spangled Banner" and at the close made his way to Madam Shaw-Ruskin's box to make his apologies for his tardy appearance. General Carrington laid his hand on his sleeve.

"Glad you showed up at last, Colonel. Began to think you'd gone A.W.O.L. on us." His voice was light but his eyes were gravely questioning. Coming on top of the wiping out of Stanhope, he had taken the contents of the carbon seriously.

"A bit of dirty work at a crossroads, sir. A crazy driver almost ran me down on my way here. Had to find a police interpreter to straighten it out." He turned to Madam Shaw-Ruskin, who was regarding him through her glittering lorgnon.

"Sorry to be late, Madam. Sorry to miss most of the singing. I heard enough, though, to know it was out of this world."

"She's good, but no better than my prospective daughter-in-law, *Pat*—ricia, Colonel Fulton. Madam Moto Marcella is coming home with me. You will join us, of course."

She swept out of the box and along the corridor with Sally Shaw, the General, Señor Cardena, Patricia and her son following like a court in attendance.

"I'll be hanged if I go. I've got more important irons in the fire," he told himself. Besides, it made him sick to see Pat kowtowing to the old autocrat.

Would she be her daughter-in-law—eventually? He made his way through the crowd toward his jeep in a parking space on a side street.

"Cam! Cam!"

He turned. Velma Dane was elbowing her way through the departing audience. He waited for her to join him.

"Wonder I didn't lose my pearls in that jam." She touched the lustrous collar about her throat as if to make sure of its safety. "Or my precious gardenias." She sniffed at the corsage at the shoulder of her thin beige frock. Her auburn hair made a glowing frame for a stocking cap of beige and gold mesh from the tip of which hung a gold tassel. "Whither bound, soldier?"

"I have been ordered to meet the songbird at Madam Shaw-Ruskin's, but I'm not going."

"That's what you think, but you are. I have been *invited* to attend by no less a person than 'her majesty'—tie that—she sent word by Monty. What do you suppose she's got up her sleeve? I'll bet it's a pay-off for the crack I let go about her toupee. I should worry. You've got to take me. The hotel wouldn't promise to send a taxi after the concert."

"Where's your husband? It's his job to get you there."

"He promised to meet me at Madam Shaw-Ruskin's and drive me home. He side-stepped the concert. Music bores him. Do your boy-scout deed for the day, Cam, and take me to the party. I'm dying to see that house and the things in it."

"Promise to behave if I do? Promise not to hurl any verbal brickbats at your hostess?" They had reached the jeep.

She folded her hands meekly on her breast, glanced up at him under a fringe of black lashes.

"This is angel-child day with little Velma." Her voice was demure but the green eyes sparkled with mischief.

"You and your angel-child stuff can't fool me. I'll bet I'm heading straight for trouble, but I'll bite. Hop in."

Was this unexpected meeting with Monty Dane's wife on the very day he had received the mysterious carbon part of the pattern? Had fate in the person of Velma taken a hand and turned him from the Barracks to the festivity at Madam Shaw-Ruskin's for a purpose? Where did a crazy idea like that come from?

"I'll bet you are dying of curiosity to know how come I am bidden to the royal presence," Velma Dane suggested as the jeep joined the procession of automobiles on the boulevard.

"Not so near death as you'll be if you don't give. You're seething with the urge to tell all. I feel it. Go on. Let's have the awful truth."

Cars were turning into side streets. Progress was faster. A voice drifted back from the road ahead.

"Flow—as! Flow—as!"

Cam stopped the car as they came abreast of a large woman in what looked to be a dark blue gunnysack with a red sash tied round her waist. She carried a basket heaped with flowers on her back and an armful of *leis*.

"Want a *lei*, Velma?" Cam asked.

"I'd love the gardenia one. Crazy about gardenias."

"The lady knows that one much better than oddas. You t'ink so, yes?" The flower vendor grinned toothless approval and tucked the money he gave her into her obi.

"You paid too much for this," Velma Dane protested as

she slipped the fragrant garland over her head. "I've been told they've about doubled the price of these things since the war."

"You wanted it, didn't you?"

"Flow—as! Flow—as!" She waited till the voice behind them had faded in the distance.

"Ohmigosh, Cam, are you the type that believes a woman should have what she wants?"

"Yes, to a degree."

"I've heard of the creatures but I've never met one before. How have you escaped matrimony all these years? Come to think of it, perhaps you haven't. I have taken it for granted you are a bachelor. There are plenty of officers your age and older—like Monty before I appeared to spoil his fun —living the life of Reilly here, with a wife on the Mainland."

"If this is a quiz, you're doin' fine, Velma. My age is goin' on thirty-one. I am not living the life of Reilly—page General Carrington, who keeps my nose to the grindstone—and I haven't a wife on the Mainland. And that sets me to wondering how a gal like you spends her days."

"What do you mean, a gal like me?"

"Hold everything, no criticism intended. I mean a girl with plenty of money to spend, loads of charm and beauty and a husband *in absentia,* most of the time."

"Talk English. I only went through junior high. What do you mean by *in absentia?*"

"It's a legal term, the papers have been full of it in reports of the Nuremberg court proceedings. 'He's being tried *in absentia,*' meaning that the man isn't present; more often than not, it isn't known where he is."

"I never read anything in newspapers but the advertising and lovelorn column. Too much work to skip from the first page to one in the middle to finish a write-up. As to what I do, I spent this morning handing out hand lotion and face cream to the war brides on the 'Diaper Special' which stopped here for twenty-four hours on the way to the Mainland. The women are not allowed to leave the dock."

"That was tough after the long voyage."

"They weren't grousing. The band played and we all admired the babies. Such healthy, lovely babies, I bet they'll grow into grand citizens of the U.S., and they were on the way to their husbands. Speaking of husbands, I guess Monty comes under the head of *in absentia* all right. When he is in the hotel he's everlastingly pounding a typewriter in the room next to mine or phoning about a business deal. My eye, does he glare when I interrupt!"

Typewriting. Cam's pulses stepped up their beat. "He's

darn lucky to have a typewriter. Mine went on the blink this morning and so far I haven't found a replacement. I feel as if I'd lost a hand."

"You are welcome to the use of mine, Cam."

"How come you have one? Did you bring it with you? Don't tell me I am in the presence of a career woman in disguise."

"Stop kidding. I was trained by Pop, who had a small grocery business, to keep accounts. He knew that when Grandpop had to let go his money I would be filthy rich. I have to turn over to the trustees of the estate a list of personal expenses for tax purposes. They look more professional typed. I always have a portable machine in my luggage. I like business. I bet I could qualify as a career woman."

"I bet you could. Here we are. Pretty snappy outfit, what?"

She stood for a moment looking at the sprawling mellow-white house with its blossoming vines, its flower hedges, at the sheer cliffs of the Pali looming behind it, at the sea that stretched like a great brazen mirror before it, at the palms, the monkeypod and shower trees.

"Snappy? It's out of this world. I like it. I'll buy it."

"Just like that." Even as he laughed at her he was sure if she decided she wanted the place she would try to get it.

"I thought I was coming to a party to meet some of the crowned heads of the Island, and only the people I see every day are here," she complained as they entered the foyer from which they could see into the long drawing room.

"Remember, this is your angel-child day. You've promised to behave. There are some persons here you don't see every day. I'll bet you haven't met that bunch of j.g.'s hanging over Miss Carey at the piano."

"J.g.'s are not in my class. Nothing lower than admirals, generals and colonels for my money. Scared blue, aren't you, for fear I'll throw a monkey wrench into the party. Relax. Watch me make the perfect-lady approach. I know the act. I did a stretch in the movies. Reception, visiting gal slinks up to shake the hand of the hostess. Here I go."

Madam Shaw-Ruskin raised her lorgnon and regarded Mrs. Montgomery Dane with very evident suspicion as she approached. Velma had spoken truly when she had declared, "I know the act." Her usually strident voice was softly modulated, her smile tailored to show appreciation—without a touch of servility—of the honor of being a guest in this most desirable of houses, her reference to the views from the great windows a masterpiece of restrained admiration.

"I didn't think she had it in her," Maida Parsons confided to Cam in a whisper. "I'll bet she's Hollywood out of New York's East Side. Relax. No fireworks at present. Our hostess is smiling—a cat that swallowed the canary smile—but one can't expect too much. She's positively beaming at General Carrington—I thought she'd have her knife out for him after being driven from Sally Shaw's into the cold, cold world yesterday. Too bad the guest of honor reneged."

"Isn't she here? What happened?"

"Cracked her voice on the high note of 'The Star-Spangled Banner,'" she said. "I thought at first she was side-stepping the party, but I guess it was the truth. She was white as a sheet and clutching her throat when I saw her. Hooray, Pat will sing. I think her voice as good as the diva's. Those navy boys are turning over the music like nobody's business. Looks like she'll have to sing a selection for each or there'll be bloodshed. Well, Monty, it's about time you realized that I am among those present."

Cam nodded to Dane and walked away. Pat and the j.g.'s were laughing and arguing over the sheet music. He paid his respects to his hostess and went on to the entrance to the *lanai* from which he could see the long room. Behind him he heard the pad-pad of feet as the Chinese boys moved about the refreshment-laden table.

Velma Dane, standing against a background of superb Polynesian embroidery, was listening to Señor Cardena with apparently ingenuous interest. The angel-child was still in the works. She met his eyes and responded with a wicked wink, before she again gave absorbed attention to what the Brazilian was saying.

What was he telling her? What did he know? Why was he here? Was his suspicion that the alleged Brazilian was in communication with Dane's *Frau* a phony? Monty pounded a typewriter at all hours, his wife had said. Had that revealing carbon come from his machine? If so, who would have mailed it if Velma hadn't? She wouldn't do it when it contained that reference to herself—or would she —to let him know that she was under suspicion and needed protection? "Watch her," the letter had instructed, "we may have to take care of her."

A few soft chords switched his attention. Pat was standing straight and slim and lovely with hands clasped. A j.g. in navy whites was seated at the piano.

"Aloha means I love you," she sang with ease, charm and infinite tenderness. Her voice was even more lovely than when he had heard it in the church with flute accompaniment. All the shock and heartbreak of that night two years ago when he had read her letter, had realized that he had lost her, surged through him in a tide of love and longing. He had thought he no longer cared.

"Aloha means I love you," he said under his breath, and knew that the last tinge of emotional numbness had departed.

They kept her singing until she protested, waved away the j.g., took the seat herself and struck the opening chords of "Hawaii Ponoi," the Hawaiian national anthem. Even Madam Shaw-Ruskin rose and sang in a high soprano. After which they repaired to the *lanai* for refreshments.

The j.g.'s hovered about Pat like bees above a buckwheat field. Velma, still in her perfect-lady character was talking with Phil Ruskin on one side and General Carrington on the other, who were listening as if under the spell of an oracle and a fascinating one at that. Mrs. Shaw-Ruskin glowered at her son. Good Lord, here's trouble, Cam thought, and approached the group in the hope of averting it. Too late. The hostess, bristling with hostility, reached them first.

"Mrs. Dane, you are irresistible, it seems, always surrounded by men, I hear. The hotel is buzzing with the spicy news that a certain Colonel, whom I won't name, lunches with you daily behind a screen of palms."

"Of course she means me." Cam swore softly to himself. Had Pat heard the crack? Would she believe him if he told her that many times meant just once? Velma looked as if the breath had been knocked from her body. What would she do with the challenge? He hadn't long to wonder. In answer she flung herself into his arms.

"Cam! Cam, my demon lover!" Her half-whispered, half-sobbed words carried. "She—she has discovered our guilty secret."

18

"NEVER a dull moment," Pat exclaimed and juggled a sharp sob into a laugh. "Was Cam's stunned expression due to surprise or guilt? He had brought Velma here. Monty's eyes had changed from amazement to hope. Would he be happy to have his wife turn to someone beside himself? Velma Dane was clinging to Cam as if he were her Rock of Ages. Color surged under his bronzed skin and turned it dark red. He loosened the hand which gripped his collar, pushed her away and laughed.

"Cut out the ham, Velma. Unchivalrous as it may seem I insist that you tell our hostess that the 'guilty secret' stuff is the bunk."

"That's what she wants to believe, isn't it?" Velma Dane's expression was of childlike ingenuousness. "Didn't you declare that you wouldn't bring me here unless I promised to be a perfect lady, Cam? I just told her what she was dying to hear, a nice piece of scandal she could roll round on her tongue." She turned on Madam Shaw-Ruskin like a red-headed fury.

"If you were referring to Colonel Fulton, he lunched with me once, there was *one* palm and any number of tables within hearing distance. Monty, take me home, but before I depart I'd like to put on record the fact that where I grew up a woman couldn't insult a guest and get away with it. There are nine men present and not one with the nerve to tell the old girl to go to—"

"Carrots! Shut up!" Her husband fairly dragged her from the room.

"Now that is *pau* shall we proceed with tea?" Madam Shaw-Ruskin inquired suavely in spite of the fact that her face was a blotched crimson.

Cam Fulton said a word or two to her and departed. Sally Shaw's face was white with indignation, her eyes suggested repressed tears as she engaged Señor Cardena in conversation. The General settled his tie and started the controversial subject of Statehood versus Territory rating for Hawaii with his hostess. It would be good for fireworks as long as he kept it up. The j.g.'s fell on the refreshments like an army of locusts on a wheat field.

"What the devil started Mother after the peppy Dane, Pat?" Phil Ruskin demanded. "Looks as if she had invited her to come for the sole purpose of handing her that nasty crack. What'll you have to eat and drink?"

"Pineapple juice and sandwiches and make it quick. The recent unpleasantness gave me the shakies. You made your mother furious by listening to Velma as if you had gone off the deep end. You know she hates her. Heaven and she only know why."

"Boy, that deep-end stuff doesn't mean you're jealous, does it?"

"It does *not*."

"Don't get mad about it. The peppy Dane is common as they come in so-called polite society, but she's fun. Sort of man-to-man approach if you get what I mean. No come-on line like Maida Parsons. Boy, she set the Colonel back. He looked as if the ground had opened under his feet and a female devil had shot up to clutch him." He threw back his head and laughed as she had never seen him laugh before.

"Then you don't believe what Velma insinuated is true?" His eyes widened in amazement.

"Don't tell me you were taken in by that demon-lover corn? I hold no brief for Fulton; I hate the guy, you like him too much—don't perjure yourself, I'm no fool—but if he is having an affair with that red-hot offspring of Mother Pele's, I'm a piker. Go into the garden. I'll bring a tray and we'll enjoy our eats in peace."

From the lower *lanai* Pat looked up at the house. Snowy white thunbergia cascaded from the roof, yellow roses had climbed round a corner to meet it. Close by two African tulip trees were flaming with color; at the same time their pods were falling and sending seeds drifting through the air. Ti leaves were waving in the slight breeze laden with the scent of heliotrope. She thought of the treasures inside, of the perfection of the setting. How could a woman with such a home take pleasure in hurting anyone?

She asked the question of her aunt as, dressed for dinner, they waited in the living room at Silver Ledges for General Carrington and Cam Fulton.

"Don't ask me why Mother Shaw-Ruskin is as she is, Pat. I've been working on that problem for years. The only solution I've reached is that she was born with an urge to hurt people's hearts. She has had everything to make life worth while, superintelligence—she is an encyclopedia of knowledge—the courtesy and devotion, if not the love, of two husbands and two sons, money to burn, luxurious surroundings, impeccable social position. As she has grown older, more and more she has mistaken pomp for power—that last lifted from Senator Vandenberg."

"She must have been a beauty when she was younger."

"She was, and is exceptionally good-looking now—another asset. I let her walk over me when I married her son—to a degree—to keep peace in the family. Never again. I didn't say 'Yes' to the General because I wanted to get away from her—I'm not that spineless—but I've waited so long to hear him say 'I love you' that I let him assume I was a tender flower which needed protection from a withering blast."

"You, a tender flower, you who have carried on like a trouper for tragic years. It is to laugh."

"I mean to forget those years, honey. Velma was right, a woman who insults a guest shouldn't be allowed to get away with it—anywhere. I'm thoroughly in sympathy with the 'peppy Dane' as Phil calls her, but had I been Cam Fulton I would have strangled her with my bare hands when she flung 'our guilty secret' into the blue."

"Then you don't believe they are—are more than friends?"

"Pat! Don't tell me that combat fatigue is beginning at last to get in its work on your brain, that your sense of values is so addled you can believe Cam Fulton is the sort of wolf who would have an affair with a married woman, or any other for that matter."

"She is terribly attractive, she's so—vital."

"So is a sleek, smooth cat, with sheathed, sharp-pointed claws. I wouldn't be surprised if we received a polite note from the Colonel regretting that matters of importance would prevent him from doing the M.P. act here tonight. He must loathe anyone by the name of Shaw."

"I don't see where you come into it."

"I come into it because all the years I have lived on this island I haven't had the nerve to slap my mother-in-law's face in public, figuratively speaking, when she stuck pins into me or my friends. It might have had a Stop! Look! Listen! effect. The Russians have the right idea. They respect combatants who stand up to them and whack back. Glad you put on that sequined gypsy print tonight. It will add a note of cheer to what may prove a gloomy evening. The General was speechless with fury when we left Mamma-in-law's. One more rhinestone bracelet on your left arm and you wouldn't have the strength to lift it."

"When I'm low in my mind glitter does things for me. Lucky our thief wasn't interested in junk jewelry. I have a ton, more or less."

"Had he realized what nice junk costs—tax additional— he would have taken it. That reminds me, you may go back to your room tonight. Parkus and his men spent the afternoon there. He is coming this evening to report."

"Report what?" Her aunt's words sent memory swooping back. Had the black brief case been found? She hadn't thought of it for the last five hours.

"He didn't say what, but his voice dripped mystery. It is his line. Isn't that Cam's voice outside? Looks as if he had forgiven me for the sins of my mother-in-law."

"What's that about forgiveness, Sally?" General Carrington asked as he entered. "Hooray, I'm glad you've stepped out of gray for once. I like you in that peacock blue, it was called, back in the days when I was young."

"All men like blue, they can't tell why. You have a nice sense of timing, Colonel. Pat and I were just wondering if you would appear tonight and here you are."

"Why shouldn't I come? Because of that blockbuster Velma dropped? Did I look guilty? For a minute amazement had me slugged." His amused eyes met Pat's. "I don't like your one-to-a-customer smile, Miss Carey; I doubt if a woman, no matter how hardened, would proclaim that she had a 'demon lover' to a room full of people. Let's forget it." He glanced at the back of the General, who was standing in the opening to the *lanai* with his arm about Sally Shaw.

"I'm not musical but your voice made a tremendous hit with me. I've got a lot to tell you. After dinner we'll walk down to the garden wall—right?"

What had he to tell her? The question kept getting in the way of Pat's appetite. Had he forgiven her for hitting and running? Would that accusation ever stop hurting? Perhaps he had news of Skinner's brief case. Perhaps Parkus had found it and was coming tonight to bring it.

"Dramatic country, isn't it?" Cam Fulton asked as they stood at the bougainvillia-covered wall.

Dramatic was the perfect word for it. Steeply towering pinnacles stood out against the phosphorescence which heralded the rise of an aging moon. Reflected lights from distant battleships and destroyers made floating islands of color on a smooth, dark sea. Big stars and little starlets turned the heavens to cloth of gold. The soft wind blowing across the garden was fragrant with the scent of gardenias.

"Wouldn't it be fun if radar scientists would contact the moon when it rises over the mountain?" Pat inquired. "The night is so still we might hear the *ping* of response." The remark didn't crackle with brilliance but it would serve to break the silence.

"I'll bet we could hear it here if anywhere. I have the most curious feeling that this Island with its tumbling hills and rugged mountain peaks, its fields of cane and pineapples; its mixture of races, its Waikiki, palms and shower trees, is like a magnificent backdrop, a stage setting for the work General Carrington and I were sent here to accomplish, nothing more—that we are not and never will be a part of it. Our mission has nothing to do with Hawaii. It just happened that it brought us here."

That first evening in the *lanai* he had asked, "Did you think I wouldn't find you?" That must have been a line. Now he spoke of a "mission."

"Has my rave over the beauties of this island sent you to sleep?"

"No. My hearing and brain are still functioning. I was wondering if that 'mission' impinged on the 'lot' you have to tell me?"

"The General et al., meaning yours truly and Sergeant McIlvray, came here with a job to do. That's hush-hush. I'm trusting you not to repeat it. But I didn't bring you here to the garden to tell you that. Figure this out, if you can."

He told of Skinner's letter to McIlvray, of the Sergeant's conviction that she was the nurse to whom the brief case had been entrusted; of his admission that he had entered Mrs. Shaw's house; of his account of what followed; of his fear that he would be mixed up in the disappearance of the diamonds.

"Of course he didn't take them."

"Believe in him, don't you? Wish you had as much faith in me. You should have seen your horrified expression when Velma Dane put on her act this afternoon."

"I was stunned with amazement. If it had been Maida—"

"Maida isn't the kind who would 'kiss and tell; for that matter, she wouldn't have a 'guilty secret.' Velma isn't either, it was a phony line to get back at Madam Shaw-Ruskin and make her ridiculous. She scored. Now that is disposed of let's get on with McIlvray's part in our mystery."

He told where and how the brief case happened to be on the bed, that the Sergeant had tossed it into the shrubs below her bedroom window intending to return for it.

"*Intending* to return! Didn't he come back?"

"Yes, but too late, it was gone. Did you find it?"

"*No.* You heard me tell Phil that I hunted in the shrubs. Nothing there."

"McIlvray swears he didn't turn your room upside down."

"Then who did? It must have been done after the Sergeant was there. Was my room torn to pieces by the man who, Skinner said, wouldn't stop at murder to get the brief case? It's a shivery thought. If he didn't get it, who did? I know. I *know.* Parkus has found it."

She repeated what her aunt had told her as to the presence of the Chief and his men in her room that afternoon, that he was coming tonight to report, concluded:—

"That doesn't make sense. In the first place, the Sergeant told you he had dropped it from the window, it couldn't have been in the room when they made their search; in the second, why should Parkus be interested in that brief case when he knows nothing about it? Another fond hope blasted."

"Don't be downhearted. We'll find it, we've got to find it. What kind of a person is Wong Chun?"

"Lilly Yee Lung's husband? Thoroughly domesticated sort. Nice to his family but a fuddy-duddy about this place. Old Cerberus, the Watchdog, Sally calls him. She has her own garden to grow the flowers she wants for the house, which he is not allowed to enter. He raises the roof if she cuts anywhere else. Why bring him into the picture?"

"I was wondering if by chance he saw the brief case under your window and picked it up."

"Could be, if he thought it was heavy on one of his adored shrubs."

"Any idea what he would do with it if he found it?"

"He might take it to the tool house thinking it was a new kind of gadget for the garden. His mental radar will never induce a responsive *ping* from another brain. Let's go look."

"Not in that frock if we are going on a secret mission. Every time you move a red or green or gold sequin catches the light and glitters. Can't I find a coat in the house?"

"Yes, my old mackintosh in the closet in the back hall. If Lilly Yee Lung hears you, tell her we are waiting to see the moon rise over the mountain, that I need a coat. You'll find a duplicate key to the tool house hanging on a nail there. Better bring it. Wong Chua probably has locked up for the night."

If they found Skinner's brief case, without the key, they would have to find something with which to pry it open, Pat figured as she waited. Would Sally hear Cam and hale him into the living room? No, he was returning rapidly across the lawn. He held out the coat.

"Put your arms in. Just made it. Heard a car drive up as I sneaked out the back door. May be Parkus. Where is the tool house?"

"Behind the servants' quarters. We better walk on the grass so old Cerberus won't hear and spring out at us."

"It must have been he who came to his door and peered out just as Ruskin slipped around the corner last night. It would be in character as you have described him."

She put her fingers to her lips and led the way. Once she stopped and clutched the sleeve of his tunic. He caught her fingers in his. She felt the contact tingling to her toes and freed her hand.

"Thought I heard a door open," she whispered. "False alarm. Come on."

A rim of moon fitted like a halo hat on the mountaintop when Cam carefully pushed the key into the lock in the tool house door.

"I'll go first."

Inside he snapped on his cigarette lighter. The faint glow revealed garden tools of all varieties in racks; a work bench, a motor-driven grasscutter in a sort of lean-to; a set of pine drawers with seed labels. A ladder mounted to an opening in a floor above. A mouse gnawed behind the wall of wood. The place smelled of fertilizer and dried herbs.

"Lo—" Excitement blocked Pat's voice. "Look!" she whispered and pointed to a black brief case hanging on a wooden peg. "Wong Chun found it."

"Don't touch it." He gripped her arm as she started forward. "It's too easy. There's a catch to it. Good Lord, see that light outside? Someone's coming with a lantern. Scramble up the ladder. Quick! Quick!"

She went up hand over hand—the educational value of the movies, she thought—and swallowed a laugh. She stepped on her mackintosh, slipped back a step. Hands seized her under the arms and boosted her ahead. She tumbled onto the floor. Cam lifted her and deposited her away from the opening. Not a minute too soon. A key scraped in the door below. A light was snapped on.

"Shure, an' it's a nice dump you have here." Sergeant McIlvray's voice. Cam's released breath made her think of the air escaping from a football. She felt limp as a rag herself. Now they could go down and—Cam caught her arm as she moved and stopped her.

"Velly nice." Wong Chun's voice. "That w'at you want?" Was he indicating the black brief case?

"Shure, an' if it ain't the identical fella. Where did you find it, Mr. Wong Chun?"

"In shrubs under Mees Pat's winda. I ask Lilly Yee Lung, 'Do Mees Pat have one?' She velly mad. Don' know w'y. She says she don' know. Say she nevva see it. How you come drop it?"

"When I came to take Sib Lou Waikiki, I'm carrying my flute case and that bag, see? Need one hand free when I'm taking out a gal—you know how it is, Mr. Wong Chun. I toss the bag into the shrubs till I get back. When I look for it, Saint Patrick, 'tain't there. Sherlock bust loose and handed me a tip. 'Mr. Wong Chun may have found it,' says he, and here it is."

"Who Shelock? He live Honolulu?"

"Shure, an' he's a guy who knows all the answers."

"You Sib Lou's fliend, you oklay. Hully an' take, I lock up. Go to bed."

"All right with me, Mr. Wong Chun. I've got it. Douse the glim— Put out the light. Lock up. Here we go."

Darkness below. The click of a lock. Cam snapped his cigarette lighter.

"We should have taken that brief case," Pat whispered.

"It's safe with Mac."

"Suppose someone is lying in wait to get it."

"That's a lovely thought. Let's get out of here. Parkus may be on the lookout and grab him. I'll go first. Take it slowly. I won't let you fall."

It seemed years to Pat as step by cautious step she backed down the ladder. Another decade before they had crossed the lawn. She threw off the mackintosh before they went in. Voices. She flexed stiff lips and whispered:—

"Has Parkus stopped the Sergeant?"

"What in thunder?" Cam exclaimed under his breath as they reached the living room door. Sergeant McIlvray stood rigidly at attention, as rigidly as he could with a black brief case under his left arm. General Carrington was frowning and settling his tie. Sally Shaw, on the sofa, was pleating and unpleating a fold of her brilliant blue crepe skirt, as she looked apprehensively at Police Captain Parkus standing in the middle of the room.

"You say you know who took the diamonds?" she asked in a voice which sounded as if she were supplying a cue for the girl and man who hàd stopped on the threshold.

"I know who took the diamonds but before I spring the trap I'd like to be put wise to what the Sergeant is doing with that brief case. My man caught him sneaking out of the drive with it."

"That's easily answered, Captain." General Carrington's attempt to infuse amusement in his voice was a flop. It was strained with anxiety. "McIlvray was put on the job of trailing down a brief case I left in a jeep. Had an idea it had been stolen. He thought he knew where it was. He was right. He has it."

"Where'd you find it, Sergeant?"

Parkus's question sent McIlvray's eyes to the General. He promptly responded to the unworded appeal.

"You needn't answer, Sergeant. This is a military, not a civil matter, Captain," he reminded.

"Oh, all right, all right, if you want it that way. Perhaps you'll allow that the snitching of the diamonds is civil, not military, and is my concern, General?"

"Certainly it is. Let's have it. Who stole Miss Carey's jewels?"

"He's right there by the door. Colonel Fulton."

Cam steal her diamonds? Pat's brain whirled for a second and steadied. She had told him where they might be, under the scarfs and dickies, if the upper drawer of her dresser had been turned out on the floor. He had remained behind in the room. He had said, "Your aunt is calling. Go down. I'll take a look-see." Had he taken the clip and earrings then? Had Parkus found his fingerprints on the white case that he was so sure? If he had taken them it was because their disappearance would in some way help his "mission"—she would stake her life on that.

"Well, Miss Carey, has the truth struck you dumb?"

She flexed stiff lips. She didn't like the acidulous triumph in Parkus's voice, it proclaimed that at last he had something on the army, between which and himself there was a jealous feud, Sally had said. She didn't like the consternation in the eyes of the General and Sally, she didn't like the eagerness of Sergeant McIlvray's eyes as they sought those of Cam's beside her, and the way he stepped back as if he had received a Stop signal. This was her chance to make up in a slight degree to Cam for hitting and running, this was where she became a go-through guy. She laughed, she hoped it sounded like a laugh of pure amusement.

"Sorry to disappoint you, Captain Parkus. You've barked up the wrong tree. Suppose Colonel Fulton did take my diamonds, what's all the shootin' about? Why shouldn't he take them? I'm his wife."

19

"NO! No! *No!*"

Pat stared at Cam Fulton in shocked amazement as he passionately denied her acknowledgment. His face was as white as bronzed skin can be before the blood surged back in a dark red tide.

"It's a mistake, Parkus, about the diamonds, I mean. I have them. Mrs. Shaw, take Pat out of this while I explain."

"Thanks for the kind thought, but I'm not the white man's burden. I don't need to be *taken* anywhere. I'll go under my own power."

She left the room feeling as if she were moving sticks for legs. Cam had denied their marriage. What did it mean? She heard her aunt behind her on the stairs and ran, but Sally Shaw was as fleet as she, reached the door at the same moment and pushed past her into the room.

"I won't be shut out this time. Tell me what it's all about, honey." She stopped to control her quick breathing and snapped on a rose-shaded lamp. "It's a long time since I ran upstairs, makes me puff. Sit in the big chair and tell me the story. You might as well. I have known for two years that you and Cam Fulton were married, but I've never known why you left him." She dropped to the edge of the blue satin covered bed.

Pat whirled from the open window from which she had been staring unseeingly at the moonlit garden.

"How did you know? When?"

"Cam wrote to me the night before he sailed overseas. In case he didn't come back he wanted me, your nearest relative, to know what provision he had made for his wife."

"Why didn't he write to me?"

"After you let him down? A man would have to be a little lower than an angel to forgive that. Why did you do it? Why didn't you confide in me, child?"

"You're asking me why I did it. Don't you think I haven't lain awake night after night trying to answer the same question? Have you never done anything crazy that stopped your heart each time you thought of it? I kept putting off writing to you, then, as weeks passed, there were times when the fact I had danced with Cam at the Post, held Maida's lilies while she knelt for the benediction, seemed like a dream, the world in which I was living was so bloody and cruel and tragically real. We were married in a small town near the Post, in the late afternoon. I had my health certificate in preparation for Red Cross work, Cam had his because he was slated for overseas. Somewhere he found a gold wedding ring. No hold up there. A special license and marriage made easy. Joke as it turned out, isn't it?"

"No joke for Cam. Don't be bitter, Pat."

"Bitter! So what? As my snappy Sergeant would say, 'I have been given the gate.' Didn't you hear him deny that I was his wife?"

"I heard what he said. Go on, what happened after the ceremony?"

"We had reservations on an early evening train for New York. We went to the inn where I had been staying to collect my luggage. An order to return to headquarters at once was waiting for him there. After he had gone I came to with a crash. It was as if I had emerged from a spell. What had I done? Promised to marry a man I had known but a week, promised to live with him as his wife. I couldn't do it. I just *couldn't* do it."

"Sounds like emotional reaction and you let it throw you."

"Call it what you like, it threw me, all right. When he phoned that we couldn't leave as we had planned, that he would join me at midnight at the inn, I felt like a prisoner reprieved. He had left one ticket with me so I could board the train if he had to make it the last minute. I twisted that fact into an omen. Fate knew I had made a mistake and provided this out. Of course it was phony reasoning, but I caught at it like a ditched aviator to a life line. I sent him a letter by messenger explaining how I felt, enclosed the ring, and left on the early evening train. I know you are thinking me a quitter. I know you are ashamed of me. Nothing you can think or say will make me realize more than I do what a short sport I was."

"You returned the wedding ring! You were thorough! Why haven't you told me since your return, honey? I have known you were troubled and why, have hoped each day for your confidence. A mother couldn't love a child more than I love you, Patricia."

"Think I don't know that? Think I haven't longed to put my head on your shoulder and sob out the truth? I told myself that the news was bound to break sometime, that meanwhile I wouldn't burden you with my mistake. You had had heartbreak enough to carry. I would take keeping silent as my punishment. I was too ashamed of welshing to tell you."

"Why didn't you talk it over with Cam when he came?"

"That's a laugh. When I saw him again I was ready to do anything he wanted, step into his life or out of it. We hadn't been on the *lanai* five minutes the first night he dined here before he made it painfully clear that I was to step out."

"Are you sure of that?"

"He said, 'I shan't make love to you. I haven't the slightest interest in you as a woman. I'm through. Cam Fulton signing off.' Would you have fallen on a man's neck after that?"

"*Auwe,* life forms amazing patterns, doesn't it? Now that the secret is out we will have some tall explaining to do. Best way would be to give a big reception—"

"You will do nothing of the sort. I'll take the first reservation I can get for the Mainland, go to Reno, after that find a job. My word, I can't. I have something of importance to finish here. I'll have to stay and face the music. It has just dawned on me what a hypocrite you have been, Sally Shaw, pretending you didn't know Cam or about this crazy marriage."

"Remember that I told you once I could keep a secret? If you didn't trust me enough to confide in me I wouldn't force you. Perhaps I have been hurt all this time, too." She steadied her voice. "Let's not turn this into a sob session. I did what I could. I wrote Sam Carrington what had happened, swore him to secrecy and asked him if he could help."

"Then he knew?"

"Certainly he knew. You didn't think the fact that

Colonel Fulton is his aide was coincidental, did you? They have been together for almost two years. I was worried for fear Cam would be reckless. I knew from his letter that he was a very special person. For the honor of the family I had to make up as far as possible for the harm my child had done."

"Have you been corresponding with him all this time? Was that how he knew I was caught in the Belgian Bulge?"

"I didn't know it myself until a long time after, remember. When I did, I passed the information on to him. I'm not ashamed of you, honey. I haven't a doubt but there are hundreds of men and women who realize now that their lives would be better, bigger and happier had the bride in their war hysteria marriage listened to an inner voice reminding her that she knew nothing of the real man inside the uniform beside her, and had the courage to stop right there. Of course, she would be called a welsher, better that than to step out later. Just the same I wish the experience hadn't come to you. Cam is such a grand person, so clean-minded, so true. Who's there?" she responded to a tap on the door.

"I want to talk with Pat, Mrs. Sally."

"Don't let Cam in, don't." Pat backed against the door. "I don't want to see you. You can't come in," she said to the man outside.

"Try and stop me." She held her breath to listen. He was running down the stairs.

"You'll have to see him sometime and talk it out," Sally Shaw reminded. "Better get it behind you."

"There is nothing to talk out. The situation is done, finished. You'd better sleep on that reception idea, Sally. From the manner in which Colonel Fulton denied my melo-dramatic announcement, it is flamingly evident that he doesn't want the news of the marriage to get on the air. That would be a break for me."

"I don't like your hard flippancy, Pat. If you feel that way about it why did you announce it?"

"Parkus seemed so darn smug and pleased—you had told me he was sour on the army—that I feared he might arrest Cam—and—and I had a rush of conscience to the brain —thought I might save him—and out it came."

"Sure it was conscience doing its stuff?"

"What else would it be?"

"I'm not psychic. I don't know what was in your mind— or heart. Listen. A car is driving away. The police depart-ment, I hope. I'm going down. Coming?"

"No. I'll see you in the morning before I leave for the

hospital." She tenderly kissed her aunt on the cheek. "I adore you, Sally. You—you can't think—" she cleared her voice of tears—"what a relief it is that you know—my guilty secret, that last lifted from the peppy Dane, in case you care."

"It could be a very lovely secret, it's all in the point of view. Good night, honey. God bless you and may He revitalize your common sense."

Just what had she meant by that, Pat wondered as she turned the key in the door which had been closed with a slight bang. No use going to bed. Cam's thundered, "No! No! No!" went round and round in her mind as if caught in a whizzing electric fan. She hung the glistening frock in the wardrobe—it seemed years since she had slipped it over her head before dinner—belted a lime-green satin housecoat and changed her sequined sandals for silver mules. She pushed back the long blue hangings and stepped to the balcony.

The broken moon was almost overhead. Madam Pele was flaunting her rosy glow above the mountain. The night was cooler and the air was laden with the aroma of earth and garden. Suppose she had told Sally that the memory of her hasty marriage to a fascinating playboy ten days after she met him, and the unhappiness that had followed, had been a contributing factor to her runout at the Post?

Cam had said this Island was merely a stage setting for the work he and General Carrington had been sent here to accomplish. Had she put a spoke in the wheel of progress when she had made that crazy declaration downstairs? Had taking her diamonds been part of a plan? He hadn't wanted her to hear his explanation to Parkus. He had curtly, if politely, told her to scram.

When he had come to the living room at midnight she had thought for a hectic minute that he had seen Phil Ruskin under her window and had come to protest. Her mistake. He didn't give a darn who came to see her or when, he had been interested only in the mystery of the afternoon break. There had been the instant when he demanded, "Shall I have to pick you up and carry you?" that had been a cutback to the man she had met at the Post. Had it been her chance to convince him she was sorry? Had opportunity brushed lightly against her when she was struggling between regret and pride, too hurt to recognize its presence?

Better change that thought wave-length and quick—it wouldn't get her anywhere. She listened. The window next hers had been flung open. She retreated into her room and seized the hangings.

"Don't pull those together, Pat. They won't keep me out.

I'm coming in." Cam followed his words by action and stepped into the room from the balcony.

"At ease, Miss Carey. Sit in the big chair and stop looking as if I were a big, bad wolf all set to devour you. I shan't touch you. In case you are interested, the next time I take a wife in my arms she won't get away." Back to the mantel, he looked down at her curled in the deep chintz-covered chair.

"This room looks slightly different from the last time we saw it together, doesn't it?" he began as matter-of-factly as if his previous announcement hadn't set her afire with jealousy. "But that isn't what I came to talk about. I have conferred with the General. He wants our marriage kept off the record at present. Until it can be announced it will be better if we don't discuss it ourselves."

"What marriage? You denied that there had been one."

"The reason for that denial is a military secret."

"How can it be kept off the record when I shouted it to the housetops? Sergeant McIlvray and—"

"Mac has known of it since he took care of me when I was wounded overseas. It seems I did a lot of babbling when delirious. Until a few minutes ago he has never given a hint that he knew. His devotion and loyalty to me is something that won't bear talking about."

"Parkus heard me."

"The General and I had a conference with him. We told him enough of our work here to make him understand how important it is to keep your admission of the marriage off the press and gossip wires. He is square. He has been given the raw end of a deal once or twice by brass hats and his professional pride is hurt. He will co-operate. He has taken the Sergeant to police headquarters to get that brief case open."

"Did you take my diamonds?"

"Yes. I hunted for them after you went downstairs yesterday. Figured that as much as you and I wanted to find the brief case the person who made a shambles of this room wanted to find it more, that if attention could be diverted to the theft of the diamonds said person would think us ignorant of his urge to possess it. Parkus found my fingerprints on the white case."

"Do I get the clip and earrings back?"

"Not until we discover who was in this room after the Sergeant left it. Do you need them?"

"Need them? Of course not. Having told me so much—or so little—will you tell me why it is so terribly important that the truth about that marriage ceremony be kept hush-hush?"

"Do you want it announced?"

"I do not. It will be all right with me if it never is heard of even after it is annulled."

"No annulment proceedings. That is a hold-the-line order."

"You needn't be so emphatic. As I am responsible for the secrecy to date I can take the delay. That secrecy has been like a sharp splinter in my heart and mind pricking constantly. I have felt like such a cheat when men—"

"Made love to you?" His mouth set in its stand-and-deliver line, his jaw muscles tensed.

"Why shouldn't they? I'm reasonably attractive—I have been told. They didn't know I was not free. Don't scowl at me. I have known. I have remembered. It hasn't been too hard. I don't like to be kissed."

"No? Forgotten that 'love-is-heaven' week?"

Color burned in her cheeks. "The answer is still No."

"That matter being settled, we will proceed to the next. Don't accept an invitation from Captain Dane or Ruskin till I call the signals."

"I don't care to go out with Monty. I haven't been anywhere with him since his wife arrived and only once before. Phil is different, he's family."

"Dane is one of the men who made love to you, isn't he? He kissed you, didn't he?"

"If he did it was before I knew he had a wife."

"But not before you knew you had a husband—of sorts. Those kisses are another mistake I'll chalk up against Dane."

"I'm surprised at your narrow-mindedness, Colonel. How about the kisses you gave the English girl you were crazy about?"

"English girl?"

"Sally Shaw told me about her, she must have had it straight from those letters you and she have been exchanging—that you were deeply in love, that you were ordered to the invasion hell before you became engaged." Too late she remembered that she had promised not to repeat it.

"Oh, that English girl. I'd rather not talk about her." His voice was depressed.

"Too bad, must have happened after you knew you had a wife—of sorts."

"But, you see— What's happened now?" He scowled at

the phone on the desk. "I'll take the call. It is for me probably. Your aunt knew I was coming here." He picked up the
receiver.

"Fulton speaking. . . . Sergeant? Where are you? . . .
Headquarters? . . . All right. It's all *right*. Cut the apologies.
What's up? My God! Are you sure? . . . I'll join you there."
He cradled the phone.

"They have opened Skinner's brief case, Pat."

"What *did* they find? I'm all creepy chills of excitement."

"Crumpled blank paper."

20

RAIN and wind beat and clamored at the windows of Cam
Fulton's quarters. Through rivulets of water running down
the panes he could see the flooded roads of the Barracks. He
turned quickly as the door opened.

"Any news about the blank paper stuffed in Skinner's
brief case, Sergeant?" he asked eagerly.

McIlvray peeled off his wet raincoat, clapped his cap
against the top of a chair and shook his red head.

"Too soon, sir. I only took it to the fingerprint fella two
nights ago. Too late for him to go to town on it. But right
off quick, he said there was such a mess of prints on the
bag itself he'd never get that straightened out. If he doesn't
do any better than he did with that furniture in Miss—
Mrs.—"

"*Miss* Carey, Sergeant. Don't forget, *Miss* Carey."

"I get you, sir. I'll remember. He only found her prints
and those of the two Chinese women on that. The guy who
turned that place upside down wore gloves. That shoots
him into the expert class." He crossed to the window.

"Shure, an' this is sunny Hawaii. I've never seen wetter
water or more of it at one time in all our travels. You
should have seen the dames wading in bare feet across
wet streets, flooded sidewalks and hopping on a bus. They
made nothing of it. Looks as if the bottom had dropped out
of the clouds that have been nightcapping those mountains
this last week. Water got into the engine, that's why I'm
late, sir."

"Cheerio, Sergeant, the weatherman promised a clear
afternoon. That will be a break. I feel hemmed in. Did you

make Wong Chun understand I wanted to see him here this morning? There are times when I suspect that Chinaman isn't so dumb as he appears."

"He'll show up, sir. He said, 'Oklay! Oklay, I go Ballacks.' It didn't trouble him, apparently, but his missus looked scared out of her wits."

That was understandable. He had impressed Mrs. Wong Chun with the fact that if she admitted to the police or anyone else she had been in Pat's room she would be questioned about the missing diamonds. Tough on her when no one had known better than he that she knew nothing about them. It was a situation which had happened often during the war, the individual had to be sacrificed for the good of the many. McIlvray leaned over the desk.

"I haven't the fingerprint report, sir, but I've partly located a new typewriter."

"Good Lord, Mac, where?"

"Señor Miguel Cardena bought one, the only new one in town, the day after he landed on the Island, sir."

"The Brazilian! Did you find out if he wanted it for himself?"

"The man who drives that black convertible he's hired for the duration—of his stay—came for it and tried out the machine good and plenty before he plunked down the chips and lugged it away."

"If we could only get a scrap of the typing."

"We have it, sir." He drew half a sheet of white paper covered with typing from his pocket and laid it on the desk.

"I gave the salesman a spiel that my boss just had to have a certain type and could I see the style of letters of the machine sold before I left an order for one like it. He pulled that from the drawer and handed it over, said they always kept samples on hand."

"Good work, Sergeant. I'll get the carbon."

He left the room and returned with the copies he had made and the black paper between two white sheets. It had been tested for fingerprints, the report had not come through. He spread the carbon on the desk and the sample provided by the salesman beside it.

"The letters and spacing look identical to me. How about it, Mac?"

"One hundred per cent perfect, sir. You did fine. Getting the lowdown on those two impressions must have been a tough job."

"Here's the story." Cam handed him the copies. "What do you make of it?" The Sergeant read them and whistled.

"We're up against a tougher lot of babies than we thought,

sir, an' we knew we weren't settin' out on a picnic. I remember driving you to the night club. The next day you told me about the dame who yelled. The guy who wrote that letter must have been awful close to—if not at—the table." He reread the carbon. "I'll bet that slick vally of you-know-who is the gunman of the outfit."

"Watch the papers for an answer to the ad for ukuele lessons. I've been over the advertising columns with a fine-tooth comb each edition since the arrival of the carbon; no answer yet. Now that you know how desperate a gang we are up against, watch your step."

"Shure, an' I will, mine, yours, and another person's too, sir. Now that I know the story that carbon tells I'm kinder stumped about something the salesman told me. He said the man who lugged off the machine said his boss was particular that it should be perfect because it was a present for a lady."

"A lady! A present for a lady? So what?"

Had Cardena given the typewriter to Velma Dane? Was she in the conspiracy to secure the stolen millions? Wrong slant. The writer of the letter had intimated a suspicion that she had been working with Stanhope, besides she had said that she always carried a portable in her luggage. Perhaps that same letter had been designed to fall into his hands to avert suspicion from her. She couldn't be an espionage agent. Why not? Women had been used to implement wars, were still on the job all over the world. The less one seemed like a spy the more valuable she was. Velma was beautiful, fearless, rich. Was she rich? Her jewels and the money she flung round so lavishly might be supplied by a "boss." She had offered him the use of her typewriter. He would ask her to let him try it out.

"I guess that's Mr. Wong Chun now, sir."

"Let him in."

"Mr. Wong Chun, Colonel Fulton," McIlvray announced as he ushered in the Chinaman. The man pulled off his wet cap and bowed.

"Mac, he tell me you velly much want to see me, yes?" He shook his head violently when the Sergeant tried to take his leather jacket which glistened with moisture and tucked his big-veined, work-hardened hands into the sleeves.

"Right, Mr. Wong Chun. Sit down." The man sat on the edge of the chair opposite Cam at the desk. "Sorry you had to come so far in this storm."

"Not solly, no. Rain much good for cane, flowas, shlubs, make 'em glow."

"Glad you take a cheerful view of it. Have you seen a

stranger prowling round Mrs. Shaw's place this last week?
That was a serious break-in."

"You p'liceman?"

"No, Mr. Wong Chun. I am a friend who would like to
help Mrs. Shaw and Miss Patricia."

"Lilly Yee Lung, she slay beflo I come, 'Don't talk. You be
allested.' "

"She's got it wrong, Wong Chun. You were not on the
place when the house was entered. You had gone to
Honolulu to get a blade for the grasscutter, Sib Lou told
me."

"Oklay. Fliend call day beflo, he say, 'Want go Honolulu
tomollo, Wong?' I say, 'Oklay, one clock time, I be leady.' "

"A Chinese friend?"

"Alla my fliends Chinese."

Suspicion set Cam's pulses quick-stepping. Was the
friend the "Chi—" of the carbon who was "Okay"? Had he
been bribed to get Wong Chun off the place that afternoon
and leave the coast clear for the room wrecker?

"Did your friend call for you in a car, Mr. Wong Chun?"

"He come in tluck."

"He means truck," the Sergeant interpreted.

"What kind of a truck?"

"Fliend, he cally fluit tlees for sale, sweet sop, bleadfluit,
flig tlees. He cally lettuce, chihili and—"

"Must have had a big load." The truck which had col-
lided with his jeep had been laden with trees, Cam remembered.

"Did you succeed in finding the knife for the grasscutter, Mr. Wong Chun? Things like that are mighty scarce
now."

"No. No knife. Velly good time. Fliend jus' paid off. Much
moneys. Go movies. Plenty ice cleam soda. Chinese dinna.
Plenty bloil steak. Not much peeples. Fliend wanta stay late.
I say, 'No,' I come back."

"Was it dark when you reached Mrs. Shaw's?"

"Plenty light. Light so I see some peeple been in schlubs
side house. Much break down. I look see. Foun' bag Sib
Lou's fliend say he want. I give it."

"When you picked up the bag did you see any scraps of
paper?"

"No sclaps. Finga."

"Finger!" Cam was on his feet. He laughed. "That
word 'finger' gave me a start, Mr. Wong Chun. I thought
for a minute the thief might have had it chopped off while
turning out Miss Patricia's room. What kind of a finger?"

"Glove."

"That may help us locate our man. Where is it?"

"Solly, too bad. Tlow it on compos' heap."

"Sergeant—"

"Yes, sir. I understand."

"Thanks for coming, Mr. Wong Chun." Cam offered a piece of folding money. "Take this for your trouble for driving so far on such a rotten day. Throw a broiled steak party for Mrs. Lilly Yee Lung and yourself."

The Chinaman tucked his hands deeper into his sleeves and shook his head.

"No take money. I come help Missy Shaw find fella bloke in house. No pay. Oklay I go?"

"Okay, and thank you again for coming. Sergeant, go along with Mr. Wong Chun if he has room for you in his car. Stop for ice cream sodas and pick up the biggest box of chocolates you can find for Mrs. Lilly Yee Lung. All right with you if I send your wife candy, Mr. Wong Chun?"

A wintry smile distorted the Chinaman's face.

"Much allee light, Lilly Yee Lung she like velly much, me too like. No much candy long time. You come, Mac? I tly find finga."

"Shure, an' I'm coming. You don't catch me passing up sodas if it is twelve noon. We'll find the chocolates, sir."

"Good. The biggest box in the shop, remember. I'm going Waikiki to see Mrs. Dane at the hotel. Wait for me there and I will bring you back to quarters. Understand?"

"Yes, sir. I'll be hanging round. Come on, young fella." Wong Chun made a deep bow before he left the room with McIlvray's arm linked in his.

Curious that he should have had that sudden urge to call on Velma Dane, Cam thought, as a half hour later he drove away from the Barracks. Had what the psychologists call the deep mind commenced work when McIlvray had announced that Señor Cardena had purchased the typewriter for a lady? When the Sergeant had said, "We'll find the chocolates, sir," of course he had meant that he would hunt for the glove finger; equally, of course, Wong Chun knew what it was all about—his, "You come, Mac? I tly find finga," proved that. Which reflection brought back the question, Was the Chinaman as childlike and bland as he appeared?

The rain stopped before he reached the hotel. The sun was peering through thinning clouds to turn the raindrops coating palm fronds into iridescent jewels. Diamond Head was sporting a soft green mantle.

He inquired at the desk if Mrs. Dane would see him. She would. She would come down at once. He waited at the *lei* stand hung with strings of every type of Island flower, at the entrance to the foyer. He had never bought one for Pat, he didn't even know which flower she preferred, though she wore pink a lot. How little he really knew about her. Would the day come when—

That subject was taboo. He had spent the night after her acknowledgment of the marriage walking the floor, tempted almost beyond endurance to go to her room and explain his passionate denial. "To love—to cherish—" the words had echoed and re-echoed through his memory. It would be neither loving nor cherishing if he allowed the persons he was after to know what she meant to him. Her life would be in danger. Her safety was more important than his desire to clear the situation between them.

"See who's here!" He turned at Velma Dane's gay greeting. The white of her cardigan, which matched her slacks, made her hair burn like flame in contrast.

"Any spot hidden by palms—that's a quotation, recognize it?—where we can talk, Velma?"

"Come up to my sitting room. I'll order lunch served there. I'm glad to see you comfortable in a shirt, Cam, you look so formal in a tunic."

"No lunch, thanks. You offered to loan me your typewriter. My man has screened the town for one to buy or hire. Nothing doing. It's a lot to ask, almost as serious as to borrow a fountain pen. May I see it?"

The windows of her luxurious room furnished with creamy mahogany and chintz of every shade of green, with an occasional splash of orange on a white ground, framed a superb picture of the beach with its snowy combers, of the ever-changing tints of light and shade as clouds floated over Diamond Head. The sun was out in earnest now, so were the sports lovers, surf riders by the daring dozen, some paddling seaward, others racing toward shore, standing with arms outspread. Two outrigger canoes rose and plunged through sheets of sparkling spray. Far out a fleet of white sails shone like mother-of-pearl. On shore coral-pink walls and towers loomed above majestic coco palms. The music of guitars and ukuleles playing "Song of the Islands" drifted into the room on a breeze fragrant with the scent of many flowers.

"It is more like fairyland than an everyday world, Velma," he said as she joined him.

"It's a great show. I've been told that this isn't a patch on what it will be when ships and planes are again in full commission for civilian travel and the Island gets back to its before-the-war state of spick-spanness. I hope that some-time the sea wall built as a war protection will be removed. The typewriter is on the table, Cam."

"Mind if I give it a workout?"

"Of course not. I offered to loan it, didn't I?"

He rolled a sheet of paper into the machine. Typed, "You had the right dope—" Smaller letters than those of the carbon. This was not the typewriter purchased by Cardena for a lady. That was a break. He liked her. It hurt to suspect that she was a double-crosser.

"Thanks for the offer to loan it, Velma. The type is too small for my work."

"Sorry. I would have been glad to help. Wanting to test it hasn't anything to do with my suspicion of Monty, has it? I told you he typed a lot."

If her terrified eyes and voice were part of an act he'd throw up his present job and retire to Montana, pronto. She couldn't register fright like this if real fear wasn't back of it. Couldn't she? Had there been a flaw in the "perfect-lady" act she had put on at Madam Shaw-Ruskin's? Hadn't she said she had done a stretch in Hollywood? He left her question unanswered.

"Any chance for me to try the tyepwriter in the next room?"

"Not now." The words were a mere breath. "Do you think this place will be big enough in which to entertain a dozen or more of Mrs. Sally's veterans this afternoon? Most of them will be in wheel chairs. Hi, Monty!" She hailed her husband, who opened the door between the two rooms quickly. "Just in time to say 'Howdy' to the Colonel. Try to persuade him to lunch with us, I've failed."

Dane smiled but not before Cam caught the hardening of his eyes, the tightening of his mouth.

"If you can't persuade him, I would be a total loss. Cardena asked me to check your engagements, Carrots. The Señor wants to pull off that supper at the Officers' Club, Haleiwa Bay, tomorrow. The weatherman has promised a fine afternoon, perfect for the glass-bottom boats. Will you be free? He seems set on having you among those present."

"Why shouldn't he want me? I don't like to talk about myself, but little Velma will be the life of the party; besides I've been crazy to see if the colored fish and coral formations are as advertised. Are you going, Monty?"

"I've been roped in. I don't like the Brazilian, but he caught me unprepared with an excuse and I said I'd go. How about you, Colonel?"

"I was invited originally. Perhaps I'll find the invitation

confirmed when I get back to quarters. I will report to Mrs. Sally that the accommodations for the tea party are out of this world, Mrs. Dane." He took a step toward the door.

"Don't let me hurry you, Colonel. I'll depart pronto, don't want to spoil my wife's fun. Do stay for lunch," Monty Dane urged. Cam ignored the sarcasm in his voice and laughed.

"Sometimes I wonder when real writers get the time to write, if they are besieged with temptations to do other and easier things as I am. I'm trying to put the experiences of the last two years into shape for publication—I had some that were unique, that had to be kept strictly hush-hush at the time, and I'm beset with social invitations, besides my army job, which is strenuous."

"Then you have an army job?"

"You don't think I'm staying on this Island to become an expert surf rider—or do you?" With difficulty Cam kept his temper on leash. The tone in which Dane had voiced his question had been nasty. "Just to make my literary walk in life harder my typewriter has gone on the blink. Try to get one repaired or a new one on this Island, it can't be done."

"Won't trouble me. I have no use for a typewriter. Carrots is an addict. You might borrow hers."

"She was noble enough to offer it but it would be cruelty to dumb animals to accept. I've never learned the touch system and I punch the daylights out of a machine."

"But you've been testing it, haven't you?" Monty Dane nodded toward the table.

Cam's eyes followed his, the slip of paper on which he had typed, "You had the right dope about—" was under the roller. The sound of the wind rushing by his ears when in the outrigger canoe was as nothing to the roar in them now. How could he have been so careless? If he touched that paper it would be a confession that he had typed it. If Dane read it he might recognize the opening of the carbon copy of the letter. Then what?

"Don't touch that paper, Monty," his wife protested sharply. "It is a part of a business letter and long ago we agreed that you were to keep hands off my private affairs." Dane, who had taken a step toward the table, stopped.

"Private business—between you and Colonel Fulton?"

"That sneer has all the hallmarks of a dirty dig, Captain Dane. I don't like it."

"Ohmigosh, you two men aren't starting a fight here, are you? Don't be a nut, Monty. I told you why I pulled that silly joke at Madam Shaw-Ruskin's when you dragged me from the royal presence—to make her mad. And did it work!" She giggled. "If Colonel Fulton has forgiven it, you'd better forget it. Going, Cam? Tell Mrs. Sally I'll give her Vets the party of their lives. It's such a darned little to do for them who have done so much for us." Her eyes glittered like emeralds under water. "*Aloha.*"

"*Aloha a nui.* I learned from my sergeant's guidebook that it means big or much *Aloha.* I'll be seeing you." He opened the door. Monty Dane's voice stopped him on the threshold.

"Speaking of your sergeant, Colonel, hope you're not counting on him to chauf you home. He just drove away from the hotel with that man of Señor Cardena's in the black convertible with the canvas top the Brazilian has hired."

21

THE half-gay, half-plaintive strains of "Aloha" drifted from the terrace. The broad leaves of the banana, the fronds of the coconut palms, bent and swayed in time to the music like court dancers treading a stately measure. Clouds had retreated to distant mountaintops, leaving a sky clear, dazzling blue. The rain-washed world smelled as if it had been sprayed with flower scents.

Dane's words flashed through Cam's mind as he crossed the drive to his car and echoed with the persistence of a radio announcer plugging a commercial. "He just drove away from the hotel with that man of Señor Cardena's." The Sergeant believed that the Brazilian's servant was the thug of a gang outfit. Having escaped recognition by the man he knew to be a former SS trooper, why crowd his luck and deliberately walk into danger?

"This is my day of good fortune, Colonel." Señor Cardena sent the greeting ahead in his stilted English as he approached. "I telephoned your office that my supper at Haleiwa Bay is set for tomorrow. It is short notice for such a busy man but I hope you will come."

"I wouldn't miss it. It's my only chance to see one of the major show places of Oahu. Lucky your party is coming so soon. Orders for me to pull out shortly have arrived."

Perhaps his announcement would speed the gang to an overt act unless already they had the "stuff" Skinner had claimed was in his brief case, always supposing that that was what they were after. They were not on the Island as spies, observation and deduction assured him of that. The suspense as to what would happen was like walking in mined territory expecting every instant that the earth under your feet would blow up.

"It is a surprise that you go so soon, Colonel. You will leave much regret behind. The charming Miss Carey will be bereft, yes?"

Cam restrained a savage impulse to remind him forcibly that he was heading for trouble. The unction with which he rolled out Pat's name, his meaning smile, made him see red. No dice. A man in a job like his kept his temper or else—He laughed.

"Who has been talking out of turn, Señor? Haven't you heard Madam Shaw-Ruskin announce that the young lady is her prospective daughter-in-law? Have you heard the two most interested parties deny it? I haven't. That arrangement comes under the head of a setup. It would take a brave man to intrude."

"But you are a brave man, Colonel. Your ribbons and stars attest that."

Cam didn't like the man's impertinent insistence, didn't like the steely glint in the eyes under the peaked black brows, didn't like the keen edge in the suave voice, but he smiled and confided:—

"This happens not to be my brave-man week, Señor. Strictly between you and me, Madam Shaw-Ruskin terrifies me. Besides, there is a girl in England. Now that you have discovered my secret, for the love of Mike, keep it under your hat—as we say in the States. I'll see you tomorrow."

He walked quickly toward his jeep wondering if Cardena believed there was a girl in England—he had Sally Shaw to thank for that idea—hoping fervently that he had switched his attention from Pat.

Why had the Sergeant gone with the Señor's man instead of waiting at the hotel? He puzzled over the question as he sent the car ahead. Had he discovered a clue to the break-in when with Wong Chun at Mrs. Shaw's? Better stop there and check on the truth of Velma Dane's message. Had she thought of it when she heard her husband in the next room or was the story of the party for the Vets straight goods?

The Chinaman was pottering around the shrubs in front of Silver Ledges when he parked his car. The parchment-like skin of his face crinkled in surprise.

"Look fo' Mac? He go hotel see you, sa."

"He didn't come. I concluded he might have found something here to keep him so came along to pick him up. Did he get the chocolates?"

"Velly big. So like." Wong Chun spread his hands to indicate size from one foot to three. "Lilly Yee Lung eat. Me too. Mac take finga."

"You found it. Bully for you. What did he do with it?"

"Put in papa, velly slow. In pocket velly easy. Say now he hunt glove, *wikiwiki*."

"Did he say where he intended to look for it?"

"No. He say 'Keep unda hat, Wong. No tell nobody but my boss.' I say, 'No tell.' He say, 'Closs thloat, hope die.' I closs thloat like he show how. Velly funny fella, Mac. Madam, she callin'."

Cam entered the house in response to Sally Shaw's hail. She met him in the foyer and led the way to the *lanai*.

"What's up, Cam?" she inquired anxiously. "Why did Sergeant McIlvray come here with Wong Chun this morning?"

Arms crossed on the top of a tall chintz-covered chair, he smiled down at her perched on the edge of a fan-back of lacy wicker.

"Relax, Mrs. Sally, you appear as if ready for a take-off."

"I am. In spite of the fact that I am radiantly happy, since the break-in my poise has been shot to pieces—reaction after the close of the war, perhaps. My nerves have risen to the surface like slices of fruit in gelatin that hasn't set."

"I don't like that redness of your eyelids. Can I help?"

"No thanks, Cam. I've just come from seeing off a shipload of my Vets, some of them amputees, all of them garlanded with *leis*, all gallant, brave and happy to go. Someone on deck started that old hymn, 'Nyland':—

> Green pastures are before me,
> Which yet I have not seen;
> Bright skies will soon be o'er me
> Where darkest clouds have been.

"A hundred voices rose in the music of the song. The ship slowly moved away. My Vets flung their *leis* on the water. 'Bright skies! Bright skies for all,' I called and waved frantically as the tears ran down my cheeks. Then I came home and cried my eyes out. Such waste, such tragic waste of youth in that horrible war. That's the story. The storm has passed."

It was lingering still, he knew from the tears that welled in her eyes. Better to turn her thoughts from the Vets.

"Mac came here to follow up a clue to the break-in. He was to meet me at the hotel and when he didn't appear I drove over to find out how come. He must have thought he had a lead and started after it. Where is Pat?"

"At the hospital. She is working too hard and playing too hard. She was out dancing with Phil Ruskin until late last night, or rather, early this morning."

"I heard her come in."

"Cam, won't you forgive her? Don't look at me like that. I know I'm barging in where an angel would fear to tread, but it hurts to see my child unhappy."

"I am not making her unhappy. Page her for the cause. How did she go to the hospital?"

"Drove in the gray sedan in a drenching rain."

"How late will she stay?"

"She will leave earlier than usual today. She had faith in the weatherman's promise of clearing weather, wore her uniform and carried her afternoon clothes in an overnight case. She planned to change at the hospital. She is to meet Señor Cardena at the jeweler's to help him select presents for his family and later in the afternoon pour at the tea Mrs. Dane is giving to cheer those of my Vets who were left behind this morning."

"When I saw Velma an hour ago she asked me to tell you that her living room will be plenty large to accommodate the number of men you plan to entertain."

"Funny she should have sent the message. Already we have checked on that."

Not so funny when one knew that Monty Dane was on the prowl, possibly listening to the conversation in his wife's room.

"Cam, are you falling in love with Velma Dane?"

"Could be, she's mighty attractive, but there is the girl in England with whom I am deeply in love, remember?"

"So Pat repeated my romantic scenario. She promised she wouldn't, but knowing the female mind I was pretty sure she would, give her time and the opportunity. I told the yarn to help your cause, before I knew if you wanted it helped. I am beginning to think you don't."

"I prefer to play a lone hand working out the mix-up—if it can be called anything so simple—between Pat and me."

"In other words, you will be obliged if big-hearted Sally will mind her own business and keep out of yours."

"I didn't mean it that way, Sally. You will never know how your letters and tenderness helped me over the rough spots of the last two years. I've got to handle the situation in a way that may seem raw. Trust me?"

"Yes. I have from the day I received the first letter from you. I didn't mean to force your confidence but anxiety for my child got the better of my common sense. Señor Cardena telephoned that the Haleiwa Bay excursion is slated for tomorrow. I don't want to go. I neither like nor trust the man, but he is giving the supper for Mother Shaw-Ruskin and me in return for our hospitality. The General says it's a must."

"The General knows. With your mother-in-law and bomb-shell Velma present I can see where Old Man Trouble also will be a guest."

"You'd better dedicate your evening to keeping the two apart and devote yourself to Mrs. Dane. I'll tip off the General to start Mother Shaw-Ruskin on an account of the beginning of her family here; they are among the first of the New England missionaries. The story is tremendously interesting and she tells it vividly. She is a fascinating woman when she wants to be. The General won't be bored but I don't know how the host will react."

"What do you mean?"

"Haven't you heard, haven't you seen that Señor Miguel Cardena is Mother Shaw-Ruskin's devoted swain? He dines with her on an average of four times a week. She declares it is her chance to practice Spanish, but there is a self-conscious smirk when she says it. She is so keen, she *can't* believe the man is in love with her, or can she? He must be at least fifteen years younger."

"Older women have been fooled before, especially those with a fortune as large as hers. Perhaps he really has fallen for her."

"Perhaps. Love moves in mysterious ways its wonders to perform. I have just discovered that he has given her a typewriter."

"A *what?*"

"A typewriter. I don't wonder you look amazed but why go white about it? He presented it soon after they began conversing in Spanish. She writes to him in his language and he answers. He said he could criticize the construction of her sentences better if they were in print. Who knows, perhaps tomorrow's party is to announce an engagement. Stranger things have happened."

"I'll try to keep Velma entertained. Swell of you to give up your General and sacrifice your own evening on the altar of peace." He bent his head and kissed her lightly on the cheek. "But then, you are a swell person, Sally Shaw, and sweet. I'll be on guard tonight. *Aloha.*"

He glanced at his watch as he started the car. Pat would leave the hospital before three to meet Cardena at the jeweler's. He would have time to return to the Barracks, change, get a bite to eat and reach the hospital before she left. If possible he would persuade her not to keep the date with the Señor. It wasn't safe, though he couldn't tell her that. The Brazilian had given Madame Shaw-Ruskin a typewriter. His nerves still tingled from the shock of Sally Shaw's announcement. Could it be the machine on which the letters had been typed? If so was the gift a red herring drawn across the writer's trail? He must test it. How? Madam Shaw-Ruskin had given him the cold eye lately when they met. Was it because he had turned down her many invitations or because the Señor had prejudiced her against him? He would persuade Pat to take him there this afternoon. Once there, he would count upon his luck to give him a chance at the typewriter.

McIlvray was not in the workroom when he entered. Tilted back in a swivel chair at his desk he clasped his hands behind his head and relived the hours since he had left his quarters. In spite of Sally Shaw's tale of the Señor's devotion to Madam Shaw-Ruskin, Dane was a prime favorite with her. Had the Captain used the machine Cardena had presented to type the letters of which he had the carbon?

Which reflection reminded him that he had not made his usual search for the answer to the ad in the morning paper. There was time to give it the once-over, before he met Pat. It was doubtless a cockeyed idea to think he could keep her from meeting Cardena but it was worth a try.

He skimmed the glaring headlines of strikes; local floods that had inundated cellars in which families were living because of housing shortage; letters to the Editor pro and con the ever-present subject of statehood for Hawaii; chuckled over the ad "You can learn to do the Hula"—could he?—glanced through court reports, came on the reply for which he was looking so suddenly that he blinked.

Will meet person who advertised fo. ukulele lessons in Bar Lounge of Moana at six P.M. Wednesday.

The carbon had instructed "Answer cipher when you've got the goods." Did that mean that the money was in the possession of the person or persons who were after it?

Wednesday! That was today. Good Lord, he had come near missing it. The most popular meeting place in the city had been selected. Finding the party of the first ad and the party of the second would be like hunting in the telephone book for a man named Brown whose Christian name you didn't know. Just the same he would be among those present. If he were being watched it might be noticeable if he went alone. Velma Dane was the answer. Would her tea be over in time?

He telephoned the hotel hoping that she would be in her room, praying mightily that her husband wouldn't be near.

"Mrs. Dane speaking."

"Cam Fulton, Velma. Are you alone? Good. How about meeting me in the Bar Lounge at six? . . . Sorry it will be early for you, but it has to be that time to fit in with a later engagement. . . . Sure, I'm a popular guy—glad you appreciate it. I'll wait for you on the terrace. Don't fail me. *Aloha.*"

Had she realized that something serious was behind the invitation? She had lowered her strident voice when she discovered who was speaking. His errand in the Bar Lounge, to trace, if possible, the meaning of the ad for ukulele lessons and the reply, wouldn't be suspected if she were with him. No man on a secret errand would choose a spectacular woman like Velma Dane as a companion unless he wanted the attention of everyone in the place focused on his table.

He was waiting in the corridor of the hospital when Pat came down the stairs in a soft green frock, carrying an overnight case. The gloves in her right hand were the exact shade of pink of the mammoth rose in her flower hat. A flat, flexible gold necklace matched the broad bracelet on her left wrist. Her underarm bag and high-heeled pumps were lizard skin almost as white as the polka dots in her dress. She saw him and took the last two steps in a leap.

"What's happened now? Aunt Sally?"

"Don't be so breathless. I'll take the suitcase. Can't I call for you without scaring you to death? Heard you were driving from here to town so came to bum a ride to Waikiki. I'm dining there and you are due at Velma Dane's Vets' party, aren't you? That's a sharp outfit you're wearing."

"I so seldom wear afternoon clothes and a hat that I feel overdressed. Thought the Vets might enjoy seeing me in something besides a uniform. Sorry I can't take you along. I have an appointment on the way."

"I don't mind waiting. I have all the time there is this afternoon."

"Lucky you. My appointments fit together snug as the scraps of a picture puzzle. To be quite honest, I don't want you."

"You are not faring forth on an adventure of which you are ashamed, I hope, Miss Carey?"

"I am not. As you insist on being nosy, I am to meet Señor Cardena to help him select gifts for his wife and daughter. Not so long ago he said that business might detain him for weeks. Yesterday he phoned he might have to leave the Island at an hour's notice, and wanted to be ready."

Cam mentally marshaled facts.

"Answer cipher when you've got the goods," the carbon of a letter had advised. The answer had appeared today. Yesterday Cardena had told Pat that he might have to leave suddenly. What would she say if he told her that he had been informed that the man posing as a Brazilian had no family? Might leave at "an hour's notice." That put the skids under Sally Shaw's suspicion that he was paying court to Madam Shaw-Ruskin. Did it indicate also that he had the "goods"? Since the Sergeant had spotted him as a Nazi, he himself had had a growing suspicion that he had come to the Island to meet the man who had the stolen money. Give him plenty of rope and they would round up all persons implicated, he had argued, when General Carrington wanted to pounce and make sure of him.

"Nice to have met you." Pat's laughing reminder recalled him to the present. She had stepped into the gray sedan. "Please move, you're in my way."

"Hold on, take me along. Why can't I drive round while you shop, pick you up when you're ready, take you to Velma's and get to Waikiki myself? You've no idea what a luxury a chauffeur can be. Break down and say yes, like a little lady."

"If I don't something tells me you will come anyway."

"That's a world-shaking concession."

"Glad you appreciate it. Come on. I'll make you drive and save my precious gloves." He slipped behind the wheel and touched his cap.

"Your servant, Madam."

They were silent for the greater part of the long drive. Had Pat objected to his company for fear he would bring up the subject so vital to both? He had told her that until the marriage could be announced it was taboo. That held, terribly as he was tempted at this moment to introduce it. As they came within sight of Pearl Harbor she said softly:—

"When I see those rows and rows of white crosses on the mountainside I remember the men under them who fought and died for a better world and I think of the mess of strife and confusion that same world is in today. I hope their spirits haunt the troublemakers."

"Unfortunately riot rousers and troublemakers are immune to spiritual messages and there are plenty of them working for the downfall of the peace plans, even some who would have known how to die valiantly in war. It is the sacred duty of every person who stands back of this country to do his utmost to block them, to stay in there pitching, whether his job is civil or military. There has been one gain. For the first time in history a small nation has dared stand up for its rights against a great nation and be sure of a fair hearing before the UN."

"Do you intend to stay in the service, Cam?"

"To stay or not to stay is one of my two major headaches. I'll bet it is almost the sixty-four dollar question for many of the men being demobilized."

"Have you two major headaches?"

"You're asking me that?"

"Don't lop off my head. I shall need it."

"Sorry, but it was such a fool question from you."

After that conversation languished and stopped. The tires rhythmically picked up the miles. Traffic became difficult on the boulevards crowded with busses, trucks and automobiles. He drew up in front of a shop whose windows glittered with gold and jewels, displayed exquisite glass and porcelain, ivory, carved wooden figures that upheld lamps and colorful *chinoiserie*.

"Here you are, I'll wait as long as the law allows, drive round and come back. Take a look at the representative of the law in front of us. A girl traffic cop with J.P.O. on the band like a diplomat's ribbon across her white blouse. Make it snappy," he advised as she stepped out. "I don't want that Junior Police Officer, cute kid that she is, to tag me."

"Don't hurry me. *I* am on important business. *You* have all the time there is this afternoon," she reminded.

The long silences during the drive had provided a chance for him to work out a plan to see Madam Shaw-Ruskin's typewriter, the carrying through of which depended on Pat. Would she consent to help if he withheld the reason for the call? He lighted a cigarette with one eye on the girl who was handling traffic like a veteran. She was looking in his direction. Did that mean he had stayed too long? He'd better get a move on.

"Cam!" Pat ran across the sidewalk. "Thank goodness, you're here. I was afraid I might have to sit on the steps until you appeared. Señor Cardena isn't coming."

"Hop in." He followed her. The sedan shot ahead. "How come he walked out on you?"

"His man, who looks like a concentrate of all the screen valets in Hollywood, was waiting to tell me that the Señor had been obliged to go to Haleiwa Bay to straighten out a mix-up about his party tomorrow."

"Don't they have telephones in Brazil? Doesn't he know how to use one?"

"He probably relies on the power of the spoken word. It's all right with me. My urge to help him select take-home gifts cooled when he told me he had gone all out for a brooch of a diamond tiger stalking through gold jungle foliage. I wouldn't have the heart to okay that for my worst enemy. But then I'm allergic to bugs and animals in jewelry."

"Perhaps the woman for whom he wanted it has a yen for diamond tigers stalking through gold jungles."

"She's welcome to it. The gold ring and bracelet, set with Mother Pele's tears—olivines to you—I intended to recommend has been sold, so that ends that. Now what? It's a lot too early for Velma's party."

"Let's call on Madam Shaw-Ruskin."

"At this hour? If she is at home she won't see us."

"Try it, will you? I have a reason for going."

"Turn right at the next crossroads."

"Good girl, not to ask questions."

Getting there would be easy. A chance to try out the typewriter was something else, he reminded himself.

Suzette, the fluttery French companion, in a frilly red frock, opened the door in response to his ring and enfolded Pat in an ardent embrace.

"It is so good to see you, *Chérie*."

Her ebullient welcome over, she explained in slightly accented English that Madam was driving, that the servants were off duty. She led the way to the *lanai*.

"*Chérie*, you look be-autiful. It ees not to be wondered that *Monsieur le Colonel* looks proud as Luciver. I have been putting away Madam's work. She works very hard at her lessons in *l'espagnol*."

Cam's eyes followed the dramatic wave of her hand. He went cold from repressed excitement. On a steel table with a pile of papers beside it reposed a typewriter.

"That's a busy-looking table, Mademoiselle."

"*Certainement*, Monsieur. Madam types, Señor Cardena uses it and when he ees here, *tiens!* Captain Dane plays the keys like eet ees a piano. You weel stay and take tea with me, *Chérie?*"

"No tea, Suzette, thank you—"

"Speak for yourself, Pat," Cam interrupted. "I'm perishing of thirst." Even though tense for fear there might be a slip he managed a smile. "If it won't be too much trouble for you, Mademoiselle?"

"Trouble!" She shrugged thin shoulders. "It is an honor to serve one who has been a gallant soldier. *Prenez la chaise, Chérie. Asseyez-vous, mon Colonel.* You like toast with your tea, *Monsieur?*"

"I'd love it. It's the English in me, Mademoiselle. Can't I help you? I'm an ace water-boiler." That was a crazy proposal. Suppose she said "Yes."

"*Non! Non*, Monsieur! Make yourself happy here. *Je reviendrai.*" She fluttered out of the room.

"Quick, Pat! Watch the door. I must get a whack at the typewriter."

For half a minute she stared at him as if a hand grenade had exploded at her feet, then dashed into the drawing room, dropped to the piano stool and played "La Marseillaise" tempestuously. Smart girl. That was co-operation one hundred per cent. Under cover of the volume of sound he picked up a half sheet of paper beside the machine, slipped it under the roller and typed, "You had the right dope—" and pulled it out. The letters looked the same as those on the carbon and the salesman's sample but he would have to compare— The music crashed into a thunderous finale. He crushed the paper in his pocket as Pat called:—

"Come and help Mademoiselle with this tray, Cam. It's loaded. Why did you get so much, Suzette?"

"Eet was already prepared for Madam's tea when she returns. Monsieur is hungry. Eet ees the nature of man to be hungry," the woman in the red frock answered and filled a cup with tea. She laughed, threw a coquettish glance at Cam. "Ees eet not, *mon Colonel?*"

"Did you have time to test the typewriter?" Pat inquired when they were back in the gray sedan, headed for Waikiki.

"Yes, thanks to you and your quick thinking. Mademoiselle is a cheery party."

"She's a dear, we are great friends. You'd better keep this car if you are not returning to Silver Ledges for M.P. duty tonight. I'm not going home for hours. Phil Ruskin will have his roadster." She glanced at the clock on the instrument board. "In spite of our detour I will reach the Dane party in time to help welcome the arriving guests."

Why had the Sergeant driven off with Cardena's man, Cam wondered as he drove on? Had the Señor given Madam Shaw-Ruskin the typewriter after the two letters had been inscribed on it to get it out of his hands? Had the Brazilian gone to Haleiwa Bay about his supper party? He had told Pat that he wanted his gifts ready in case he had to leave the Island suddenly. Suppose that supper party was a cover-up? Suppose he was planning to leave the Island tonight?

"Answer cipher ad when you've got the goods," memory reminded.

"'Tention, Colonel. Here's the hotel entrance. You're so absorbed in thought you almost passed it."

"Sorry and sad to have been such a dumb companion. I'll leave the car in the parking space here. You may want it."

"You never can tell. Happy landings." With a gay wave

of her hand she slipped into a fold of the revolving door.

Two hours to spend before meeting Velma. He could use part of it trying to contact the Sergeant from the Officers' Club near by. He would feel a lot easier in his mind if he knew that Mac was safely back at his quarters.

"Oh, Colonel Fulton," the doorman at the Club greeted him, "message for you. A lady has been buzzing the last half hour. Said she tried to reach you at every place she thought you might be. You are to wait here till she calls again."

A lady! For the last half hour? Pat in trouble? That was out. He had left her not ten minutes ago. Could be Sally Shaw but it sounded more like Velma Dane with one of her SOS outbursts.

"Here comes a boy now, Colonel. I'll bet it's you he's after."

He was right. As Cam closed the door of the telephone booth he wondered if this call could be tied up with the cipher answer.

"Cameron Fulton speaking."

"Are you alone?" It was a woman's voice, soft, mysterious.

"Yes. Who are you? What do you want? . . . Wrong slant, I don't fall for mysteries. . . . If it isn't a mystery what's it all about? . . . Information . . . Shoot . . . Suppose you have heard I am interested in getting a new typewriter—so what?" He could hear the loud thump of his heart, icy chills crept up his spine and slithered down as he listened.

"Yes. . . . Yes. . . . I understand. . . . I'll be th—" A click at the other end of the line cut off the word.

For a moment he glared at the box on the wall as if trying to hypnotize it into revealing the identity of the person who had spoken. Was the information straight goods or was it a trick to land him in a trap?

There had been a familiar note in the woman's voice. Pat was out as a possibility. Too soft for Velma Dane; besides, she would be busy welcoming her guests. Sally Shaw, Madam Shaw-Ruskin and Maida Parsons were the others whose voices he knew well enough to recognize, but they would have no way of getting the information which had been handed to him. Could it have been Lilly Yee Lung? That was a crazy thought; even had she been told what to say there had not been a trace of accent in the words. That canceled out Sib Lou, Mac's Chinese eyeful, and—

Mac! It had been Mac, with his dulcet imitation of a femme secretary! Mac, who had left the hotel with Cardena's man this noon. Mac, who had giggled like a girl when he said that the beau who had taken him driving wore a glove with one finger missing. Mac, who had told him where to locate a typewriter of the same make as the one Cardena had bought, where to be at seven-thirty tonight, no earlier, no later.

22

THE party had been a smash hit, Pat assured her hostess after the guests laden with baskets and packages of fruit and confections had been wheeled away by hospital attendants. Sally Shaw had gone with them to make sure of their comfort.

"It was so little to do, Miss Carey. You were the outstanding attraction, you and your music," Velma Dane declared cordially. "They knew you, and felt at ease. No wonder they fell and fell hard. You're looking out of this world in that green dress and flower hat."

"Thanks a million. I'd like to believe it."

"Why not? Believe everything nice said to you, and raise the roof about anything you don't like, that's my rule of life. It works. You'd be surprised. Now that we are alone it's my chance to tell you that I came to the Island determined to break you for stealing Monty. Don't get mad. Let me get it out of my system. I'd be a dumb bunny not to know you are not that sort. I think you're grand. Let's leave it at that. I'd like to be friends. Shall I phone down for your car to be brought round?"

Pat caught her surreptitious glance at the crystal clock on the mantel. A few minutes before six. Had she a date? Was it a date that had been on her mind this afternoon? Twice when the telephone rang, during the party, her face had whitened. After she had answered her color had returned.

"Thanks, no. I am to meet Philip Ruskin downstairs, after which we are stepping out to dine and dance. Hope I haven't detained you by lingering here?" Phil wouldn't appear for half an hour but in the face of her hostess's evident desire to get on with what she had ahead she had better depart at once.

"You haven't detained me, there's loads of time before I change to keep a dinner date. Are you dining at this hotel?"

"No, we are to try something new in a shrimp concoction at a Chinese place. You rate a decoration, several, for giving those Vets so much pleasure. It was tough for them to be left behind when others sailed this morning. The afternoon will be a red-letter memory as long as they live. *Aloha*."

Sally Shaw will be relieved when I report the peppy Dane's confession of faith in me, Pat thought as she went slowly down the broad stairs. Velma asked me not to answer, why would I? She had said it all. Why should she be interested in where I'm dining? Why change from that adorable aqua shortie she was wearing? It was special enough for any occasion.

Whom was she meeting? Cam? He had said he had a date at the hotel. During the long drive together this afternoon they had been as silent as two strangers wondering what to say to one another. Strangers wouldn't have had to be silent, there would have been no *kapu* sign for them as there was for Cam and herself. They were strangers, except for one short week two years ago; the memory had a dreamlike quality now. How little she had known of him then. That was why she had welshed, wasn't it? She had had time and opportunity this afternoon to clear up the misunderstanding. Misunderstanding. That was an understatement. It was a chasm so deep and dark they never could bridge it. It wasn't her move to bring it up. She had done her part when she had brazenly announced the marriage. Would she ever forget Cam's passionate "No! No! N—"

"Hi, lovely!" Monty Dane hailed her. "What are you doing here alone at this time of day, descending those stairs as if you were floating down in a dream?"

"I have just left your wife's party, I'm not dreaming and I won't be alone as soon as you stop blocking my path. My word, you're in civvies. When did that happen?"

"I told you I was here on terminal leave."

"I remember. Dark blue is tremendously becoming, but you know that, don't you?" While she was waiting for Phil why not ask Monty a few questions which were pricking in her mind? Whither Señor Cardena, for one; the trip to Haleiwa Bay didn't sound convincing, why hadn't he phoned his message? There was the little matter of the brief-case key. Had he picked it up in the parking space at the Barracks? That was out. Cam had said never to let him know she had lost a key. She glanced at her wrist watch.

"I'm half an hour ahead of my date, Monty. Are you meeting someone or will you make this your be-kind-to-Pat week and treat me to a drink? Sorry, I can see that you can't. Forget it."

"You're too quick on the trigger, lovely. I had to think ahead for a minute. Of course I will. Come on."

The sound of surf, the smell of the sea came through the

great open windows of the terrace—balanced on one end by a huge dining room and on the other by the Bar Lounge— which offered a superb view of the beach, of rollers breaking into foam far out on the coral ledge, of Diamond Head. The palm-bordered terrace was colorful and glittering with smartly dressed women and men coming and going like a continuous style show.

"Still on the fruit juice wagon?" Dane inquired after they had been seated at a table in the softly lighted Lounge with its gigantic ferns and tinkling wall fountains.

"Yes. Make it iced pineapple. I used to dream of it when I was overseas. Since my return I can't get enough. The Royal Hawaiians are playing 'For You a *Lei*.' I would know their music if I heard it at the North Pole. Isn't the woman being seated by the maître d'hôtel the photogenic Congresswoman? I heard she was on her way to Japan to report on conditions there. That gives me an idea. When this Territory becomes a State I'll run for Representative. 'A Nylon on Every Leg' will be my battle cry. I've never seen this place so crowded."

"The Clipper that was held up by bad weather leaves Rodgers Airport at nine. Departing passengers are taking a farewell fling. Why all the conversation? Why so breathless? Not like you to be so talkative, lovely. What's on the little mind?"

Her face turned warmly pink in response to his quizzical eyes. Her tongue had been throwing off surface sparks while her mind was formulating the questions she hadn't given herself the chance to ask.

"And I thought I was being entertaining. *Auwe*, one never knows how one appears to others. Wasn't there a poet named Burns who said something like that only better? I have been on the move since 7 A.M. Perhaps I'm like a mechanical toy wound up to go. Perhaps I'll run down in a few minutes and give you a chance at the conversational ball."

"Have you been in that rig all day? The flower hat is a knockout. You look as smooth as if you'd just been unpacked from tissue paper, a lot of it."

"What a wonderful thing to say, Monty."

"I can say something a lot more wonderful, if you'll break down and listen."

"That will do, thank you. Anything more would go straight to my head."

"I'm aiming at your heart."

"Haven't one. In case you are interested I donned this so-called knockout costume to meet Señor Miguel Cardena."

"Where did you go with him?" His voice was rough with anger.

"That's the point, Monty, I didn't go. We had planned to shop for take-home gifts for his family. I was met at the jeweler's by his sleek servant with the message that his boss had gone to Haleiwa Bay to straighten out a mix-up in the arrangements for his supper party tomorrow night. I was left holding the bag, as it were. I'm beginning to think he is a sort of mystery man. Do you believe he is after Madam Shaw-Ruskin and her fortune?"

"*Marry* her, do you mean? You're crazy."

"Haven't you heard the rumor? All the little myna birds are whispering it."

"I haven't and I don't believe you have. I bet you made it up to get a rise out of me. You know I'm dead set to get her permission to copy—Well, see who's here!"

Pat's eyes followed his. Velma Dane and Cam were being seated at a table across the room. So this was the dinner date? She had changed to a brilliant emerald-green frock shot with gold. The necklace of diamond roses blazed around her throat, a matching rose quivered and glinted in her auburn hair.

"Sure to see things like that when you haven't a gun." Monty Dane tempered his evident anger with a laugh. "Not that I want to shoot the Colonel. I'd give him a bonus to take her off my hands, then I could have you, lovely. There would be no qualms about a deserted wife to hold you back."

"Captain, your assurance pos-i-*tive*-ly takes away my breath. A discarded husband is not good enough for me. If for no other reason I would be sure that were Velma to beckon with her little finger she would get you back, she is so beautiful and *rich*."

"Is that a crack? I certainly couldn't marry a woman without money, I need moolah in the business I want to do. You'll have plenty, won't you? I understand your aunt wallows in wealth, that you are her heir."

"My word, you have been busy with research since your arrival, haven't you?" The hint of contempt in her voice sent a tinge of red under the bronze of his face.

"Why not? But I wasn't wise to it when I fell for you overseas. Who knows, I may acquire enough money to marry you if you haven't a penny."

"Now, that's what I call noble. King Cophetua and the Beggar Maid circa 1946. I've always hoped I would be loved for myself alone."

He wasn't listening to her satirical nonsense. He was frowning at his fingers twirling the stem of a glass. She glanced covertly across the room at Cam. Did he want to marry Velma Dane? Was that back of his passionate denial of the marriage that night at Silver Ledges? Was that one of his major headaches? "It was such a fool question from you," he had flared. Was she supposed to know that he wanted to marry?

"Call for you, Captain." A Filipino waiter set a telephone on the table.

Pat laughed.

"It won't bite, Monty. You are staring at the phone as if it were a rattler coiled to strike."

"Just my natural caution. It may be a holdup for a hand-out. I'll take the call in a booth, waiter. Back in a few minutes, lovely."

Her eyes followed him as he walked away, then flashed to Velma and Cam. They were watching his exit. Had they noticed who was with him at the table? Awkward sitting alone in a place like this. The strains of "They Say It's Wonderful" drifted from the terrace. She hummed the tune softly under her breath. Monty was returning. He must have cut the call almost before it started.

"Wrong party," he growled as he sat down. "Did Fulton speak to you while I was out of the room?"

"Speak to me? Why should he? He is absorbed in his charming companion."

"Been watching them, have you?"

"If you can call a casual glance their way, watching, I'm guilty. That scooped-out neckline of your wife's frock is the latest word from Paris. My eyes fly as straight to her sensational necklace as a jet bomb to its target. You ought to speak to her about wearing it in a place like this. It isn't safe. Remember her scream at the night club?"

"Sure, I remember. She said it was a mouse but I've always thought Stanhope, the guy she picked up on the Clipper, made a try for it. Any clue yet to your lost diamonds? Was anything else stolen? This must be call-the-Lounge night. There goes a phone to the Colonel's table. Velma is answering."

She was not only answering, she was leaving. Even from across the room her face looked white. Was this the call of which she had been afraid when she had answered the two rings this afternoon? Cam, who had risen, was following her with his eyes. They came back and met hers. He moved his head the fraction of an inch in the direction of the terrace. Did it mean he wanted her to follow Velma? If she was ill why didn't he tell her husband, who was giving a repeat order to the waiter? Because he wanted her to go, was the answer. Could Velma's sudden departure be mixed up in the mystery of Skinner's brief case, or Cam's anxiety to test the typewriter at Madam Shaw-Ruskin's? He was signaling again, a little impatiently this time. Apparently he had mistaken her for a mind reader. She rose quickly.

"Thanks for the party, Monty. I'll have to run. Phil is on the terrace looking black as lava smoke above Mauna Loa."

"What's the rush? Afraid he'll beat you if you're late? Is his mother right? Has he tied you as well as himself to her apron strings?"

"He has not, but I wouldn't put it past him to make a scene here. Please don't come with me."

She apologized to Phil in her thoughts as she walked toward the terrace. He was sulky and temperamental, but he had a horror of scenes. She had made him the whipping boy because a man had signaled to her to follow the woman he was entertaining, whose husband had been intent on ordering another drink when she left the table. In a minute Monty would notice his wife's absence. Then what?

Velma was not on the terrace. If she was ill she would probably bolt for her apartment. Pat caught a glimpse of green inside an elevator. There she was. The door closed. The cage shop up. Wait for another? She had come down by the stairs a short time ago. Only a short time? It seemed hours since Monty had hailed her.

The door of Velma Dane's living room was unlatched, open enough for her to see the light within. She tapped. Was that sound a muffled answer? She entered and closed the door softly behind her. No one here. No one in the dressing room. Velma might be lying down in the bedroom. She glanced in, shook her head. The pale green spread was smooth and undented. Evidently one side of the room was given over to closets. A panel had been pushed back, the sleeve of a silver fox jacket showed in the opening.

Again in the living room she fitted together the events of the last five minutes, or had it been ten? Velma had looked white when she left the Lounge hurriedly after a phone call. She had stepped into an elevator in the foyer. Hold everything, had she? The only proof was a glimpse of a green dress. There might be a dozen women in the hotel tonight wearing green. She was not here. It would be a joke on Patricia Carey if at this very moment she was seated across the table from Cam explaining her absence.

Not exactly a ha-ha joke if she herself were seen coming out of this apartment by a person passing in the hall and later some of the peppy Dane's fabulous jewels were reported missing. Could be. It would account for the door on the latch as she had found it when she knocked. Cheerful thought. This was where she had come in. This was where she went out and made it snappy.

A sound. A stealthy sound. She stared at the knob of the door between the two rooms as if hypnotized. It was moving. The person who was turning it was in the room Velma had explained was her husband's when it had been open this afternoon to give more space for the party. Suppose it were Monty? Suppose he were to find her here? He wouldn't hesitate to turn her presence into evidence to be used in the divorce he wanted. That was another cheering thought.

Whoever was at the door was hesitating about opening it. Afraid that someone might be on the other side? Perhaps it wasn't Monty. Perhaps it was the same person who had broken and entered at Silver Ledges. Her nerves buzzed a warning like bells along a one-party country telephone line. Was this tied up with the murder of Stanhope? Velma had been his friend. Was she in danger? Had a warning whitened her face when she had left the Lounge? Had she been kidnaped?

Now she was crazy. Crazy or not she mustn't be found here by the person on the other side of that door. No use making a break for the hall. The window! Her best bet. She had wheeled one of the Vets to the balcony on which living room and bedroom opened.

Hardly daring to breathe she tiptoed out. Flat against the white wall of the house she hitched along till she reached the side of the bedroom window. Lucky her frock was not dark. Lucky that the lamps inside were so placed that no light shone out. She drew a long breath and tried to unknot her nerves. She pulled off her hat and hung it on her wrist by its ribbon strap. It was a wonder she had kept the tiresome thing on so long. The lizard bag was clutched under her arm. Chalk that up to force of habit.

Perfect night. The star-spangled sky shed an opalescent glow on the white frills of the waves as they broke gently on the sandy shore. There were strings of silver lights on the terraced hills. A plane with its gargantuan green and yellow eyes twinkling like racing stars hummed overhead and vanished beyond a mountain. Long, pointed rays of searchlights swept the heavens.

She could just make out the time on the dial of her watch. There was still ten minutes' leeway before Phil was due, twenty if he ran true to form and was late. How long would she be marooned here? The person who had fumbled with the doorknob wouldn't be likely to spend the evening on his job, whatever it was. Was Cam wondering what had become of her? Perhaps he hadn't signaled to her to follow Velma, perhaps the motion she had thought was a signal had been her imagination.

The strains of "Going My Way" drifted up to her. Could she escape under cover of the music? She listened. It had stopped. Only the pound of surf broke the stillness. A sound in the bedroom. She counted the hard thumps of her heart. Was someone after Velma's jewels? Could she save them? She had been afraid to have Monty find her here but she wasn't afraid of a thief.

Cautiously she moved till she could see into the room, not far, but far enough to see a closet panel slide back and a dark sleeve, a man's sleeve. Whoever it was was kneeling, reaching for something on the floor. The hand came out with a good-sized white paper package. She set her teeth hard in her underlip to keep back the sound of her quick breathing. Had it been taken from Skinner's brief case? Had Monty picked up the key to it? Had he hidden the contents here? Whoever it was mustn't know he had been seen. If he could be followed his accomplice could be caught, always supposing there were one—the officer who had blackmailed Skinner into stealing the "stuff," perhaps.

If only she could see who it was. She moved. The crackle of paper stopped as if the person handling it had paused to listen. Suppose he came to the window? She flattened herself against the wall, held her breath till she was dizzy. The crackle was on again. Silence. Light out.

She slid along the wall till she could see into the living room. It was dark except for the slit of light which came through the partially open door to the corridor. A dark figure stood as if listening. There was a jaunty tilt to his broadbrim hat. The band below sounded off with "Washington Post March." The person waiting took advantage of the burst of music and slipped out, leaving the door partly open behind him.

Quickly, lightly, Pat crossed the room, pulling on her flower hat as she went, and stepped outside. A man in a wide-brim Panama, with brief case like that of a State Department courier's under his arm, was starting down the stairs. Two chatting, giggling women kept just behind him. She followed step by slow step, her eyes on the man ahead. When he crossed the terrace she was a few paces in the rear. He didn't look back once. She'd hand it to him for nerve. Had she been escaping with stolen "stuff" her head would have been hung over her shoulder in fear of pursuit.

He swung through the outer revolving door. She followed after a second's interval. He was walking leisurely along the drive. No mistaking the Panama and the brief case under his arm. Now he was putting on speed. She crept along in the shadow of the palms. She lost him as he rounded a curve of the drive. Cautiously she made the curve herself, expecting a hand on her shoulder at any minute. There he was again, heading for the parking space. He stepped into a roadster on the outer edge. The lights switched on. Her eyes widened in unbelief. She brushed her hand across them and looked again. She had been right the first time. It was Phil Ruskin's car.

The person taking it must be followed. What would happen to her if she tried to stop him? Never mind that. Skinner's brief case had been left to her in trust. If this man had the contents it was up to her to get them. Her car was here. Cam had said, "You may want it." Little either of them had thought for what she would use it. Had he locked it? Her heart stopped, picked up and thudded on. The key was in the bag under her arm.

With a desperate urge to race to the gray sedan which she could see, she held herself rigidly in the shadow as the man at the wheel of the roadster maneuvered it till it was free of the car in front. She must let him get started before she moved.

He had reached the hotel drive which was as far as she could see. She pulled off her flower hat, and tossed it under a palm. It was the first time she had worn one in days, she couldn't be bothered with it now. She darted to the gray sedan. Stopped to look at the departing roadster. Still going. She jerked open the car door. Stared in horrified unbelief. A woman in green was huddled over the wheel. Velma Dane.

23

CAM stood on the terrace of the Moana looking out at the expanse of sea and looming mountains. A frigate bird with huge wings flapped like a dark spirit against the pink afterglow and disappeared in a purple canyon. Since hearing Sergeant McIlvray's disguised voice on the telephone he had turned the information over and over in his mind, formulating and rejecting plans for carrying out the closing suggestion:—

"Meet me at seven-thirty at the night club where we had dinner with Mr. Ruskin, will you, dearie? Seven-thirty. No earlier, no later. I'm crazy to see you again. You'll find a jeep in the hotel drive, when you're ready." Before he could answer the saccharine request the line had gone dead.

Why was he so sure it had been Mac? Because no one else knew that the person who had rifled Pat's room had lost the finger of a glove. This noon the Sergeant had driven off with Cardena's servant, who had worn a glove with one finger missing; that was a point cleared. The blank paper in Skinner's brief case was still a mystery or was it, if Captain Dane had taken the bag from the shrubs? Had he seen Pat place it on the seat of the gray sedan? It was one hundred to one that he had picked up the key she had dropped at the hospital. The answer to the cipher ad which was to appear when the "goods" had been secured had named this hotel Lounge as the rendezvous. No line yet on the person who had typed the letters, or sent the carbon. Velma had complained that her husband was everlastingly pounding the typewriter, but, dislike and distrust Dane as he did, he couldn't believe that he had written:—

"Just then a woman screamed. She may be in his game— we may have to take care of her."

That was too raw even for the unstable Captain. There must be a fourth person involved in the scheme. Not likely that Cardena and his servant would write letters to each other and nothing would convince him that Dane had pointed the finger of suspicion at his wife. Had the Sergeant discovered the missing scrap of the puzzle? Was that behind his cooed request for "dearie" to be at the night club?

Dane was crossing the terrace. Dane in a dark blue suit, out of the service. Was he here to turn over the "goods"? He had stopped at the foot of the grand staircase, Pat was coming down. His heart broke into quickstep. She had been and was still the only woman in the world for him. Had he lost her to Ruskin? Why was she here? Velma's party would have been over long ago.

They were entering the Bar Lounge. How come? She had said she was to dine and dance with Phil. Perhaps she was filling the time while she waited for him. Was that heel Dane dragging her into danger? Evidence pointed to him as the finger man who had cleared the way for the person who had torn up her room. Could he get her out of the Lounge without letting her know—or anyone else—that he feared for her safety?

"Hi, Cam!" Velma Dane hailed him. "I've spoken to you twice but you were watching that couple crossing the terrace so intently you were deaf to my voice."

"Sorry. I was surprised to see your husband in civvies. Boy, oh, boy, but you're gorgeous. Why the snazzy green and gold costume? Why the Aga Khan's weight in diamonds in your hair and round your neck for a date with a mere colonel? Only a four-star general rates that display of what my sergeant calls 'cracked ice.' "

She waited till they were seated at a table in the softly lighted Lounge and a swarthy-skinned waiter had taken the order before she explained.

"You are not the only pebble on my beach, Cam. I have a dinner date. Besides, my hotel public expects me to be sensational."

"And have you a public. It isn't necessary to tell me that—" his eyes were attracted by a sparkle on her left shoulder, a diamond tiger stalking through gold tropical foliage—"that you are the number-one femme of buzz-buzz speculation here."

"Sure, I'm a conversation piece—I learned that from you —and am I giving it a workout, for the leisure class here, it is still with us, believe it or not. Let's get down to business. Why this sudden urge to have a cocktail with me when you don't drink 'em? You haven't touched the one you ordered." She leaned toward him. Her green eyes were clouded with anxiety. "They haven't pinned anything on Monty, have they?"

"No. Soft-pedal your voice, Velma, or you will be overheard. The rain this morning got into my bones. I decided I needed to contact someone attractive and gay. Right off quick I thought of you. What is the band playing?"

" 'For You a Lei.' I've hired a phonograph so I can bone up on Hawaiian music. See what I see across the room? Did you know that Pat Carey was coming here with Monty? Is that why I got the bid?"

"No, to both questions."

"Then if it isn't bad news or a dame, what's the answer? That chatter about an urge to contact something attractive and gay is just the old oil. Why make me the goat?"

He couldn't tell her that he had invited her because he needed a valid excuse to come himself, not after spotting that diamond tiger at her shoulder. Pat had said that Señor Cardena had wanted to buy a brooch like that. Had he given it to Velma Dane? She wasn't the type of woman to accept jewels from a casual acquaintance—or was she? What did he really know about her? Why be so sure that the alleged Brazilian was a casual acquaintance? They had arrived on the same Clipper. Stanhope had been a passenger. Stanhope was no longer living.

"What do you know about that!" Velma whispered. "Monty has a phone call. He is not taking it at the table. He's going out. What's happened?" Here eyes were wide with anxiety. "Ohmigosh, have they got anything on—"

"Don't!" His low protest set color burning in her cheeks. "How was the party for the Vets? I'll bet they had the time of their lives."

"Pat Carey declared it a smash hit. I think it was. When those cruelly disabled men laughed and cracked jokes it was all I could do to keep from bawling, but she and her aunt kept right along with them, their spirits apparently high. They wouldn't let the boys down."

"I'm glad it went over big. That's a gay sextette at the round table. The three women are bogged down with *leis*. Looks like a celebration."

"It's a farewell party. They were to leave this morning on the Clipper but it was held up by the storm. The announcement this noon that it would take off at approximately nine this evening created a near panic for those having reservations on the next plane out. One of the women told me they had assumed it wouldn't leave until tomorrow and had made evening engagements. There was a great scurry to cancel last-minute parties and—"

While he appeared to listen he was mentally checking on her information. Clipper leaving for the Mainland tonight; take-off not announced till noon; scurry to cancel last-minute parties. Suppose Cardena had counted on leaving tomorrow? He couldn't leave by air or water without clearance papers, but he could get those easily by showing the credentials with which he had arrived. Suppose he had side-stepped his date with Pat because he had to change his plans in a hurry? Not so good. Wasn't he giving a supper at Haleiwa Bay tomorrow? He wouldn't walk out—good Lord, suppose the celebration in honor of Madam Shaw-Ruskin and Sally was a red herring? Suppose he had planned to make his getaway under cover of that? "Answer cipher ad when you've got the goods."

"What's happened, Cam? You got up as if you were about to bolt and then dropped back into your chair. You haven't been listening to me either."

"Sure, I've been listening, Velma. I can repeat everything you said." Here's praying she won't ask me to. "Your husband has returned. The call couldn't have been as important as you feared—he looks mad as a hatter, but not depressed. This must be phone-your-friend night. It is our turn. For whom is the call?" he asked as a boy set a telephone on the table.

"Mrs. Dane."

"Who, *me*?" Her hand shook as she picked up the receiver. She had been tense and apprehensive. Why? Had she been expecting this call? "Mrs. Dane speaking. . . . Yes. . . . Yes." She rose hurriedly.

"Excuse me for a minute, Cam? I'll be r-right back."

"Not bad news, I hope."

"No—no, the—the surprise call gave me a jolt—you know what I'm scared about. I've got a touch of migraine. Ate too much at my party. Please don't come with me. I'll go upstairs till it passes. Wait for me here."

He watched her as she walked to the terrace. Was she dizzy or had she left to answer a summons? First her face had gone white, then deeply flushed. Pat was looking at her as if wondering if she were ill. What a chance, what a miraculous chance to get her out of the room and away from the Captain.

Now, she was looking at him. Could he make her understand? He moved his head in the direction of the terrace. She glanced at Dane before her eyes came back to his. This time she understood his wireless. She rose, looked up at the Captain and laughed, and walked away.

He dropped back in his chair with a sigh of relief. She was going out with Ruskin, who, probably, was waiting for her on the terrace and would insist upon leaving at once. For the first time since he had seen the man he was devoutly thankful that she would be with him. What a crowd in the great room. Men and women of many different races had gathered at this Crossroads of the Pacific for different reasons. How many plots and plans, besides the one in which he was involved, were being begun or finished here, some good, some bad, some involving treachery, passion, perhaps tragedy?

"For you, sir."

A Chinese boy in dark blue jacket and broad trousers, whose eyes glinted like black beads between slanting lids, handed Cam a note. He untwisted the paper, and read the scribbled words:—

I won't come back, Cam, I'm all in.

He gave the boy a coin and tore the note into shreds. Should he tell Dane that his wife had gone to her room because she was ill? Too late. He was leaving the Lounge. Had his phone call and the one to Velma been from the same person? Seemed to be nothing more for him to see or do here. Better move on and quick.

He tried desperately to stroll nonchalantly as he crossed the terrace and the foyer to the telephone booth, while every nerve prompted him to run. Time was marching on and the

Clipper left at nine, Velma had said. It seemed as if hours passed before his call was answered but the hand on his watch showed but five minutes' progress when a voice announced:—

"Haleiwa Bay. Officers' Club."

"Sorry to trouble you, but I'm a colonel newly arrived on the Island. I've mixed my dates. I'm ashamed to let my host know I'm so dumb so gave you a jingle. Is Señor Cardena's supper set for tomorrow or the day after? . . . Sure. I'll hold the line."

Through the window of the booth he watched the people passing back and forth in the foyer while his thoughts raced. If his hunch was right, if Cardena was leaving in the Clipper, would Philip Ruskin be on hand to give him a send-off? That was a fool question. The caballero was going on the q.t., wasn't he? There was Ruskin now hurrying toward the Terrace to meet Pat. She would be safe. He could dismiss her from his mind.

"Right here . . . What? . . . No reservation in that name? I am dumb. Are you sure? . . . Don't get mad about it. Of course you know your own business. My mistake. Sorry."

That was that. Cardena was set for a secret getaway. Now for the night club. If he reached there promptly at seven-thirty, he would have time for a light meal—unless Mac had other plans—before he went on to the airport; it wouldn't do to be waiting there when the Señor arrived. What was he stepping into, he wondered, as he left the hotel and walked along the drive under a sky so thickly sprinkled with stars that it looked like gold mesh. The Haleiwa Bay party had been a bluff. The cagey Señor had planned to leave on the Clipper this morning. Where had he hidden all day? Was Velma Dane wise as to his departure? Had the phone call at the table been from him? Where and how did the diamond tiger fit into the pattern?

The jeep was where Mac had told him it would be. He had hoped to find him in it waiting to give him a line on what was ahead. No Mac.

"Here we go—to what?" he asked himself as the tires picked up the road.

It was just seven-thirty when he entered the night club. The orchestra was playing "Moon Over Waikiki," as it had played the evening of Phil Ruskin's party here. The great eyes of a plane skimmed across the star-bright sky, he could hear the soft lap of the tide as he had heard it that night.

"Colonel Fulton, it is a pleasure to welcome you here again." Pedro's white teeth glistened, his black eyes gleamed in his dark face as he greeted him. "Come this way. I have a choice seat for you, sir."

Cam followed him to a table for two at one side of the *lanai*. He drew out a chair with a flourish and laid a mammoth menu on the table.

"You have not been here since the beautiful Madam was frightened by a mouse, is it not so?"

"That was days and days ago. You must have hundreds and hundreds of guests, why remember me?"

"It is my business to remember. If I forget"—his shrug was gracefully restrained—"I lose my job, quick. The steak is especially good tonight."

"I remember it was perfection when I was here before. An order of steak and whatever you recommend with it. No wine. Coffee."

"You do not drink wine, Colonel?"

"Sure, but—" He looked up at the face of the man taking his order. "Watch dark horse." Stanhope's words blazed in his memory like an electric sign suddenly turned on. "But this is my night for a coffee binge," he finished the sentence, hoping that the catch in his breath had passed unnoticed.

"Then you shall have your coffee very hot, very strong. You like it so?"

"That's right. Make it quick, will you? I'm due at the Barracks for a conference. Too early for your usual crowd, I suppose."

"A little, but they are coming in now. I will send a good man for your order." He dashed away to greet a group of men in white and women in evening clothes who stood in the doorway.

Cam smoked and thought back to the evening Phil Ruskin had given the party. Pedro had hovered obsequiously, almost to the neglect of the other guests, he remembered now, though it hadn't registered at the time. He had attributed the attention to the fact of the Shaw-Ruskin eminence in the *Who's Who* of the Territory of Hawaii, and to concern over Velma Dane's scream. When he had looked up into Pedro's face a moment ago, he had understood why Stanhope had been here that night. He had discovered that the joint was a front for espionage and had paid the price of his knowledge. Mac had implied that there was a typewriter on the premises of the make of one he was trying to locate. Suppose the letters had been written here? Who would mail a carbon to him?

"Your steak, sir."

A tall, lank waiter, in blue livery, who looked *kalmaaina*, as if he might be a descendant in a straight line from one of the original missionaries, set a silver-covered platter on the table. "This is a cold seat, sir. I will let down the reed curtain to shield you from the wind, it's blowing strong."

"Let it alone!" Cam regretted the sharpness of the command. It might put the man wise to the fact that he was suspicious of the place. He had no intention of sitting where he couldn't see behind him. "I like plenty of fresh air," he added by way of explanation. "What time does the floor show start?"

"At eight-thirty, sir. Shall I pour your coffee?"

"I'm not ready for it. I like it hot. Quite a large plant you have here." Not that he gave a hoot as to its size but he had a feeling that it would be a good idea to keep the man beside him till he knew what—if anything—was about to spring.

"Yes, sir." He became absorbed in carving the steak as the maître d'hôtel approached.

"Everything satisfactory, Colonel?" Pedro inquired solicitously. His eyes flashed to the waiter and returned to meet Cam's.

"Perfect, even to the man you sent to serve me. I haven't been on the Island long and I have been pumping him for information."

"He is a good man to pump. He has worked in this place —is it five or six years, Jon?"

"Seven come next September, sir."

No chance that he was F.B.I. planted here by Stanhope or his boss. Cam hadn't realized until this moment how much he had counted on his help.

"Take good care of the Colonel, Jon. We want him to come often," Pedro called over his shoulder before, with hand held high, he waved to a couple standing in the doorway. Steel, ukulele and guitar, swayed into "The Beautiful Blue Danube," and men swept their partners into a waltz.

"This is quite a plant, sir." With the dexterity of an experienced waiter Jon deposited a snowy parsley potato on the plate beside a slice of steak reddening in its juice. "You'd be surprised at the number of typewriters in use in the office."

"Is that so? There must be a huge business turnover to need so many."

"There is, sir. Will you have more mushrooms? These are especially choice. Believe it or not, sir, sometimes the waste-baskets run over with sheets of used carbon paper."

This was Stanhope's man after all. He had been here "seven years come next September." Stanhope's information about the joint must have come from him.

"Funny you should speak of car—"

"Take care, sir." The words were a mere whisper.

"Everything satisfactory, I hope, Colonel?" The maître d'hôtel had appeared with the suddenness of a rabbit conjured from a magician's hat.

"Corking. Never ate such steak!" Cam glanced at his wrist watch. "Good Lord, I must get a move on. Give me the check, waiter, or do I pay at the desk, Pedro?"

"At the desk. It is the manager's custom to offer our army guests a liqueur in his office, Colonel. He would be pleased to have you drink a toast with him. Will you come this way?"

"Sure. I try always to observe the customs of the country in which I am billeted." He laid a bill on the table. "Thanks, Jon, for a mighty good dinner and advice about the Punch Bowl excursion."

"Thank you, sir. We'll be glad to see you here again, sir." The waiter pocketed the money and unhurriedly began to clear the table.

"This way, Colonel."

He followed the maître d'hôtel as he threaded his way between tables, filled now with laughing, noisy groups of men and women, to an ornately furnished room the door of which he closed behind them. Many framed photographs hung on the mahogany walls, beside a long window. A decanter overlaid with silver and matching liqueur glasses were on a silver tray on a table. Pedro looked about the room in surprise.

"The manager was here a moment ago. I will call him."

"Make it fast, will you? Remember I have an appointment at the Barracks."

"You'll have plenty of time to get there. Sit down." Pedro produced a small automatic and twirled it casually. "We think it is desirable that you spend the evening here, Colonel."

"Is that so? Just why this passionate urge for my company?" Cam perched on the edge of the table. If necessary he could hurl the decanter at the man's head.

"Put both hands in your trousers pockets, Colonel," Pedro directed as if he had divined his thoughts. "That's right. If you take them out"—he twirled the revolver suggestively.

Cam glanced at the clock. Why the dickens had he let himself in for this—he could have refused the liqueur. The answer to that was easy, he wanted Pedro to show his hand. He'd shown it, all right. Mac had said seven-thirty and here he was. What was it all about? At this minute he should be on his way to the airport the other side of the hotel; this night club was Honolulu way.

The typewriter on a desk was the make of the one the Señor had given Madam Shaw-Ruskin. Was this where the

letters had been written? Was Pedro or the manager the
fourth in the gang? This was a scheme to prevent him from
holding up Cardena at the airport, of course. How had it been
discovered that he was after him? He must go. He'd make a
break for it and—

"Put your hands back in your pockets, Colonel. I mean
what I say. I will shoot you."

"That's your lookout, Pedro, you'll have the whole U.S.
Army on your back if you do." The maître d'hôtel in-
dulged in a graceful shrug.

"I am not afraid of—"

A crash of glass. A face split by a broad grin at the
window. A glint of steel.

"Drop that gun, fella, and make it quick," said Sergeant
McIlvray.

24

PAT shook her head as if to clear her eyes and looked again.
This wasn't a nightmare. She was awake and the peppy Dane
was huddled over the wheel. Had she been about to start the
sedan? She felt of the woman's wrist. The pulse was beating.
Thank God, she wasn't dead. She lifted her head. Choked
back a cry of dismay. There was no diamond rose in her
hair, her throat was bare of glitter.

Now what? Had the man escaping with the courier's case
taken them? Not recently for he had not approached the gray
sedan. Perhaps he knew what was in it. Whether he did or
not he must be followed. She couldn't stop to get Velma
back to the hotel. Evidently she had fainted from fright. She
opened the windows wide, the cool air would revive her. She
would take her along and leave her at a house on the road
to be cared for. First she would have to be moved from behind the wheel. Good heavens, she was heavy. With the door
on her side locked she could rest against it. There she was. If
only her head wouldn't wobble as the heads of the dead
men had wobbled when moved in the Bulge.

Why did this have to happen? The man would get a tremendous start. Steady. Steady, she warned herself and cautiously sent the sedan forward. Nothing to be gained and
everything might be lost by getting panicky. Allah be praised,
the drive was clear. How loud the surf sounded, or was it
the pound of her heart? It seemed hours but it hadn't been

many minutes since he started. When she saw Phil's roadster she could follow. The tail light would show the license number she knew as well as she knew her own. There it was, turning into the highway. A moan. Thank heaven Velma was regaining consciousness, she wouldn't have to stop and leave her somewhere when every second counted.

"You wo—n't get—key—" The voice was so low Pat bent her head to hear. Did she mean the key Monty had picked up?

"Who won't get what key, Velma?" she prodded.

"He—he fooled me—" The green eyes were open now but dazed. "He said Monty—would be safe—no—that wasn't it—he wouldn't be suspect—if I helped." Her eyes closed.

"Helped about what, Velma? Tell me. Tell me," Pat implored.

"Cam knows I'm—I'm afraid—He said Monty—promised the German girl—"

"Don't stop, Velma. Who is 'he'? Go on, try to keep your mind steady, you fainted, that's all. You'll feel fine in a few minutes. Tell me," Pat pleaded with her eyes on the car ahead. The driver was taking the road to the airport. Monty had said that a Clipper took off at nine. If the man who had taken the white package from the closet counted on escaping from the Island in that, he had another count coming to him. Did Velma know of the theft?

"Who told you about the German girl, Velma? Cam?"

"Cam. Cam—doesn't know. Do you know—Cam? He's a right guy."

"Who told you about the German girl?—Try, try to remember."

"The Señor said Monty played—round with one—over there—I hate—her—I'll br—eak her."

"What did Monty promise the girl, Velma? Please, *please* grip your mind and hold it steady. I must know."

"Well—you needn't—cry about—it."

Tense as she was for fear the man ahead would escape, Pat chuckled. Velma was returning to normal.

"I won't cry. What did Monty promise the German girl?"

"Promise? Monty?"

"Think! *Think!* You said the Señor told you—"

"Señor Car-de-na. Oh, that man? He said Monty made a GI steal papers—" She lifted her head and looked up. "Funny place. How did—I get—here?"

Pat knew now what the term "wringing hands" meant. Frustration would set her to wringing hers if they were not needed on the wheel.

"Velma, *try, try* to keep your mind on what the Señor told

you, please, *please*. If you do we may save Monty. You remember Monty? He's your husband. You want to save him, don't you? Who stole what papers?"

"Don't ask me—so many questions—you tire my—head. It —it hurts," she whimpered.

"Did Monty steal papers?"

"I told you—he made a GI steal them."

Pat's quick-drawn breath was half sob. The GI was Skinner. Velma had confirmed his story.

"Why? Did the Señor tell you why?"

"The German girl—to send—to brother—somewhere in South America—they were worth—money—lots—and lots—and lots of money," she singsonged.

"Is Señor Cardena her brother?"

"No. *No.* My—but—you're dumb. *He* came to help Monty —watch for the brother—coming to meet the GI with the formu-las. That's the word—gas for-mu-las. He said Monty'd go to prison if—if Cam found out. Cam wouldn't—send Monty—" Her head dropped against the back of the seat. Pat restrained a desperate urge to shake her. Still only one car ahead. The driver was increasing speed. She must make the most of this time. There would be any number of automobiles soon on the way to the airport. She couldn't stop to figure out what she had heard. She pressed her hand hard against Velma's shoulder.

"Open your eyes and listen." She cleared her hoarse voice. "Your diamonds have been stolen. Get it? *Your diamonds have been stolen.*" That opened the green eyes. That got through to the dazed brain. Velma raised one shaking hand to her throat.

"Ohmigosh! Gone! Stolen!" Shock had cleared her voice. Her eyes shone like emeralds in the dim light. She straightened out of her slump, tried to sit erect. "My necklace! Who are you? You stole it? You're taking me off to dump me— like Stanhope—they dumped him—Hel—" Pat slapped her squarely on the mouth and stopped the scream.

"Quiet, or you'll have us both wiped out. If you yell again I will dump you for fair. *Listen.* I've *got* to follow that car. See the red tail light? The driver is the guy who snitched your jewels."

"Who are you? It's dark. I can't—see you." She shook her head. "My eyes—are blurry. How do you know who—who took my diamonds?"

Pat didn't but her statement had stopped hysterics. Better not tell Velma who she was yet, in her dazed state she might go back to the idea that she wanted Monty.

"I saw him leave this car and jump into that roadster

ahead." The last four words were true. "I almost passed out when I opened this door and saw you slumped over the wheel."

"I—I don't believe you. You're one of the gang—"

"That's enough from you. Out you go." With eyes on the red light in the distance Pat reached across her to unlock the door. She hadn't supposed it was in her to be so hard-boiled but with so much at stake she had to appear heartless. "You're so weak you'll probably lie in the road till you're run over, but I can't help that."

"Don't throw me out—I—won't make any trouble—I promise. My head aches like the—the devil—but I can see better. I know who you are—when you leaned across I could see—you're Pat Carey. Of course you wouldn't take my diamonds. I—can—see the red light—now—" She dropped her head into her hands. "Ohmigosh, how it aches—what did he hit me with?"

"Hit you? Did someone *hit* you? I thought you fainted. Who hit you?"

"I don't—know. I'm so—so cold." She shivered. "I'm—going to—be sick."

"For heavens' sake, Velma, you *can't* be sick. Don't you *dare* be sick." At the risk of running off the road Pat reached into the seat behind and pulled forward a robe. "Put this round your shoulders. No wonder you're cold with your neck bare halfway to your waist."

"My neck doesn't go—halfway to my waist." She giggled as might a person coming out of ether. Pat restrained a responsive laugh.

"Don't waste breath wisecracking. Rest your head against the back of the seat and you won't be sick. Don't talk. I've got to plan. Think back over what happened before I found you in this car. We've *got* to save Monty." This last was an inspiration. Perhaps, after all, fear for the safety of her husband would clear Velma's mind more quickly than fear for her diamonds.

"What do you know about—Monty?" The demand was fiercely suspicious.

"Only what you told me." Pat repeated what she had said, always with her eyes on the light ahead.

"Forget it. I was nutty. A person will say anything after—a crack on the head."

"Usually they talk about what was in their mind at the time of the crack. I happen to know what you said about the stolen papers is true. Unless we reach the airport and catch the man who stole them your husband will be arrested. What will happen then is anybody's guess. The government isn't patting the heads and 'good-boying' traitors."

"Monty isn't a traitor. He was trapped by a Mata Hari—you know, a girl spy. He isn't the first man who has gone—crooked because of a woman."

"Unfortunately he isn't, but that won't help him. Feeling better, aren't you?"

"My stomach has settled down but my head throbs. Ohmigosh, you don't suppose it's a concussion?"

"I don't. Never mind your head." If conditions were different she wouldn't have to appear so darn hardhearted, but she must get the story. "Tell me what happened tonight. I know you were in the Bar Lounge with Colonel Fulton. Why did you leave? Where did you go? I'll remind you once more that if you tell the truth we may catch the man who was behind your husband's theft. If you don't—I don't know whether the government shoots or hangs traitors. I guess it doesn't make much difference to the traitor in the end."

"How can you talk like that? Proves you—you never loved a man." She caught back a sob. "I guess I needn't have worried about you and Monty."

"I guess you needn't. The only person about whom you need worry is your husband. See the glow in the sky ahead? That's the airport. If I don't know what brought you to this sedan before we reach that—after all, I believe they hang 'em. Hear the car behind us? Passengers for the Clipper are beginning to leave the hotel. Look out the back window. What is following? For goodness' sake, stop groaning every time you move."

"It looks like a black convertible with a white top." She faced front and gripped her head. "Ohmigosh, you'd groan if your head ached as mine does."

Pat's heart thumped in her throat. Cardena had hired a convertible with a white top. Was he following Velma? That stuff about helping Monty sounded phony. Why the jitters? There was more than one car like that on Oahu. This wasn't the time to lose her nerve. She'd give Velma a few minutes to get her grip, then she'd probe again for her story. Better think of something else for a minute and relax her muscles and nerves which were tied in hard knots.

Beautiful sky. The stars were thick as if sewn together like the yellow Mamo feathers in the golden cape of King Kamehameha the Great. Had the Sergeant really made notes of the information she had given him that day by the statue? "Don't speak to the guy coming out the door. He's poison," he had warned. Later he wouldn't tell her whether he had meant the Señor or his servant. Velma had said a few minutes ago that Cardena was trying to save Monty. If only that adorable red-headed Sergeant would drop from the blue at this minute she would fall on his neck. He wouldn't. This wasn't miracle week. It was up to her to carry on.

"Fog clearing, Velma?" she asked.

"Yes. Sorry I went nutty about you. I like you. Have we been driving for hours? Was the party for the Vets only this afternoon? It seems years since your aunt left with the boys. She sure has them on her mind. Had a tough life with her husband, didn't she? I've been told he had a rovin' eye and drank himself to death. That's why she doesn't serve anything stronger than sherry, isn't it?"

"You'll have to ask her." Haze was giving way to garrulity. Perhaps now she could get Velma's story. "The control tower's searchlight at the airport is sweeping the sky. Is the convertible following?"

"Yes. Glory be, it didn't hurt so much to turn that time."

"That's to the good. Pull yourself together. Concentrate. Go back to the beginning and tell me why you think Monty is mixed up in a crooked deal. I know you do, don't waste time denying it. I'll be third-degreed when we reach the airport for I intend to get that man with—with your diamonds if I never do anything else. If you don't come across with the truth I'll tell everything you've said to date."

"You don't have to threaten me. My mind is clear as a bell now—a cracked bell," she giggled. "Your nasty threat about hanging 'em or shooting 'em swept out the last wisp of fog. I'll tell all. I'm no fool—except about Monty. Watch the man in front. I'll keep my eyes on the convertible following. I don't like it. Something about it starts the heebie-jeebies along my spine."

She twisted round in the seat till she could see the window and talked, punctuating sentences with an occasional groan. She revealed that almost from the day of their arrival on the Island Señor Cardena had begun to hint that he knew Monty hadn't been on the up-and-up—nothing definite, just enough to make her uneasy. Monty hadn't helped allay her doubts, he had been jumpy, had had mysterious telephone calls, had been everlastingly typing. Yesterday Cardena had said that her husband had hidden stolen papers in her apartment, had followed with the story about the German girl; had warned that if she repeated what he had told her the person who was after the stolen stuff would get Monty—and quick.

"Don't stop to groan, Velma. That was up to yesterday.

Don't talk while this big car is passing. I can't hear. Passengers for the Clipper. They're noisy enough. I can't see that roadster we're following. Yes, I can. Go on."

"This morning Cardena sent me a brooch of a diamond tiger—what's the matter?"

"I didn't speak. Just cleared my throat. Go on."

"He wrote that I was to wear it this evening." She put her hand to her shoulder. "My eye, the heel took that, too."

"Never mind, you don't want the ugly thing, do you? Why were you to wear it this evening?"

"He said that an F.B.I. would be on the alert for it. That at a phone call I was to go to my apartment, unlock the door and leave it partly open, then scram—he didn't use the word but that's what he meant. A detective would slip in and when the party who had been alerted to get the loot arrived he would be caught, and he, himself, would swear that Monty knew nothing about it, that it had been planted to catch the guy who had come from South America for the loot."

"You believed all that stuff?"

"I guess I was a fall gal. Just remember, I love Monty. I was all for anyone who would promise to help. The call came while I was in the Lounge with Cam. I followed instructions and set the door of my living room ajar. On the way down to return to the table I had a rush of suspicion to the head. Why not check at the parking space to see if Cardena's suspect made his getaway, he might escape the F.B.I. I would stop him. Little Velma at the controls. I scribbled a note to Cam that I was ill and wouldn't come back. I slipped along the drive in the shadow of the palms. Saw a mass of parked cars—I knew nothing more till I came to, here. Make what you can of that."

"I'll bet Cardena is the man from South—my word, I've lost that red tail light. I was so excited over your story I kept my eyes on you. Is the convertible still following?"

"Can't see it. There are several pairs of headlights way back. What'll we do now? Perhaps—perhaps the man with my diamonds has drawn up beside the road and is lying in wait to knock us out."

"That's a cheery thought." Pat leaned forward, brushed her hand across the windshield as if to clear it, though she knew she was fooling herself. It didn't need clearing. The roadster was not in sight. "We've got to go on. We'd better make time, too."

She drove swiftly, but cautiously. Was there a trick about the sudden disappearance of the black roadster she had been following? Phil's roadster? Where was he? Would he be furious because she hadn't kept her date? Had Cam expected her to return to the Lounge?

"Look out!" Velma's scream and her own awareness of something drawn across the road in front were simultaneous. "Ohmigosh! My head! Why did you stop so suddenly? You about snapped it off."

"If we'd struck that truck loaded with trees, it would have been snapped off—and how. Is there room on your side to go round it? There isn't on mine. That fool Chinaman is jacking up his wheel in the middle of the road. He's shaking his head. He didn't like the bleat of our horn to make him move. I'm going round him. Hold on, Velma. If you feel we're tipping into the gutter, lean against me and lean hard. Here we go."

Palm fronds brushed into the open window as the car squeezed past. Velma leaned hard. Pat held her breath. Would they make it? They would. They were again in the open road.

"Hear the horns behind us. Those passengers bound for the airport will come back and beat up that man if they're late. Now we'll head for the black roadster, *wikiwiki.* I'll bet the man driving bribed that Chinaman to block the road." Pat's spirits were mounting. "Realize that you are part of an adventure with a capital A, Velma? Excitement ahead of us and—what's *that?*"

"That's your excitement behind us instead of ahead. A busted tire. Ohmigosh! There goes the other. I'll bet the guy who robbed me punctured them. Slow leak since. Feel us sink. They're flat as pancakes. What'll you do now, change?"

"Change when there's an escaping thief ahead? It's 'half a league, half a league, half a league onward.' "

"Hold it, Pat, you're getting hysterical."

"I'm not. My spirits always kick the beam when I'm in danger—not bloody danger."

"Are we in danger?"

"Be yourself, Velma. What do you think when the tires of a car are punctured? It's to stop pursuit, isn't it? We'll have to limp along. Headlights behind us. Another driver has squeezed past the truck. On second thoughts we won't limp. We'll hitchhike. I've always been crazy to try it." She stopped the sedan close to the bordering palms.

"Step out, Velma, and for goodness' sake keep that robe over your shoulders, that expanse of bare neck would scare any decent driver from giving us a lift."

"It's the latest daytime neckline from Paris."

"Maybe, but the fashion hasn't reached the Island yet.

Come on, step into the road and hold up your thumb. You know how to do it. You've seen it on the screen times enough if not on the road. John Rodgers, here we come."

"Ooch, my head hurts when I move." Velma clutched the robe round her shoulders. "Who's John Rodgers? The guy who stole my diamonds?"

"John Rodgers Airport. Here's the car. Step out into the road. Quick. Do your stuff."

Headlights illumined the two girls standing with upraised thumbs. Brakes screeched. A roadster stopped. The driver leaned toward them.

"What's the trouble?"

"Two flats." Pat indicated the sedan beside the road. "We've got to make the Clipper." As the man's eyes swept them from head to feet she added hastily, "We've just come from a farewell dinner. We're on our way to see off my brother who's been demobilized and is leaving on that. Will you give us a lift?"

"Hop in. There's room enough for both on this seat."

They drove on in silence. Pat was aware of the driver's occasional furtive glance at her seated next him. Never having hitchhiked before she didn't know if conversation was in order or if one should maintain a demure silence. Page Emily Post. She would take a chance on the last. The car took a hump on high. Velma groaned. The man's suspicious eyes flew to her.

"Far as we go," he announced as he stopped at the gate in the iron fence which enclosed the brilliantly lighted airfield. Pat heard his prodigious breath of relief.

"Thanks, thanks a million." She jumped out. "Come on, Carrots." Velma alighted more slowly, clutched her head and groaned. The robe fell away from her shoulders.

"That must have been *quite* a farewell dinner," the driver observed. "Better tell your *brother* about it," he added, and drove on.

"I guess you didn't get that farewell dinner story across, Pat."

"I guess I didn't." Pat picked up the robe and flung it across Velma's shoulders. "Try to keep this on. I'll bet that man was glad to get rid of us. He looked scared stiff when you groaned, he probably pictured himself in court answering to an assault-and-battery charge brought by 'brother.' Come on. We won't be allowed to get by the passengers' gate—we'll have to work out the how of that when we get inside this fence."

They passed the parking enclosure. Eureka! The roadster

with Phil's license number apparently was the latest arrival. Their man was here.

"What do we do next, Pat?"

"Keep out of sight in the shadow of the waiting room and
watch for a man with a courier's brief case—it's bigger than
the ordinary kind. Probably he figured they'd think he was
from the State Department. When he starts for the gang-
plank we'll have to charge the gatemen—both of us—unless
someone else stops him. Feeling steadier? This fluorescent
lighting makes you look ghastly."

"It doesn't hand you much, girlie. The way I look isn't a
patch on the way I feel. I'm a brilliant, vivid Paris green inside. Between my worry about Monty, my diamonds, and
my aching head I'm due for an attack of the willies."

"Cut out the willies, we have a job ahead. How huge that
plane is. It shines like burnished silver. Look!" Pat's fingers
bit into Velma's arm. "There he is. Keep back in the shadow.
See him with the fat brief case behind the two GI's? Can't
see his face. He's pulled down the brim of his hat."

"*Him!* Is that the guy we've been chasing like mad? It's—
Don't pinch me. My eye, haven't I enough trouble? Are you
sure—?"

"Don't mention a name. Keep your voice down no matter
what hap—" A gulp of excitement snagged the word. "It's
up to us to stop him. No one else knows what he has. There
goes the crew preparing to board the plane. One motor is
being warmed up. I've got to stop him! No, I haven't." She
pulled Velma back against the wall of the waiting room.
"Cam—" her voice broke in a sob of excitement—"is on the
job."

"How do you know he isn't here to give him a send-off?
How can he have heard the heel has stolen my diamonds?
I'm going to yell—"

"No you won't. General Carrington is with Cam. They are
not here to say *Aloha*. Hold your breath. Something's going
to happen."

"Do you see Monty? Is Monty with them?"

"No. Cam and the General are walking toward the man
with the courier bag. They're laughing. Are my wires crossed?
Have they come to give him a send-off? Perhaps they still
believe he is the important person he claimed to be. He's
pretending not to see them. He's getting near the gang-
plank. A scond motor warming up. Why don't they hurry?
Don't they know Cardena is a fraud? Why don't they hurry?
Don't they know what he has done? It's up to me now—"
She started forward, gripped Velma's arm and pulled her

back as blue and khaki uniforms closed in on the man with the courier's brief case.

"They've got him! They've got him," she whispered hoarsely. "Skinner's papers are safe." She drew a long, frightened breath.

"My word, what's happened to my knees? They've come unglued." She made an ineffectual grab for Velma's arm and dropped to the ground.

25

LATE afternoon sunlight had turned the velvet lawn at Silver Ledges to green gold, deepened the tints and shades of the pink, blue, yellow and lavender flowers in the borders and the bougainvillia blossoms on the rock wall. It pointed up the small iron door, almost vine-covered now, of the bomb-proof shelter among the golden shower trees and set ashimmer the broad horizontal bands of lime, melon, and pale blue of Pat's surah frock as she sat on a bamboo stool at the front of the *lanai* absorbed in a newspaper. She reread the glaring black headlines.

TEN HUNDRED ONE THOUSAND DOLLAR BILLS

Get it? Sure, it's a million. This reporter never had seen a one thousand dollar bill, to say nothing of ten hundred of them but, there they were, pretty things, ten packages with one hundred of the thousand dollar smackers in each with a paper strap around them just as they had left the bank. A little soiled but boy, they'd traveled, under a GI's shirt, probably. The scenario? Here goes. Discovered; the cache of a wanted Nazi ersatz-gas industrialist; stacks of U.S. greenbacks; millions of them. Enter German *Frau*; ditto U.S. Captain; *Frau* weaves spell; U.S. Captain teams with her; blackmails GI; GI steals above mentioned packets from hoard. Don't ask how. No one knows. *Frau* contacts brother (?) in S.A. in best Nazi tradition; GI arrives Honolulu; is smashed in accident. Tipped off by Intelligence two army officers and a noncom follow to lead the manhunt; U.S. Captain arrives on hunt for GI with the ducats. Enter Nazi SS trooper disguised as Brazilian grandee; social whoopee for gay caballero. GI in hospital while hunt for him and T H O T D B (see headline) is on; no one but U.S. Captain knows who stole the dough. GI repents; turns over brief case with loot to nurse; tries to name U.S. Captain; dies without telling. U.S. Captain sees nurse leave hospital with brief case; learns that the GI he is after is dead; clears way for theft of brief case from nurse's room by Nazi's valet. Slight case of murder, Strategic Service man, the valet again. U.S. Captain hides loot in wife's apartment. Local night club manager involved. Nazi SS—alias Señor Miguel Cardena—caught with above mentioned million as about to enplane; police retrieve diamond necklace, flower and pin, property of wife of same U.S. Captain; versatile fella, that valet. Two empty seats on outgoing plane as caballero and valet are removed to guardhouse. Curtain.

Pat dropped the newspaper, leaned her head against the vine-covered vertical behind her, and watched the shadows on Diamond Head change pattern with every drifting cloud. It hurt to know that Monty Dane was the heel whom Skinner had tried to name; she had liked him, had been proud of his war record. Would that help him now? The reporter didn't know that when the "U.S. Captain" had discovered that Cardeña was getting away with the cut-in promised him, he had admitted, while in custody, that after the valet had torn the nurse's room to pieces in his hunt, and had discovered what he was after in the shrubs, the brief case filled with blank paper which had been substituted for it had been provided by him. The General, who with Cam and Sergeant McIlvray had flown to the Mainland with the three accused men, had written the gist of Monty Dane's confession to Sally. They had been away a week.

It had been a strenuous week. Madam Shaw-Ruskin had heard of the identity of the Señor who had paid assiduous court to her and of Sally's approaching marriage, and had angrily accused her daughter-in-law of introducing a criminal into her house—forgetting his gilt-edge letters of introduction—of bringing Dane and his cheap wife there and of daring to marry, go to Germany and leave the Island property without care. She had added vindictively, "John had no right to leave it to you anyway."

It hadn't seemed the auspicious moment to tell her that Mrs. Montgomery Dane was taking over the place and Sally's Vet Club also till her return. She had courage to settle here with Madam Shaw-Ruskin her enemy, but Velma had courage, she had demonstrated that in the way she had taken Monty's departure. He would be tried by a military court-martial in the European theater of operations. Señor Cardena and Dane were already on their way to Germany, the General had written.

That wasn't all the week had developed. Phil Ruskin had been furiously angry because Pat had side-stepped their date the night she had chased the man with the courier's brief case—then, repentant, had asked her again to marry him. She had refused with a finality which left no doubt in his mind. She thought of the days she had put in helping Sally prepare for her long journey; it had meant giving up the Nurses' Aide job—she would have had to do that later. Velma wanted her to stay with her but as soon as Sally was off she would go to New York and find something to do.

"Hi, Sarge!" Sib Lou's laughing hail brought Pat's attention to the present. If the Sergeant was back Cam must have returned. "What you doing here?"

"Shure, an' I've come to say *Aloha* to you and Lilly Yee Lung and Wong Chung. Me and the boss are shovin' off stateside tomorrow."

"Gee, Sarge, I'm going to miss you something terrible." They were crossing the lawn toward the vine-covered white cottage, the girl's hand tucked under his arm. She giggled. "There's a Chinese boy who won't miss you, he'll be glad to see you go. He needn't have gone nuts, though, I knew you thought I was just a kid, but it's been fun, hasn't it, Sarge?"

"Shure, an' it has. You're a cute trick, an—" His voice thinned in the distance and was lost among the golden shower trees.

Pat drew a little breath of relief. Sib Lou had shown no sentimental regret at his leaving. Sergeant Mac had played fair. Cam must have returned to the Island. Was he planning to leave tomorrow without saying good-bye to her?

"Here she is, Sally." General Carrington spoke from the opening in the glass wall. He followed her aunt into the *lanai* with Cam behind them. Cam, in gray tropical wool suit and blue shirt and tie which made his bronze skin appear even bronzer. He laughed.

"Greetings, Pat. You looked stunned. Hope my appearance isn't too much of a shock? It's quite a drop from silver eagles to mufti. An officer is permitted to wear it when the fighting is over, particularly when he is about to be demobilized."

"If I appear stunned it is because I thought you had decided to remain in the army."

The General settled his tie and rested an arm on the top of the fan-back chair in which Sally Shaw, in turquoise blue linen, sat among the pink and amethyst cushions.

"Let me answer that, Colonel. Patricia, I strongly advised Cam to return to his home to begin the lifework he planned as a boy. We need enlistments in all branches of the service, must have them if we are to fulfill our commitments, but more and more in the occupation zones military administration will be replaced by civilian. There are plenty of able men ready to go and plenty of officers ready to stay. Young men who have seen and experienced the horror of war are needed here to take an active part in government, to work tooth and nail toward the fulfillment of the nation's promises of benefits and acclaim to be given returning GI Joes and Joans for their share in saving this country and its way of life from devastation. That program is lagging. I am pinch-hitting for Cam, I'm going to Germany for two years. It will be tough on Sally, she's used to luxurious living; conditions there won't be easy, but she thinks she can take it." It was a long and eloquent explanation from the General who was not given to expressing his thoughts.

"Think! I know I can take it and love it—with you, Sam. Do you want to go home, Cam?"

"Very much, now that my conscience is at ease about going. I want to get into the fight to establish integrity in high places. That's a quote in case you're interested."

"You'll both stay for dinner, won't you?"

"Sorry to drag away your favorite Colonel, Sally, but we have a date. Cam has moved from quarters to the Moana to be ready for an early start tomorrow. The Intelligence chief is to meet us there in half an hour to hear our report on the evidence we laid before the provost marshal general. I'll be back as soon as we are through and you and I will take in a movie. Come out to the car with me."

"Are you really leaving in the morning?" Pat asked after her aunt and the General had left the *lanai*.

"Yes, on the *Matsonia*. I've crossed the Pacific three times by air, decided to make this trip by water. Did you see the newspaper account of our late unpleasantness?"

"Yes, but I didn't understand the reference, 'night club manager involved.'"

"That was Sergeant McIlvray's good deed for the day. He was waiting for me at the Moana when Cardena's man asked him to help change a tire. Mac was all set to tell him to go find a garage when he thought of the glove finger Wong Chun had found in the shrubs and promptly traded his help for a ride to town. On the way he discovered that the man beside him was wearing a glove minus a finger. When he pulled up at a night club with the excuse that he'd have to stop a few minutes on business, Mac remembered what I had told him about the evening at that same spot when Mrs. Dane thought someone tried to steal her necklace. He smelled a rat and began to investigate. His suspicion proved to be correct. The sleek Pedro was a pistol-toting guy. Cardena was in hiding there all day before he started for the airfield."

"And what a day it turned out to be."

"Right. I thought when I wirelessed you to help Velma that night in the Lounge that I was sending you out of danger; instead, I plunged you into it."

"How did you know?"

"Mrs. Sally air-mailed a blow-by-blow account of your experience to the General."

"Did you find out who hit Velma? I've had a nervous chill each time I've thought of the crazy chance I took taking her with me after that blow on her head. I was too excited at the time to even think I was taking a risk."

"Cardena's man cracked under a lie detector, confessed that he saw her run into the parking space, suspected she knew his boss's plan, knocked her out to save his own neck, took her jewels and put her in the gray sedan. Then he met Dane coming from the hotel with the money, took Ruskin's roadster and picked up Cardena along the road."

"I must have lost the man I followed through the hotel—it was Monty, wasn't it—when he disappeared round the curve of the drive. He probably delivered the goods to Cardena's man then. A million dollars! I don't wonder Skinner warned me to take care of his brief case. It sounds like a Crime-Club special, doesn't it?"

"It does. I must go. Whatever you want to do about—us, Pat, will be all right with me. Wear this for good luck. *Aloha.*"

Pat's eyes followed him before they looked down at the white case he had placed in her hand. She opened it. Inside were the gold ring and bracelet set with rare greenish crystals, Madam Pele's Tears. He had remembered that she wanted them.

Sally Shaw was unusually silent at dinner. When the General came for her she lingered on the threshold of the living room.

"I hate to leave you alone, honey."

"Good heavens, Sally, I shan't have time to miss you. I have so much to do I don't know which job to tackle first. Run along. Don't keep the man in your life waiting."

Heavenly night, she thought, as two hours later she leaned her arms on the iron rail of her balcony, looked up at the multitude of stars and watched the searchlights sweep across the sky. Cam was going. Didn't he care at all? Had he completely forgotten the "love-is-heaven" week at the Post?

"He won't ask me. I was the quitter. He'll wait for me to say, 'I love you,'" Sally had said about the General. Was Cam waiting for her to say that? The question set her blood tingling. I told Sally I was all set to break loose and do something crazy, she reminded herself. "Whatever you want to do about us, Pat," he had said. Suppose I go to the Moana and ask Cam what he *wants* me to do, that would be about the craziest move I could make. If he wants to marry the English girl I'll play fair and set him free as soon as possible.

The steeple clock was striking. She counted. Ten. Life at the hotel would be taking on speed. Not too late to go there—or was it, two years too late? That thought started the shivers but they couldn't throw her this time.

With the sense that she was chasing the rear end of a disappearing express train she pulled off the silk frock and dashed to the closet. What to wear? It must be something very special. The black? She had bought it on her New York shopping binge; it was so long, so sleek, so sophisticated that she hadn't worn it.

"Perfect for you, Madam," the saleswoman had lured as the model paraded before them. She had rolled her eyes ceilingward and clasped her purple-nailed hands in ecstasy. "In that, you will be the woman men remember." That settled it. She would wear the black.

Dressed, she stood before the mirror to regard the result. The model's hair had been in a snood, hers, which had been given the new short cut last week, had a satin sheen. No diamonds—Cam had returned hers by messenger last week —two strings of near pearls about her throat and studs in her ears. A daring V neck. A huge bunch of pink carnations at the waist of the long tunic was matched by gloves that reached almost to the short cape sleeves. She twisted, as the model had twisted, till the looking-glass girl's slim beige leg showed in the high slit of the sleek black skirt.

"Hussy!" she flung at her reflection, caught up the large black underarm bag, sequined to match her high-heeled sandals, a pair of spotless white driving gloves to draw over the pink, and pelted down the stairs.

"Gone to find Cam. Expect me when you see me," she scribbled on a pad at the living-room desk and hurried out.

As the gray sedan sped along the road the heavens were bright with the still lights of planets and the twinkle of stars, a breeze from the mountains was ginger-scented. She turned on the radio. With piano accompaniment a man's voice sang:—

"You never know where you're going till you get there."

"There's a lot in what you say," she answered and laughed. Why be so tense? After all, she wasn't on her way to be shot at dawn.

In the hotel parking space she stepped out of the car, flung her white gloves to the seat and closed the door. She stood motionless, her face lifted to the stars, breathing in the mystic fragrance of the night. Did this sense of peace come from the assurance that she was playing fair? Up through the golden glory of the heavens her spirit climbed to God.

"Please let Cam love me," she prayed. "Let us work together for the highest and best. Please let the world be a little better because we have lived in it." From the open door of memory floated the tender music of a flute, "Amen."

On the hotel terrace in a perfumed sea of arriving and departing women in jewel-tone frocks and men in white or uniforms she lingered, asked herself, "Now what do I do?" Waves of laughter and gay chatter beat and surged about her.

"I've been looking for you," said a voice behind her.

"Cam!" Little icy chills slithered along her veins as she turned and met his dark, intent eyes. "Sounds as if you expected me. Am I glad to see you? A minute ago I felt as lonesome as Robinson Crusoe on his desert isle."

"Here's your man Friday right on the job—or are you here to meet another?"

"No—I just took a chance—of seeing someone I knew and liked."

"You did?" He looked at her as if really seeing her for the first time. "What the dickens have you done to yourself? You look so—so, I guess artificial is the word I'm after."

She lifted one shoulder daintily as the model had lifted hers and smiled the model's smile.

"In case you care, 'I'm the woman men remember.'"

"You're telling me." He cleared his husky voice. "Let's get out of this."

From somewhere came the music of ukuleles and guitars and a woman's voice, tender and sweet, singing, "Aloha Means I Love You." At the desk he stopped for a key, said something to the clerk, who turned startled eyes on her, then grinned as he answered. Cam kept a tight grip on her arm in the elevator and as he unlocked the door of a sitting room and closed it behind him.

"Give me the bag you're clutching." He dropped it to a table. "Why did you come here, Pat?"

His stern eyes tightened her throat. He intended to make her go the whole way. She rated it.

"Because of that girl in England. I wanted to—"

"Go on."

"To play fair, and tell you that it will be all—right with me."

"So you can marry Ruskin?"

"Don't be so—so wooden. I came because I couldn't live through another night without telling you I'm sorry I reneged, that I haven't had a really happy moment since that—that night. I was panic-stricken and ran. Haven't you ever been frightened, Cam?"

"Yes. There was no girl in England or anywhere else." His hands came down hard on her shoulders. "I want the truth. Like me?"

"I'm here. I love you, Cam."

"Trust me?"

"For ever and ever."

"This is in my way." He pulled off her long pink glove and drew a plain gold ring from his waistcoat pocket.

"Want it again?"

In answer she held out the third finger of her left hand. He slipped it on. "Looks a little lonely, but I have something in another pocket to go with it. I'll give you that later." He pressed his lips on the ring and then against her hair.

"Softer even than I remember it." He released her quickly and picked up her bag. "Take this. Come on."

"Come on? Come *on?* Where? I've just arrived."

"Back to Silver Ledges. I'll help you pack. The ship leaves early. We'll take what you need on the trip, Sally will send the rest to Montana."

"Am I g—going?"

"Sure, you're g—going," he mocked tenderly. "What a question to ask. Remember what I told you that night in your room? I see that you do. I've had our reservations for a week. You didn't think I would leave you behind, did you?"

"But you didn't know until I—came that—"

"Right, but I was giving you till midnight to come; if you didn't I was all set to go for you." He started to put his arms about her, stopped and kissed her gently on the lips. "Come on, we've got a lot to do."

"Just a minute, Cam. Did the clerk know when you took the key that I—I am—"

"My wife? Sure, I told him. Didn't you hear him say, 'Lucky guy'?"

"Are you a lucky guy, Cam?" she asked wistfully.

"Lucky! The luckiest in the world to have the only girl I've ever loved."

His eyes and breathless laugh set her heart pounding. He caught her hand tight in his and drew her toward the door. "More about that later, Mrs. Fulton. Come on or we won't make the ship."

EMILIE LORING

Women of all ages are falling under the enchanting spell Emilie Loring weaves in her beautiful novels. Once you have finished one book by her, you will surely want to read them all.